Across the Seas

Across the Seas
Book 2
in the
New World Series
By
Griff Hosker

Across the Seas

Published by Sword Books Ltd 2019

Copyright © Griff Hosker First Edition 2019

The author has asserted their moral right under the Copyright, Designs and Patents Act, 1988, to be identified as the author of this work. All Rights reserved. No part of this publication may be reproduced, copied, stored in a retrieval system, or transmitted, in any form or by any means, without the prior written consent of the copyright holder, nor be otherwise circulated in any form of binding or cover other than that in which it is published and without a similar condition being imposed on the subsequent purchaser.

A CIP catalogue record for this title is available from the British Library.

Cover by Design for Writers

Dedication

To Davina, another dear friend taken to the Otherworld.

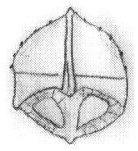

Prologue

I am Erik Larsson. My people now call me Erik the Navigator. I am honoured that they do so for I am young to captain a drekar. We are the Clan of the Fox and we are wanderers. We fled the rapacious King Harald Finehair of Norway when he took our home in Orkneyjar. We made a new home in the land north of Mercia and there we prospered. Larswick was a good home until my father was killed and Finehair came for us again. My brother, Arne Larsson, became jarl of the clan with Snorri Long Fingers, our uncle, as a foster father. We held a Thing and the clan, most of the clan, decided to take our drekar, snekke, and two knarr to seek a new home in the land of ice and fire. It was not an easy choice for we were leaving a rich and fertile land but none of us would bend the knee to the Norwegian king. We had sailed north to the land of Føroyar and hunted the seals from those islands to help us survive. We had voyaged across the Unending Sea. We did not know where this land lay but my people trusted their navigator. When I smelled the brimstone then I knew we had arrived. We had found a land free from the rule of kings but what else did it bring?

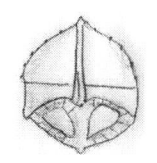

Chapter 1

We had reached the island but we saw no sign of a beach. The Norns were spinning. The winds were from the east and the south. The men were tired and so I let the wind take us north and east as we sailed along the coast looking for a beach. That changed our future. Who knows what might have ensued had we gone the other way? Eidel was the lookout. The eldest of my ship's boys, he perched precariously atop the mast. The pennant occasionally fluttered across his face and he waved it away. I kept us eight hundred paces from the coast for I did not want to rip out our hull. We had no idea what lay beneath the surface of this sea. Our three consorts trailed behind. They were ducklings following us, their mother. The other lookouts lined the larboard side as they watched for the white water of rocks.

It was Stig, who was standing with me by the steering board who spotted that *'Sea Bird'*, one of the two knarr, was in trouble.

"There is trouble astern Captain, Padraig has taken the snekke next to *'Sea Bird.'* She looks to be low in the water."

I handed him the steering board, "Keep her on this course." I turned and cupped my hands. "Sighwarth, what is the trouble?"

I had a good voice for he was three lengths astern of us and he heard me. I saw him cup his hands, "We are taking on water. The strakes have sprung. We need to land soon or we will perish. We have women and children aboard."

Padraig shouted, "We will take the bairns off and pass them to *'Raven'*." That was our other knarr.

"Good, we will seek a place to land. So long as there is a beach it will have to do." My brother, Arne, joined me. He had been by the mast with Snorri. I told him our troubles. "I had hoped to use this wind to circumnavigate this part of the land. I have seen no habitation but there may be people here."

"Just get us to land. Our folk are ready for it and the Norns have spun." He leaned in. "Already there are some who say we should never have left."

I had heard the moaners too. "Eidel, is there any inlet close by? I care not if there is a beach just so that we can close with the shore." He did not answer but peered landward. I edged the steering board over to close with the shore. There were cliffs which rose from the water. Savage rocks, like the island's teeth, guarded their base.

Eidel shouted, "I see an inlet. It looks to be a mile ahead. I can see no beach."

"We will head there. Arne, tell the others what we do. Stig, tell the lookouts to be vigilant. We risk unknown waters here."

I heard Arne shouting to the three ships which followed us. We had been lucky to have travelled so far and to have stayed together. It was inevitable that we should have damage to one of our ships. It had been Heyannir when we had left Føroyar. That had meant longer days. I suspect we might have lost ships had it been later in the sailing season.

We crabbed our way to the cliffs. The cliffs were not as high as in Norway but they were higher than any we had seen in the land of the Angles or our islands. I wondered if there was arable land here. I saw smoke rising from a nearby mountain. It seemed to tower over this part of the island. Below the wreath of smoke, I saw snow and yet this was high summer. What would winter bring?

Stig returned, "The water looks deep, Captain."

"I can risk edging closer?"

It was a question Stig did not wish to answer for if he was wrong then we might strike rocks and all would be lost. He took a deep breath, "I would say so, Captain."

We closed to within two hundred paces of the shore. I would go no closer but, if **'Sea Bird'** did begin to sink, we had a chance of salvaging something from her.

Dreng shouted, from the prow, "I see the inlet. It is as wide as a sea!"

"Arne, we will need to take **'Sea Bird'** in tow. We will have to use the oars."

My brother nodded, "The men are tired but the end is in sight. Let me know when we row!"

I said, "Stig, find the best rope we have. We will take our ships in tow." As he hurried off, I turned but kept my hand on the steering board, "Padraig!" he waved his arm to show that he had heard me, "We will take *'Sea Bird'* in tow. Have *'Raven'* lash herself to one side. You take the tow, row and fasten it to the prow of *'Sea Bird'* and then lash yourselves to the other side of her. We will let *'Njörðr'* show her strength! The clan will pull you all to a safe anchorage."

Our snekke was like a little greyhound and Padraig brought her close to the stern. Stig threw the rope and Padraig allowed *'Jötnar'* to fall off and drift back to the knarr." I looked back to the shore. I could see the inlet now. We edged a little closer. When I turned we would lose the wind. I glanced back and watched as the rope was secured to the prow of the stricken knarr.

"Arne, take to the oars!"

"Aye, brother. "Right, Clan of the Fox, we have one last row. Let this new home of ours hear our voices so that it knows the Clan of the Fox has come!"

The oars had just begun to bite when Padraig waved to show that the tow was secure. I felt the hull judder as we took the weight. It would become easier once the snekke was tied next to the knarr for her sails would help to push us.

The Clan of the Fox has no king
We will not bow nor kiss a ring
We fled our home to start anew
We are strong in heart though we are few

Lars the jarl fears no foe
He sailed the ship from Finehair's woe
Drekar came to end our quest
Erik the Navigator proved the best
When Danes appeared to thwart our start
The Clan of the Fox showed their heart
While we healed the sad and the sick
We built our home, Larswick

The Clan of the Fox has no king
We will not bow nor kiss a ring
We fled our home to start anew

Across the Seas

We are strong in heart though we are few

When Halfdan came with warriors armed
The Clan of the Fox was not alarmed
We had our jarl, a mighty man
But the Norns they spun they had a plan
When the jarl slew Halfdan the Dane
His last few blows caused great pain
With heart and arm, he raised his hand
'The Clan of the Fox is a mighty band!'

The Clan of the Fox has no king
We will not bow nor kiss a ring
We fled our home to start anew
We are strong in heart though we are few

    I headed for the centre of the channel in the inlet. I saw that the inlet was a fjord. It twisted and turned as it headed north. The smoking mountain lay ominously close to it. I was more hopeful. The only smoke I saw was from the nearby mountain. Perhaps this coast was uninhabited. We were prepared to fight for land but if we could land unopposed and establish ourselves first, then that would be so much better. Trees lined the fjord. None were huge ones but they meant timber. Once the timber was cleared, we could farm. As we turned and the wind worked against us a little so we slowed and the men had to row harder. Our song helped. With good fortune, this would be the last time that the men would need to row for some time.

    "Keep watch for beaches."

    I was the navigator. We needed a beach first but I was looking for natural harbours. Within five hundred paces of turning into the fjord, I saw a perfect harbour and a beach but Sven shouted, "Rocks to larboard!" I took us back to the main channel. The beach and harbour could be investigated by foot once we had landed. The men were tiring and we had travelled three more miles up the fjord when Eidel shouted, "I see a beach and a river! They are to larboard!"

    A river meant there would be no rocks. There might be mudbanks and shoals but those we could deal with. I turned and shouted, "Head to larboard!" When the three ships put their steering boards over then it became easier for our men. I saw the beach. It was neither white nor golden sand but black flecked. It looked, however, to be rock free. I had to time this just right.

Stig, go and organize the boys. I want us secured as soon as we are close."

"Aye, captain." I kept edging west to the beach. When I saw the ship's boys clinging to the sheets and stays, I shouted, "Larboard oars in. Steerboard, back water!" With three ships acting like an anchor the drekar began to edge into the shore. I felt a creak as her keel touched the sand and then there were six splashes as the ship's boys jumped into the shallows. I had time to glance astern. Padraig had the snekke on the beach already for he had untied himself from the knarr. The water was lapping along the gunwales.

"Arne, as soon as you can get the men ashore and drag *'Sea Bird'* to the beach. She is about to founder!"

"Aye, Erik the navigator! The Clan salutes you!"

I smiled and nodded. I knew I had skills and it was my duty to use them for the clan. As the boys tied us to the shore, using the rocks which lay there I looked at the landing site. This was not a good place to build a home. The better home looked to be the first place we had seen. Here the river made the land muddy and it looked to be liable to flooding. We would need access to fresh water but there had to be springs and natural waters we could find. I cupped my hands, "Ship's boys, take the water barrels and refill them from the river." The decision about our new home would not be mine but my advice would be sought.

Gytha and her husband, my uncle Snorri Long Fingers, came to see me as the men slipped over the side and headed to the stricken ship. I heard Arne shout, "Unload *'Sea Bird'* get the folk off!"

Gytha was a powerful volva. She was the one who spoke. "We have found land but not our home."

I nodded, "We passed a good place but there were rocks. I will see my brother, the Jarl, and ask to go and scout out the other. This would make a good place to camp."

Snorri nodded, "My brother would be proud of you, Erik. He had faith in your skill as a navigator and it has been justified. I see trees for homes and there is some land for crops and animals." He waved a hand at the waters, "The sea teems with fish and I see, on the other side of the fjord, basking seals. We can make a home here."

Gytha stroked his hand, "But this will not be the home which Erik will find. That is still in the distance. I have dreamt it but I have not seen it. You still have far to sail, Erik the Navigator." A woman coughed and I saw that it was my mother. Gytha shook her head and said, quietly, "But for some, they will never leave here." I wondered what she knew.

While our people and animals were taken ashore, I went over my ship with the ship's boys. We had animal dung to clean. It would not be wasted. The animal waste would fertilize new fields. The animals themselves were lean and needed fattening. Our camp would enable us to do that. When the upper parts of our ship had been cleaned and checked I slipped over the side. The icy waters were a shock to my system but I had to check the keel below the waterline. The knarr's plight showed us that we could take nothing for granted. By the time I climbed back aboard I was blue with the cold but it had been worth it. Our drekar was sound. I saw fires lit ashore and freshly caught fish were being cooked. Children were exploring the land and the women were, once again, preparing food. I changed into warm clothes and, even though it was summer, slipped into a fur to warm me through.

"Eidel, I want two boys on watch at all times." I had good ship's boys. They were more than boys. Eidel, Halsten, and Stig were almost men. They each had a beard. Sven was also close to becoming a man. Even Rek and Dreng, although younger, could soon take an oar if they so chose.

"Aye Captain."

Before I left the drekar I stored my hourglass and compass in my chest. Without them, we would not have found the land of ice and fire. I walked down the black beach to the knarr. She had been hauled clear of the water. Sighwarth shook his head, it was his knarr. "She has the worm. We checked her before we left but…"

Arne put his arm around the warrior, "She got us here. We will use her for a hall when we find where we will live."

I said, "Gytha thinks that this is not the place."

"We need to rest and to recover, brother. We cannot go sailing again. Many of the families are unhappy and the sight of the smoking mountain does not enthral them!"

"I know." I pointed south to the mouth of the fjord, "I spied some likely places there. I would go on the morrow to scout them out. The animals will need rest and we can collect fish and seals from the seas around here."

Butar Beer Belly said, "I have seen birds but no animals." He pointed to the sand. "The only tracks I saw were those of birds or seals."

Arne was young but the clan had chosen a clever jarl. "Then it is good that we brought animals to breed. We have a bull and cows. We have sheep and pigs. All that we lack are horses."

While the men went to build shelters, I spoke with the other captains. The other two ships were in good condition. "Padraig and Aed, I would have you come with me on the morrow to see if we can use the natural harbours. If not, we will sail the snekke further into the fjord." They nodded. "How was the voyage here?"

"There were times when we thought we had lost you but the light brought us safely to you and we trusted your skills with the compass. This is a strange land."

I turned to look at it, "You are right and it is well named. I see trees and then all is fire and, even though it is summer, ice." I nodded. "We had better haul the knarr from the water."

We managed to drag *'Sea Bird'* on to the sand. Water began to drip from the sprung strakes. She was now a ship in name only.

The animals happily grazed on what passed for pasture but Arne took the precaution of using the children from the clan to watch over them. I went to see my mother and Edmund, our thrall. They were both Saxons and, since my father had died, increasingly alone. My younger brother, Fótr, was all that she had left. Arne and I had our own lives.

I put my hand on her shoulder, "Gytha said that you are unwell?"

"It is just a cough, my son."

Edmund shook his head, "I just cannot see it improving here! This is a bleak place. We should have stayed in a god-fearing land." Since my father had died Edmund had become increasingly belligerent. I feared that Arne would punish him. He sometimes went too far.

He would not have spoken like that had Arne been there. He was too familiar for a slave. I did not mind, I quite liked Edmund. He watched over my mother and Fótr. Before I had left the hall, he had cared for me too. "We have our freedom and this stark land is a price worth paying."

"It is a godless land!"

I shook my head. Edmund was a devout Christian. My father had tried to beat it out of him but failed. "Now that we are ashore you can have hot food and that will make the cough disappear."

My mother smiled, "Perhaps."

While the rest of the clan would sleep ashore, I chose to sleep aboard my ship. After I had my food and eaten, I returned to the ship. I had not managed a good night's sleep at sea. Each time I had closed my eyes I was ready to be woken at a moment's notice. I went to sleep while it was still daylight and I could hear the children playing. The nights were so short as to last but a few hours. It was daylight when I woke but few were up. We had seen no sign of any danger and so we had not set guards. We had some fowl with us and they would have woken us. I made water and then went to look at the beached knarr. The water had stopped flowing. She would dry out. As a ship, she had served her purpose but her hull could be inverted to make a hall. All that I needed to do was find a site.

Arne had also risen early. "Brother, I will come with you and the Irishmen today. You might have an eye for a harbour but I am jarl and I will choose where we defend!"

"Of course." I pointed north. The fjord was a long one. "There may be better places further north."

He shook his head, "You have good instincts. If we have a hall at the mouth then we can control who uses our fjord. Other Vikings will follow. Not all will be as successful as we were but they will come. This is our land and we will control who lives close by us. We are the Clan of the Fox."

We ate some scraps left from the night before and then, after donning our capes and taking weapons we went to find Padraig and Aed. They were ready and we headed down the coast. We walked as close to the cliff as we could. There were trees but closer to the sea they were a little stubbier than those closer to the nearby mountain. We watched the ground as we walked. There was no trail. There was no game. The only tracks we saw were those of foxes. I guessed that they preyed on the seabirds. As we walked, we heard the birds. They roosted along the cliffs. Arne nodded, "I will send the boys out later to collect eggs. If they take their slings and their bows then they can hunt some of the birds too."

Aed said, "The birds will learn and choose somewhere else to roost."

My brother had an answer for everything. "And by then we will be harvesting our first crops."

It was not an easy walk. Unlike the land of the Angles or Orkneyjar, here there were no trails and we found our way by instinct. We made mistakes and had to back track occasionally. We crossed streams which fed from the mountain. Aed said, "The snow there means these will never dry up." He tasted the water. "It is not the best but it can be brewed if there is grain."

We were nearing the mouth of the fjord. It had taken us half a morning to reach it. What I saw, I liked. There were three small and natural harbours. The middle one had a beach but the other two, although they had rocks, looked like we could build a quay along their rocky arms. It had helped us when we had been on the Loyne. As a sailor, it was what I wanted but Arne was our leader and he would decide.

He pointed to the sea. "Go and check the approach while I see if there is a site we can defend."

When I went with the two Irish sailors to the rocks, I saw that the sharp rocks were on the first bay but only on the eastern side and the south. We could build a quay on the western side and would not risk the drekar. When we looked at the centre one, I realized that if we built a quay in the first bay we could land from the beach on the other side. The two bays gave us alternatives to land and yet were easy to defend. I sent Aed and Padraig to look at the third bay while I sought Arne. He was a dot in the distance. I followed him, wondering why he had wandered off. When I reached him I saw the reason why. There was a large patch of water. I knew it was drinkable when he scooped a handful and drank it. He stood and walked towards me.

"This is where we build. The water has a taste but it will do. We can build a stronghold close to the sea." He pointed to the southwest. Through the trees, I saw that there was another huge bay there. We had seen no landing places when we had passed it but it would be used for shelter if our fjord was inaccessible. "The ground just three hundred paces from us has a view of the bay. This is good. We can have another Larswick."

I shook my head, "That would be bad luck. We burned the other."

He clutched his Hammer of Thor and nodded, "Aye, you are still the thinker. We will come up with a name later. Does this mean you can sail the ships here?"

"It does. We can use the beach to land. When we build a quay then the first bay will be perfect. Tonight, we will do our best to seal the damaged knarr. We sail the drekar and the knarr here. That way we use the knarr for a hall." I saw Padraig and Aed heading for us.

"That is good. We will keep the women and the children close to the camp until the hall is built. We can set the others to collect food. Padraig and Aed can sail across the fjord and take men to hunt seals. I think that we will need to lay in as much food as we can. It is summer now but it still feels cold."

We headed back to our camp and reached it in the late afternoon. Arne gathered the men and told them of our decision. We did not need to hold a Thing. When we had built the hall then they could have the choice to come with us or find farms on the rest of the island. I went to see my mother. Gytha was with her accompanied by her son, Tostig. Helga, Freja, and Gefn were also with Gytha. She was the matriarch of the clan. They were tending to my mother.

"What ails her, Gytha?"

"She has a cough but she is a Christian. She has given up on life."

Edmund shook his head, "Christians do not give up. It is the climate and this island!"

"Edmund! You are a thrall! Go and collect firewood. This is not your concern!" He was about to say something but I think the tone of my voice dictated his course of action. I knelt next to her, "Mother, what is this? We have a new home and we have no enemies here! Come, rouse yourself."

She shook her head, "I was never one of the clan. Your father loved me and while he was alive that was enough. You and Arne do not need me and as for Fótr? He is a Viking. Like his brothers, he will soon grow and not need me."

Gytha's voice was commanding when she spoke, "He needs you now. You are a mother! Rouse yourself for the child! You make me ashamed to be a woman!" Her words were harsh but they worked. My mother rose. I put a hand out to help her. Gytha shook her head, "None of that, Erik. She does not need it. She seeks sympathy!"

My mother's eyes narrowed, "Pagans!"

Gytha laughed, "I take that as a compliment."

Helga always got on well with my mother and she said, "Come Maeve, I will help you. My child is not yet due and this will be good for the unborn babe." The two of them went to Fótr who had been watching the interchange with his mouth open. Such arguments were rare.

Gytha smiled as she turned back to me. It was as though there had been no argument at all, "Have we a new home?"

"We have. It is the first bay we passed. There is fresh water close by. There are plenty of trees for houses and ships. We will need to build fishing ships. When we cut them down, we will have land to farm. We have time to plant barley before winter and oats too."

Gytha's eyes bored into me. She seemed to read my mind. "You are not a farmer. Your path is across the water. This is but a halt on your journey. I see you in the land where the sun does not set over the sea but on mountains and forests. I have dreamed. Take my advice and use the snekke to sail around this island. It will help your brother. The only law here will be the law of the sword. Arne is jarl and he needs to know where others are settled." She saw my eyes flicker to my mother. "Forget your mother. I have done what I can to stir her but I have looked into her eyes and I have seen death."

Despite Gytha's words and the power of her witchcraft, I could not abandon my mother. That evening I ate with her and Fótr. Freja must have told Arne of the argument for after they had spoken with the men he came over. "Mother, what is this we hear? You are giving up. Father would not like that!" His words did not come out as the words of a son but the jarl. I saw little comfort in her eyes.

"I will do all that a mother should do for the one son who needs her and then my work on this earth is done."

Arne did not listen to the thoughts beneath the words and he nodded, "Good." He turned to me. "Can you manage with just your ship's boys and twenty men tomorrow?"

"Aye."

"Good. For I intend to have half of the men drive the animals to the new settlement. When the hall is erected, we can sail the other boats with the grain and all else that we need."

"Do you have any preference for the men I take?"

"I think that you should take Snorri Long Fingers. I do not consult with him as much as I think he would like. "

"I do not think he minds, brother. It was our father who wished to be a leader. Our uncle seems happy with his wife."

"You may be right but take him anyway." I turned to go but my brother gripped my arm, "I heard that Edmund spoke up against you."

I shook my head, "He was being Edmund. You know how he is with mother. It was nothing."

"Brother, we do not suffer injuries and slights from Saxon thralls."

I laughed, "We have few enough as it is. I was not slighted."

"I am content."

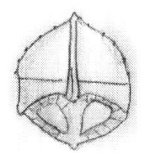

Chapter 2

Sighwarth insisted upon steering his doomed knarr. I knew how he felt. A man's ship was almost an extension of him. It would be like losing a limb. The ship was to have one last voyage and they would share it. We stripped all that could be used from the interior. The mast, sheets, stays, decking, all were taken. We left in the ballast for that would be used to help build the hall. The fact that it was stone from our home across the seas was important. We had noticed that there was a current down the fjord. It was not a strong one but it would aid our journey. We also rode high in the water for we had neither cargo nor mail. Our shields lay at our camp. We had seen no foes. Our weapons would remain in their scabbards.

We had hewed some trees already. When the snekke and knarr sailed to our new home they would tow them. Men would continue to take trees from further up the fjord until we sailed. The tow was secured and we rowed steadily down the fjord. Having walked the coast, I knew it slightly better. I studied every blade of grass, every sedge, and every heather as we headed to the fjord's mouth. This was our new home. I needed to become familiar with it.

As soon as I passed the first bay, I had the ship's boys take in the sail. The way went from us for the knarr was taking on water again and was lower in the water. I put the steering board over and had the larboard oars stop their rowing. This time I wanted us in a circle so that we faced the fjord again and the knarr was inshore of us.

"Release the tow!"

As we turned the knarr was released and Sighwarth let her ground herself gently on the beach.

"Back water." I used the steering board to help the drekar push the knarr gently up the beach. There was the slightest of creaks from the wood of the knarr and then the sound of sand grating beneath her keel. "In oars. Ship's boys, secure us." We would have to clamber over the knarr until we moved her. "Uncle, take charge of the knarr if you would."

"Aye navigator! That was neatly done."

By the time we were tied to the shore the men had begun to take out the ballast from the knarr and to climb the slight slope to the two crossed pieces of driftwood Arne had left as a marker for the hall. Sighwarth was carefully dismantling the steering board. It was a fine piece of work. I know he hoped for another ship. The board would be a thread which tied the two ships together. After carrying them to the two crossed pieces of driftwood, we laid the ballast stones in a rough knarr shape. We had brought tools. I had my compass with me and we laid out the stones so that the knarr would be on a north to south alignment. Leaving the ship's boys to begin to cut the turf we would use we went back to the now empty knarr. There were spindly trees which were close to the shore and we cut them down to make rollers. We could have carried the knarr but we would need timber for building in any case. One knarr would not house our clan.

It took all morning to drag and roll the knarr to the ship's boys. By that time, we heard our animals in the distance. They were being driven to their new home. We had brought food and we ate. My uncle sat with me on the pile of freshly cut turf. "If it were not for the smoking mountain behind us then this patch of land could be our home on Orkneyjar."

"Aye, you are right but this has more to offer." I pointed to the whales who were passing the headland. "We can find more that we need from the seas. They look rich."

"Aye, but can we grow grains?"

My uncle was right. We had brought sacks of seeds but would they grow here in the land of ice and fire? If not then we would have to raid and that meant crossing the seas back to the land of the Saxons and the Hibernians. We would not know until we had spent a winter in this land. We had eaten and drunk our water on the voyage. We could refill the barrels here. We had some flour for bread and we had some barley for beer but we had no ovens nor brew house yet. We had much to build before we could enjoy some creature comforts.

Snorri rose, "This is not getting shelter for our women. Off your backsides let us lay Sighwarth's ship to rest. "

The boys had already dug two holes for the prow and the stern post. They would secure the knarr to the ground. They were very large holes so that we had a margin for error. We would then need to dig a line so that the knarr's gunwale lay below the top of the soil. The ballast stones would be laid along the edge. I thought that would be all that we would achieve this first day. The most delicate part of the operation was turning the knarr. We had to do so gently as though the knarr was an invalid. The ship was already stricken. We had men with ropes holding the side of the knarr and resisting the pull as the majority of the men hauled her over. My uncle was not pulling. He was at the prow and watching both sides. He had Eidel and Halsten with him and they were used to pass instructions to the rest of us who, clad only in breeks and boots strained and heaved. We held the ropes for so long, at one point, that I felt my arms begin to burn. When the command came, "Lower!", there was a collective sigh of relief. With the slightest of creaks, which sounded like the knarr's sigh of death, the boat slid into her two holes. We all cheered. All that is save Sighwarth. I saw sadness on his face. Would I feel the same when *'Njörðr'* or *'Jötnar'* was laid to rest?

We were just embedding the hull when Arne arrived with the animals. While the men he had brought used some of the rolling timbers we had used to build a pen he came over.

"You have done well, uncle. This means we can bring our people down on the morrow."

Uncle Snorri looked pleased with the work. "And now we have animals." Lowering his voice, he said, "This is good for a home but how many farms can it support?"

He was right. We had many families. Some would have to find land and clear it themselves. They would not be close to the settlement. Arne and I had already noted that between our camp and the new settlement we could only see land for, perhaps three farms.

"You are right and that is why I wish my brother to sail up the fjord and see what lies there. Tomorrow will be the day for moving but the day after I would have you and two of your boys explore the land to the north of us. It may be that the clan farms together."

I nodded. I did not mind. I enjoyed being on the water and it had been some time since I had sailed *'Jötnar'*. Unless we moved or went to war then the drekar would not be needed but the snekke was the best to explore and to fish. It was dusk by the time we had secured the hall and begun to lay the first turves upon her roof. Leaving four men to watch the animals we boarded the drekar and sailed up the fjord. When we reached the camp, I would have the mast stepped and the sail stored. There would be winter storms and the ship would suffer less damage without a mast and sail.

There was food already cooked for us. It was a shellfish and seal stew. There were wild greens which grew close by and they had been added to the stew. We were so hungry it mattered not. Butar Beer Belly shook his head, "The first thing we build, jarl, is a brewhouse! A man cannot live without beer! I cannot lose my name and I will be wasting away to nothing soon!"

We laughed but Snorri counselled, "We cannot brew all that we want yet, Butar, for we have bairns to feed and crops to plant. It is summer now but when winter comes it will be worse than on Orkneyjar."

With that sombre warning ringing in my ears, I retired to my ship. The six boys all slept aboard too. We had stepped the mast already and the drekar looked lean, almost naked. "When we have moored our ship tomorrow then I will take three of you to explore this land. The other two will need to secure the drekar for winter."

"Who will you take, Captain?"

I smiled, "Let us see who impresses us tomorrow!"

The next day it rained. As we later discovered there were more days with rain than without, even in summer. It made the journey for those who walked to the new camp, both muddy and unpleasant. We took the women carrying unborn babies and the old. Edmund was forced to walk for he was a thrall. He was not happy to be separated from my mother. I took just six men to row. It was not far. The snekke and the knarr took other women and young children. The campsite looked empty and desolate as we left. There were the blackened fire pits. The places we had used to leave night soil and the places the animals had relieved themselves would become fertile but most of the dung we took with us along with that collected on the voyage. The soil would need to be improved and that was the start.

Arne had begun the men to building a second hall even before I arrived with the drekar. I had wanted my quay to be built but I understood the need for shelter. The rain which began to fall emphasized that. A door had been cut in the hull of the knarr and soon the interior would be made habitable. While the women began fires to cook for the clan the men not cutting timber for the second hall began to build the bread ovens. The whole settlement looked as though a nest of ants had been disturbed.

I needed our three ships to be secure. If there was rain then there might be wind and a storm. I took an axe and my six ship's boys. I chose a fair-sized tree. I did not need a thick one. I wanted six posts to drive into the ground to hold the three ships until we could build our quay. It took us until late afternoon to cut the tree and trim the branches before sawing it into six lengths and sharpening the end. The ships were held by rocks and that was not good enough. The boys began to dig the holes while I hardened a point on one end of each of the six stakes in the fire. Each trunk was as wide as my thigh and it took some time. The holes dug, we used the smith's hammer to drive them so that just the length of my arm remained above ground. When the ships were tied, I was happier.

I took the six boys to the side where we would build the quay. Halsten and Rek were the two who would be staying behind while I took the snekke up the fjord. When we reached the first bay I said, "I am not sure how long we will be away. It could be just one night or longer. You two have one task. Take as many stones as you can from the beach and bring them here. I want the rocks building up so that they can support a walkway."

"You are not going to drive piles into the sand, Captain?"

"No, Eidel. It is made of rock. We will use netted bags of stones to hold them in place. We will make those when we return. Your job is to lay as many stones as you can. It should be able to accommodate three drekar."

"We only have one."

"That may change."

Once again, we slept on the deck of the drekar. I rigged a piece of canvas up to shelter us from the rain. The rain did not help my mother. I heard her cough as I drifted off to sleep. Arne came to see us off on the snekke. We had spears, slings, cloaks, and furs. I had my yew bow and ten arrows. We wore our sealskin capes and we had a water skin. I had decided that we would forage for food. "Jarl, I will try to explore beyond the fjord. I may be away for two or three nights. It could be longer. We do not know the size of this fjord."

"Just so long as you come back safe. We know not what sort of animals live on this island,"

"We have seen little evidence of any." I nodded towards my mother, "Our mother is not well."

"I know. I will have Freja watch her."

Before I boarded *'Jötnar'* I went to speak to my mother. She was helping the other women to grind barley and oats for bread. Within the next day or so the oven would be finished and we would have bread. It had been some time since we had smelled and tasted bread. "Fótr, my little brother, watch over your mother!"

"I will, Erik. One day I shall sail with you. I would be a navigator."

"Then you have a little time to grow. By Einmánuður you should be big enough to try the snekke." He looked overjoyed. I could have taken him now for he was of an age with Rek and Dreng, but I did not wish to offend my six ship's boys. It had been hard enough to leave two behind as it was.

I liked sailing the snekke. It had been the ship I had first steered. It could hold eight and so the five of us were quite comfortable. I allocated two on each side. Eidel and Sven were at the fore. The four of them were to watch for hazards in the water and to look for possible farmstead sites. It was as we passed our former camp that we spied our first animals on the island. There were a pair of foxes rooting around the camp. I wondered what they would eat. I realized that we must have brought rats and mice with us. They lived aboard every ship I had ever seen. Grain and food found its way to the bottom of the ships and they proliferated. When we hauled the ships out of the water and applied pine tar they would leave, but once they were back in the water they would return. I had no doubt that those aboard *'Sea*

Bird' had fled as soon as we had taken away their home, the ballast.

I saw that the mountain which loomed over our bay dominated the land to the west of us. It looked alarmingly close. There was high ground to the east but it was not as high and was not snow covered. There also looked to be flatter ground there but, with all the trees, it was hard to tell. I had some bark and a piece of charcoal. I began to make a crude map as we sailed up the fjord. The wind was not in our favour and I had to tack back and forth. The slow speed meant we had a good view of the land at our disposal.

One piece of information which I discovered was that the rivers were more like becks. We saw many as we passed up the fjord. It looked like many were fed from the snow and glaciers we could see on the mountains. They would not be an obstacle to travel. I also spied, as we tacked west on one leg, that there appeared to be smoke coming from beneath the ground. As there was snow laying on the ground, I found this fascinating. Dreng and Stig had lines trailing behind us and it was they who caught our food. By the time it was noon we had travelled a fair way up and I saw that the fjord had narrowed to less than a mile. I put the steering board over and headed for the unexplored eastern shore. "We will cook the fish and explore the land here. This afternoon we will head further north."

There was no beach for some way north of where I intended to land. The snekke had a shallow draught and I was not concerned for it was just a shelf of rock rather than ragged teeth. We dragged the snekke onto the beach. I saw evidence that seals had used it for basking. There were fewer trees here and all I saw were lichens, heathers, and grasses. We had brought some kindling. "Get a fire going Dreng. Eidel and Stig, come with me. Bring your slings and a spear each." I picked up my bow and strung it. I had finished it some time ago and tested it. I was able to draw it three-quarters of the way back. I needed to practise more for it was a powerful weapon. I had just six metal heads. Four were barbed for hunting but two I had made of a head without barbs. That was to penetrate mail. Two of the arrows I had brought had stone arrowheads. Made of flint they could cut but they were an arrow of last resort. My two mail arrows were on the drekar. We had not come to the island for war.

We would forage for food wherever we could. I saw above us the gulls which hunted herring. They made good eating. Although a little oily and tasting fishy their flesh made a change from our normal diet. My father had told me that although some sailors did not eat them as they thought they were the spirits of dead sailors who had not gone to Valhalla, he believed that if we ate the birds then those dead sailors had a second chance to go to sit with Odin. Arne had been sceptical but to me it made sense.

The surface over which we passed was hard. Kneeling, I took Raedwulf's dagger and slid it into the earth. The rock was less than two fingers' depth beneath the surface. This was not farmland. As we headed east, I saw trees. The soil there would be deeper. The trees were either spindly or stunted. The land might only be fit for grazing. I began to fear that this land to which we had fled was good for little save fishing and a few animals. I could see why, until recently, few had ventured here. Of course, we could have found the worst place on the island to colonize. The wood stretched for some distance. We did not explore further but I noted it was a suitable site for a farmstead. The smell of Dreng's fire drew us back to the shore.

It was as we neared the water, on our way back, that we saw the solitary seal. It was basking on the rocks. "Prepare your spears. I will try an arrow or two." I nocked one of my hunting arrows. My two boys flanked me with spears held before them. The seal had jaws which could take an arm. The seal heard us when we stepped onto the rocks. It did not seem bothered. When we had been on Føroyar the seals there had learned to respect us but this one was oblivious to the danger. I pulled back my string when I was thirty paces from it and released. I was aiming at its head but I hit, instead, its body. It struck nothing vital and he lurched towards us. "Stand firm!" I nocked a second but, in the time it took to do so, the seal had closed to within six paces of us. I released and my arrow went into its open mouth. "Strike hard!" I dropped the bow and drew my dagger. My two boys did as I had bid. It was Eidel's spear which struck the killing blow. He drove it through the eye and into the skull. The beast fell dead. I knelt, "You fought hard. Go to your Valhalla. You were a warrior."

We rammed two spears through it and we manhandled it back to the camp. The fish was cooking. We laid the carcass down and went to eat the juicy fish. "When we have eaten, we will gut it and get rid of that which we do not need. When we camp tonight, I will show you how to butcher."

After I had eaten and I had got rid of the guts into the sea I added to the map I was making. We put the dead seal in the centre of the snekke and headed north. It soon became obvious that the place we had eaten was halfway along the fjord for I saw the land rising at the end. The land on the east looked to be more fertile. There were larger trees growing there and I was more hopeful that it could be farmed. The light was fading quickly for the fjord had a north to south alignment. I discovered that when I spied the head of the fjord and the river which emptied into it. This river was slightly wider than the others had been. Tiny becks and brooks emptied off the main branch to make an estuary eight hundred paces wide. We camped close to the northeastern side of it. We had fresh, incredibly icy water to drink. As Eidel and Stig lit the fire I showed the others how to butcher the seal.

"We were lucky when we killed it. There are no holes in the main part of the seal. We will cut carefully so that we can use as much of it as we can." I showed them how to cut the fat from the animal. We had brought one large pot and we put the bones in it with water on the fire. I had made a flat piece of metal with a funnel cut into it. We put the lumps of fat onto that. We put it on the fire too. I had had the foresight to bring a small barrel. We placed it beneath the funnel and, as the fat was rendered, the precious oil dripped into it. The crispy pieces which remained were eaten by the hungry boys and their captain. I also cooked the heart and the liver. They were delicious. Finally, we drank the broth from the seal bones. It was satisfying and cleansed the bones so that we could use them.

The fjord was cold, even though it was summer and we wrapped ourselves in our furs. There was little kindling left. On the morrow, we would have to search for dead wood and cut small branches for our next fire. As we lay there Rek asked, "Do we sail back tomorrow, Captain?"

"No, we need to explore the river. Our people need farms. This is not as fertile a place as the one we left."

We rose early and I left Dreng and Rek to render down the rest of the fat and cut kindling. I took the other two to head up the valley. It was disappointing. The land to the west of the river and along its eastern bank was rocky and we could not even walk on it. There were trees and shrubs for two miles on the eastern side but then the ground became too rocky and steep. For most of the way, we were in shadow. This would not be good farmland. There was just the one site we had found and that had been where we had killed the seal. On my map I had it marked as Seal Point."

We were able to leave early the next day. We had cooked all of the seal fat and had a small barrel half filled with the oil we had rendered. The meat we had yet to cook but we would do that at the new settlement. I had spent part of the evening taking the heads and feathers from the arrows I had used to hit the seal. The shafts had been broken but the heads were reusable. We had to reuse as much as we could.

It took most of the day to sail back down the fjord for I sailed close to the eastern shore to explore the potential of farmsteads. I wondered if we had found the wrong place to land. One thing was certain before winter came upon us, I would have to explore the rest of the island in case there were other sites which were better.

As we neared the drekar I saw that, what looked like the whole clan, had gathered around the hall. Leaving the boys to tie us up I hurried towards the crowd. I heard raised voices. I pushed my way through. I was the brother of the jarl. It was as I neared the centre that I heard Arne, "And I have lost a mother too, Leif Yellow Hair."

Lost a mother? I burst through between Asbjorn and Butar Beer Belly. Butar's hand was raised until he saw it was me. He shouted, "It is Erik!"

All faces turned to me. I saw a body lying on the ground and covered in a cloak. Arne's face told me that what I had heard was true. "Our mother died. It was this morning. She just did not wake."

"Then why are people angry! They should be sad. We should mourn the wife of our jarl!"

Leif Yellow Hair jabbed a finger towards Arne. "And we have lost too. Your thrall, Edmund, has cracked the skull of my son, Wiglaf!"

I was totally confused. Gytha and Snorri swept into the centre of the mob. She was a vǫlva and none stood in her way. Her eyes glared and she looked, for all the world, like a dragon. "Why is the clan turning on itself over a thrall!"

Leif could not hold back his words, "Because my son is fighting for his life and the thrall belongs to the jarl!"

"You have not been in the clan long enough yet Leif Yellow Hair and you are a fool. Your son lives. I have just come from him. Your wife has more sense than you do! He has opened his eyes!"

The man was belligerent and would not back down, "Yet the thrall who did this has escaped justice. What does the jarl intend to do about it?"

I saw my brother clench and unclench his fists. He was trying to control himself but I knew that all he wanted to do was to hit the man whose family had joined us less than two months before we left our river.

"What I will do when you behave like a man and not a hysterical girl is to go, with my brother, and hunt down Edmund. First, we will bury our mother and then we will leave."

Leif laughed, "And he will have escaped justice!" His eyes narrowed, "I do not think that you are fit to be jarl."

Behind me, I heard Butar Beer Belly, "Draw your weapon, Yellow Hair, and I will give you the closest haircut you have ever had!"

Arne showed then that he truly deserved to be jarl, "Enough! I will bury my mother, find the slave and when I return then I will settle this matter." He turned to Snorri. "Until I return, I trust you to watch over our people and Fótr."

"Fear not, Jarl, all will be well until you return."

Chapter 3

As Arne and I prepared to leave I asked, "Our mother is buried, now tell me what happened?"

He shook his head, "All is hearsay and gossip. Our mother, it seems, died in the night. It was Edmund who was with her when she died. Fótr awoke and heard Edmund crying. Our brother said that Edmund was saying, 'My daughter! My daughter!' When he saw that Fótr was awake he dashed out. As he did so, according to Fótr, he knocked over Wiglaf. The youth stood and began to berate the thrall. Edmund picked up one of the smith's small hammers and laid him out. By the time Fótr had given the alarm he had gone."

"But if Fótr heard right then Edmund is…"

"Our grandfather. Aye, I know but it makes sense. Now I think of it I can see similarities. He stayed all these years. He could have run for he had no yoke. It matters not. We have to fetch him back or the clan will be destroyed."

I looked over to where Leif was speaking with some of the other men, "It is too late for that already, brother. You have a challenger."

He shook his head, "Leif Yellow Hair is just a loudmouth. He moaned all the time on the voyage. He is the one stirring the others to return to Larswick. It is his way."

I was not so sure. "Which way did our... Edmund go?"

He turned to me, "It matters not if he was our mother's father. He was a slave. He kept that news from us. We hunt him and when we find him, we punish him." I nodded. Arne pointed to the mountain. "He headed up there. I suspect it was because he feared you might see him if he went up the fjord. We will soon find him. He is an old man."

"An old man with a head start." I knew that he was many hours ahead of us. We were fitter and younger. We would catch him but it would not be a quick hunt.

Although the days were long, we still left while it was dark. The clan was about to be riven apart and we had to do something. Gytha said she would watch over Fótr. Our young brother had not said much since the funeral. He had lost a father, now a mother and, when we caught him, a grandfather. He was growing but our mother had kept him a child for longer than Arne and I. What he had seen was much to bear. I took my bow and my dagger. We would not need my sword for Arne had his strapped about his waist. We wore our seal skin capes. Arne said that the slave had been seen heading up to the snowline. It would get cold.

We found his trail, even in the dark. He would have been better to have run through the woods but he had chosen to run across the heather and sedge. We could see his footprints. The moon shone down and illuminated them as though it was daylight. "What do you think he means to do, brother?"

Arne was ahead and I saw his head shake, "He is a Christian else I would have believed he ran off to die. It is a sin to kill yourself in the religion of the White Christ. Perhaps he hopes to find other settlers. He could pretend to be a freedman and start a new life."

I was not sure. I suspected his grief was such that he just ran away to be alone. If he had not hurt Wiglaf we could just have let him live but he had hurt the youth and Edmund was a slave. As the sun came up, we saw that we were approaching the snow line. We both wore seal skin boots. Edmund had simple leather shoes. He would struggle to walk in the snow and the cold would get to him. He had no food with him. The snow was not solid. It was summer. The hard surface crumbled easily. I saw that Edmund's feet had sunk into the snow. I saw steam rising ahead and, as we moved closer, I saw that Edmund's trail led us there. We hurried. Arne drew his sword and I nocked an arrow.

When we crested the rise and looked at the footprints, we saw that they led to a blue patch of water from which steam was rising. As we headed down, I found myself clutching my Hammer of Thor. Was this witchcraft? There was snow which had not melted and yet I could see steam. When we saw the footprints heading away, we knew that Edmund had left. We were both intrigued and we descended to the steaming pool. I put my hand towards the water and it was hot, almost boiling! I withdrew my hand quickly. The smell of brimstone told me that this was heated by fire.

"What is this magic?"

I shook my head, "I know not but reading this puzzle I think he came here and bathed his feet to warm them. You could see the imprint of his body. At least we are on the right trail."

We pushed on. Edmund looked to be moving further up the mountain and I knew not why. The top was wreathed in smoke and perhaps he thought to evade us. His footprints negated the effect of the cloud. We knew where he was heading. My mind always worked more slowly on the land and it took a few hundred paces before the thought hit me. "Arne, did he take weapons?"

Arne stopped, "He took the smith's hammer."

"Then perhaps he means to do us harm. He knows not that it will be us who trail him. He may believe that it is Leif."

We moved more cautiously after my warning. Every rock which reared over us threatened ambush and attack. The day moved on and I wondered where the old slave had got his strength. If he was our mother's father then that made him old. He had no hair and, like many Christians, he scraped his face. He could have seen more than fifty or sixty summers! The sun had passed its zenith when we saw him. His footsteps continued ahead but, as I glanced down the steep slope, I saw him. He was lying four hundred paces down the slope. He had fallen and rolled many hundreds of feet.

"Arne, I see him!" I pointed. He was lying with his legs at an unnatural angle. If he was dead then we could return home.

Arne was reading my thoughts. "Dead or alive we have to take him back, or Leif will believe that we are complicit in his escape."

He was right. Arne was no coward and he led us down the snow-covered slope. We were higher up and the snow was harder here. He slipped and slithered six paces down the ice when he misplaced his foot. "Arne, we should not walk directly down. Follow me." I imagined that instead of walking down a steep, ice-covered slope, I was sailing my drekar with an unfavourable wind. I walked along the slope and then turned to walk back and down. When I passed Arne, I helped him up. We passed the place Edmund had tumbled. His fall had smoothed the snow to an icy sheen. Eventually, we began to near the thrall. He did not look to be moving.

I reached him first but I was wary. If he was alive and had the hammer with him then he might just react and hurt us. His eyes were closed and I saw that his right hand lay beneath his body. I took a chance as Arne knelt on the other side of him. I put my hand on his chest. He was warm and breathed still. He opened his eyes and, seeing me, smiled. As he did so a tendril of blood seeped from the corner of his mouth. "Erik, I am pleased that you have found me."

Arne said, before I could speak, "We have to take you back, Edmund."

"My back is broken. You will take a corpse with you. Let me lie here and expire."

I had to ask, "Are you our grandfather?"

He nodded, "I am. Being your thrall was the only way I could stay close to your mother. My sons, wife, all my family died in the attack. My daughter, my eldest, was all that was left to me. At first, I thought to take her away one night and escape. Then she became pregnant. Once you were born, Arne, she would not leave. I watched you grow, all three of you, and I had a new life." He suddenly winced. "I do not have long. Hear my confession as I heard my daughter's. I have been a sinful man and I have lived a lie. I go to God on my knees and hope that he can forgive my transgression. I beg you bury me by my daughter. She was my life and..."

He got no further. We would never know why he climbed the mountain. Arne was ever practical. "We cannot stay up here with him. We need to get as far down the mountain as we can and find somewhere to sleep."

I was still in a daze. I had only known that he was my grandfather for a day and yet I had known him all of my life. I had seen him almost every day and spoken to him and yet I had not known that which he did. We were of the same blood!

"Come, brother. Like you I have thoughts buzzing in my head like honeybees but we have to move him. I will take his shoulders and you take his legs."

I nodded. As I straightened his legs, I saw that he had broken his left one and bones stuck out from his flesh. The cold and death had congealed his blood but, as I picked him up, the blood stained my hands. It was as we lifted him that I spied the hammer. It must have been in his belt at the back. Falling on it would have broken his back. I reached down to pick it up. We had few enough tools and we could not sacrifice this one.

We managed to make it below the snow line before darkness fell. We folded his arms across his body as we had seen Christians do. We buried our dead hunched over their knees. It was in death as in birth that our dead went to the Otherworld. I was, despite the exertions, far from hungry. If I was hungry for anything it was for knowledge. He had been Edmund the thrall. I had not bothered with his story but I wished to know more. My mother had never spoken of her family. I had never asked. Now, as I looked at his body, I wanted to know all!

"Do you think our father killed his family?"

"Probably! Brother, you think too much. Put this from your head. We can do nothing about it now. If our mother had wished us to know his story then she would have told us."

Arne was a practical man and he was moving on. He was jarl yet something kept nagging at me, "Arne, the Norns have spun. We knew our threads and our mother's were entwined but now they are entwined with Edmund's and his actions."

He gave me a sharp look as he clutched his hammer of Thor, "You mean Leif Yellow Hair?"

I nodded, "Leif and his family came with us late at Larswick. We know them the least. You did not stand in a shield wall with him. When I stood watch on the drekar sailing through the night I remember Leif and his son. They spoke with others. What if he truly means to take the clan from you?"

Arne laughed but it was a nervous laugh, "Snorri, Butar, the others, they stand with me."

"Aye, they do but what of the incomers? What of those who were not there as long?"

He lay back with his hands beneath his head, "Speculation is idle. We will discover if this is a sinister plot when we reach our home." He was silent for a while, "We should name it. It is bad luck not to do so."

"Maevesfjörður. We honour our mother by naming it after her and she is the first to be buried there."

In the dark Arne said, "I like that name. If I am still jarl this time tomorrow then we shall so name it."

We reached Maevesfjörður by noon the next day. Edmund's body had stiffened and it was slightly easier to carry. When we reached the hall, we saw that the clan were gathered and they were interring someone in the ground close to our mother. They did not turn as we approached. Who had died?

It was Fótr who spied us. The clan was stood in silence. Fótr's voice rent the air like a crack of thunder. "Arne!"

We laid Edmund's body down and Arne said, "What is amiss? Whom do you bury?"

Snorri, nursing a bruised face, spoke, "It is Pridbjørn." He pointed to the bay. The knarr was gone. "Come, the two of you, I need to speak with you." He turned to the clan, "We have honoured our dead. We have a hall which needs to be built. I will speak with my nephews."

Gytha said, "Fótr, come with me. You can speak with your brothers later."

Snorri's tale made me shiver for I could hear the Norns and they were spinning. After we had departed Leif had gathered some of the other men who had recently come to us. After they had conspired they challenged Snorri about the leadership of the clan. My uncle had tried to be a peacemaker but it had come to blows. No weapons were drawn but the camp and the clan were divided. Only three families had supported Leif and he and those four had withdrawn to the beach. My uncle was a broken man for he had not anticipated what would happen next. In the night Leif and three other men had overpowered and then killed Pridbjørn as he slept on the knarr. Having taken some animals, the four families hoisted the sail and left the bay. Things could have been worse had not my ship's boys awoken and raised the alarm. Who knows what mischief the killers could have done?

Snorri shook his head, "I knew I was not meant to be jarl and now I wonder if I am fit to be a foster father."

Arne looked at me as he said, "My brother had it right. This is the Norns. We will find Leif and these murderers. We will have vengeance for Pridbjørn and his family but first, we make Maevesfjörður our home."

Snorri frowned, "Maevesfjörður?"

"Aye, my brother named it and as he found us this haven then let us honour him, and my mother, by its name."

We buried Edmund; there were now three graves in our cemetery and we had only just landed. I took it as a sign but I kept my thoughts to myself. We worked on the hall. This time we had my ship's boys as lookouts. They had all proved their worth. I had spoken with them and discovered, as I had expected, that the knarr had headed out to sea. Leif was seeking his own fjord.

It took more than a month for us to build our hall. In that time some of the women gave birth, Helga, Freja, and Gefn all had children. Lars Arneson, Elsa Siggisdotter and Snorri Padraigson were the first to be born on the island. That was significant and Gytha insisted on Arne making a blót so that they would have good lives. The three deaths we had suffered and the three births showed a symmetry. The Norns had been spinning. We had lost two men and a woman and gained two boys and a girl.

It was Tvímánuður and the days and nights were almost equal in length. Snorri had begun to come out of the dark place in which he had hidden. That was the work of Gytha. She had used their youngest son, Tostig, to force her husband to rejoin the clan. Gradually he became the man he had always been.

Our new settlement afforded us views over the sea as the sun set and the men had taken to sitting outside the hall to watch the sun set. We had cleared trees and prepared some soil. We were ready to plant our first crops. Some of the animals were carrying young and we would need to build a third hall for them. The trees we would hew would give us more ground for planting but that would have to wait until the next year. I was not looking forward to this type of work.

Arne and the others had been talking and I had been, largely, silent. As the sun became a sliver of red on the horizon Arne said, "You are quiet, brother. Speak. I would know that which is in your heart."

"Nothing, save the renegades have left us. We both know that this fjord will not support us for long. Already we are growing.

When Maren gives birth, we will increase our numbers again. Already other women are carrying new warriors. I should do as Gytha suggested. I should sail around the island see where there may be better places. We both know that others will come to this island. Finehair's tyranny ensures that. I should leave sooner rather than later. We know not what winter brings here so far north."

"Brother, the seas will be more dangerous now for we know that Leif is out there and he bears a grudge."

"And he sails a knarr. If I cannot outsail him with my snekke then I should take up farming." I looked at Fótr. He looked a forlorn figure. "Our little brother has said he would sail with me. I am happy for him to do so but, for this voyage, I think he should stay here with you."

"You are right and I can begin his training as a warrior. We have been remiss and that was our mother's fault. I will begin when you sail. It will take his mind from the disappointment of not sailing with Erik the Navigator."

Gytha waved me over as I left my brother, "This voyage is meant to be, Erik. Your journey does not end here in this land of ice and fire. I have dreamed. Look to the west. You, alone out of the clan, do not fear the ocean and Ran knows that. You are meant to find new lands. I have dreamed of the clan in a place which is green and filled with animals. I have dreamed of a land where food leaps from the earth. I have seen a land with things growing that I do not recognize and I have seen people who are not as we are."

"But I am young."

"And you have been touched by the sea. Ran favours you. I do not believe that even your father or Ulf North Star could have found this island as quickly as did you. I will await your return." She handed me a piece of material no larger than my hand. She had woven it. "In this are hairs from your mother. They contain part of her father too. They were both Christian but they are in the spirit world. I have added some of my hairs. The spell was a good one and it will protect you. Keep it close to your heart."

I slipped it beneath my kyrtle. Perhaps it was my imagination or I wished it so but my body felt warmer when the piece of cloth touched me. *Wyrd.*

Eidel Eidelsson had been growing as had the other elder ship's boy, Stig Folkmarsson. Both were happy to sail with me but their fathers now had land to farm and needed them. They were training to be warriors. I chose to take just four boys with me on the snekke. I would have gone with just two but they insisted upon accompanying me. The night before I left, I spoke with Fótr. I knew he was still grieving over our mother and finding it hard to deal with the news that Edmund had been his grandfather.

My brother was of an age with Dreng and Rek and yet they seemed so much older. My mother had kept him too close and for too long, "Fótr, the next time I sail the snekke then you shall be one of my ship's boys. Our mother kept you close for you were her youngest and she was loath to lose you. Arne will help to make you a warrior. You need those skills. I will teach you how to sail then you can choose the path to follow."

"But when you have sailed around the island what then? Will you not stay at home or just fish?"

"Perhaps but that is not the dream of Gytha. She has seen me somewhere which is verdant and green. Our new home is neither of those things. The Norns are still weaving our threads."

He nodded, "But what if you fall off the edge of the world?"

I knew that many of the clan felt as he did. They believed that we were on the edge of the world. Any further west would see us fall. "You know when the men sit at night and watch the sun go down?" He nodded. "We have yet to sail as far as we can see. I am happy to do so. My snekke is fast. When I see the edge of the sea I will turn around and come and tell the clan what I have found but that will not be this voyage. This voyage will see me return cold and weary but with the knowledge of where we are and our place in this land."

"Then I will try to learn how to be a warrior but I pray to the Allfather that you return here safe."

It was the winds decided which way we went. The wind was from the west and south. We headed north. I had prepared as best I could. We had barrels for oil, in case we found seals. We had fishing lines and nets. We had furs and seal skins. The snekke could hold a great deal. I took no mail. I did not take my sword. I had my bow, my spear and Raedwulf's dagger. We had travelled less than a mile when I saw another bay and a further mile saw us pass two fjords. The gods had sent us where we would find shelter. We had been meant to come here. The further north we sailed the less hospitable was the land. I saw ridges and mountains topped with snow. This was still late summer. These were not places in which we could settle. As the sun began to set, I sought a place to land. I had kept an accurate record of our travels using the hourglass and the compass. By my estimate, we had travelled a hundred miles in one day. That sort of speed could not last but I was happy for we had seen no smoke. There had been neither drekar nor houses. We had no neighbours. Leif had not come north.

We found a tiny south-facing beach. The arm of its bay created this strange feature. We could not have landed the drekar but the snekke just fitted. After dragging the boat above the high-water mark, I sent Dreng and Rek to find kindling while the other two were set the task of collecting shellfish. We had caught four fish on the voyage north and we would enjoy a fish stew. I collected some heathers and added it to a tiny part of the kindling we had brought. I lit a fire. Even though high summer was less than a month behind us, already there was a chill in the air. We would need fire. Dreng and Rek found some driftwood and some branches broken from the woods in a storm. The fire made us feel better. When we had the stew going then the smells made us much happier.

As we ate Halsten asked, "Captain, how big is this island?"

"That is what we will discover. I hope that we can circumnavigate it. In Norway, so I have heard, in the winter the seas freeze over. It is too early for that but I am hoping that soon the coast will turn westwards."

The next day saw the same winds and the same progress. When we camped for the night, I saw that the coast had turned west but, in the distance, I could see more land. This was a bay. The land had been relatively fertile. There were trees but it was north facing and there were mountains behind. So far I had seen nothing that was as verdant as Gytha's dreams.

"Tomorrow I intend to leave the coast and sail due west. I believe that the headland yonder will continue to head west. I think we have found the northern part of the island."

"Yet we have seen no one."

"That is not a surprise. Few settlers have reached this island."

Halsten was perceptive, "You wish to find a better land, do you not, Captain?"

"You are shipmates and I can speak the truth. Aye, for Gytha has planted a seed. I see a verdant land and not a rocky wilderness of ice and fire. I seek land with animals to hunt and fertile soil. I do not think that this is our home."

Halsten nodded, "But we are safe from the King of the Norse."

"We are."

The boys were nervous when we set off. Unlike Padraig and Aed they had not sailed the snekke beyond land. It had been different on the drekar. *'Njörðr'* was big and she was solid. Their families were aboard. I was confident. The wind had changed slightly and we had to tack for half of the distance. As we closed with the coast, I saw that I was right. The coast headed west. We had reached the island's northern shore. I almost cheered. The wind slowed us down so that when the coast turned south, I looked for somewhere to land and we found a river. Had this coast not been north facing then it would have been a good place for a home but I could see that crops would struggle to grow.

The sun had been hidden for the last day. It was only when it set that we had an accurate idea of our position. We found a beach as the sun set, its glow marking the west. There was driftwood to be had and we lit a fire and cooked the day's catch. So far I had seen nothing that suggested we could find or make a better home. The landing we had made must have been directed by the gods.

Dreng asked the question which was also in my head, "Where are those who came here first, Captain? We have seen no footprints on any of the beaches except our own."

"I know not. Perhaps this island is bigger than we first thought. I had thought it to be like Mann. I know now that cannot be true for we would have already reached our home. We will sail on and will look for their homes and their smoke."

Rek nodded as he tasted the stew, "Then Leif Yellow Hair must have sailed west and not east."

If Rek was right then it meant that we could still run into him.

For two more days, we edged west with winds which seemed determined to stop us discovering that part of the island. We sailed around a huge headland connected by a narrow neck of land and it was there that we first began to sail south. There was nothing to the west of us. That night, as we camped, I added to the map I had been making. The island was big. Yet most of it appeared to be mountainous. The smoke wreathed mountains dominated the island but I suspected they were closer to our home than this northern part. Soon, the winds which had hurt us would come to our aid and we would travel quicker. When we sailed, the next day, I saw that there was a huge bay before us. I say bay for, in the distance, I saw seabirds flocking. That suggested land to me.

Halsten said, "Captain, to the east I spy smoke."

I turned and saw that he was right. We had found other settlers. I headed south and east. I did not wish to approach too closely. My task was to find out who lived on the island and not make contact with them. We were a small sail and I hoped that we would not be seen. The sun chose that day to break through the wall of white clouds. Was that the Norns? Were they playing a trick with us? Whatever the reason I saw the turf houses in the small bay. Standing while Rek steered I stood on the gunwale and shaded my eyes. There were two ships. They had no masts. They could have been drekar or they could have been knarr. I knew not.

I returned to the steering board. I would go no closer but the fact that the settlement was west facing meant it would have more sun than our land shaded, as it was, by the mountain. They could grow crops there. I would mark that on my map. I would use some of the fish blood to mark it in red.

We sailed across what I now saw was a huge inlet. The birds had been flocking on the sea. As we passed where they had been, I saw that there was the carcass of a young whale. Sharks had eaten most of it but the floating remains had provided a feast for the birds. I was careful when I chose our campsite for the night for, as we neared the coast, I saw more smoke from the eastern part of the inlet. It was getting on to dark and I could not discern a ship but I pushed on a little further and we made a darkened landing on a strip of shingle. I estimated that we were at least five miles from the last smoke we had seen but I did not risk a fire. We ate the fish we had caught raw. There was no water nearby and so we drank from our skins. We were all colder than we had been on our voyage of discovery. The cold woke me. I made water and then roused the boys. We would make an early start.

"We need a fire tonight. I intend to find a campsite with water and wood. We may have a shorter voyage this day!"

That decision was fateful. The Norns were spinning. As we sailed with darkness to the west and a glow of light from the east, I felt the wind begin to change. The air felt colder. It was coming from the north. It helped us to travel faster. I kept the land to the east of us but stayed far enough away from the coast to run if I had to. As the sun rose, to the east of us, I spied smoke. Worse, I spied ships. We were less than half a mile from the coast and the sun, which had been hidden for so many days now broke over the smoke-wreathed mountain and bathed us in sunlight.

Rek shouted, "To the southeast, Captain. There is more smoke and I see ships!"

I was looking east and Rek south and east. There were two settlements. I spied not just houses but what appeared to be a hall. I saw ships tied to what looked like a quay and one had a mast and sail. It was a drekar. We had found where the first settlers had landed. I spied fields which had been tilled and cattle grazing. I put the steering board over. I could have approached and seen more but a tingling at the back of my neck told me to sail away as quickly as I could. The smoky mountain I had seen suggested that our new home was less than two days away. I turned to sail due south.

Dreng shouted, "Land ahead, Captain!"

I now saw that this was a huge west facing bay and I headed south and west to sail around the headland. I would give it plenty of sea room. I did not wish to fall foul of the rocks around the coast when I was just a couple of days from my home. I now had the news we needed. The best land was already occupied. What we had was as good as it was going to get.

The Norns were spinning. Halsten stood on the gunwale holding on to the stays while he peered at the land. His voice was urgent as he said, "Captain! A ship has put off from the shore. It is a drekar."

I glanced up and saw him shading his eyes against the sun. "Can you see her sides?"

There was a pause and then he said, "Aye, Captain! They are lined with shields!"

The settlers were coming to chase away or capture the intruder. We were in danger.

Chapter 4

It was not only us who were in danger. The drekar following us would not know of Maevesfjörður. If I headed home then they would know they had neighbours. They might well wish us harm. The sky was cloudless. I said, "Rek, take out the hourglass. Halsten, take the compass and mark the sun." I stood to allow them to do so.

Sven asked, "What is it you intend, Captain?"

I pointed to the south and west, "I intend to head into the empty sea and hope that they fear the unknown more than we do!"

I saw my ship's boy clutch at his hammer of Thor. I put the steering board over and we leapt forward across the almost blue sea. The gods had sent the wind for a purpose. It was to help us escape but escape where? What lay beyond the horizon? "Halsten, when you have marked the sun take my map and use the charcoal to mark our position." I stood again so that he could take the chart from the small chest by the steering board. He looked at the incomplete chart. There was a cross which marked Maevesfjörður and between it and where we were was unmarked. Taking the charcoal, he put a circle off the coast. "Mark the two settlements. Make the sign of a sword."

He did so and replaced the chart. I sat and smiled, "Well boys we had better prepare for a sea chase. Run out the fishing lines. Sven, rig the spare sail forrard. We can take it in turns to shelter from the sun and, if it rains, we can use it to collect rainwater."

"But captain, there is not a cloud in the sky!"

"Aye, Rek, but we know not how persistent the drekar will be. Let us assume the worst and that way we will not be disappointed."

I think that the drekar intended at first to try to catch us quickly. They ran out the oars. I had Dreng watching them. When he reported the oars, I knew that they meant us harm. Why else try to close with us? "Let me know their rate of approach."

We were heading due south. I would not head east until they were out of sight. The two choices left to me would be to head south or west.

"They are eight lengths behind us, Captain."

I nodded.

When he said, "Five lengths!" then I made my fateful decision. I should have known the Norns were spinning for, as I put the steering board over to head south and west, I saw a cloud appear from the west. It was a solitary cloud but it was a cloud nonetheless. As soon as I put the board over, we leapt away from the drekar. I glanced astern and saw that we had taken them by surprise. We gained a length and I knew that the rowers would be tiring. By the time they had altered course to follow us, we had a seven-length lead. Dreng's chant became repetitive. The gap remained at seven lengths. I saw that we were heading into a cloudbank. The clouds had grown and changed from white to black. The seas began to rise.

"They have turned!"

"Good. We will stay on this course until they are over the horizon and then we will turn."

The first drops of rain fell. They became heavier. The wind began to swing to come from the north and west. I turned to head south. The drekar was still in sight but it was heading away from us. "Reef the sail!" I gave the order just in time. Standing I said, "Put the compass and hourglass in the chest!" We would not be needing them until the sky cleared and that would not be for some time. The Norns were spinning and the storm hit us. We had to let the wind take us. The sky all around became black and the seas rose to make cliffs and troughs. *'Jötnar'* was a hardy little snekke but she was tested to the limit that day. Halsten took my sealskin cape from the chest by the mainmast and put it about my shoulders. I was already soaked but this would keep me warmer. Already the sail we had rigged at the prow had filled with rainwater and Dreng and Rek poured it into a barrel. Time had no meaning. My face, hair, and beard became rimed with salt. My hardy crew clung on for dear life. The sun must have passed its zenith but we knew not. We ploughed on south with the wind pushing us into the unknown.

Sven brought me some water. My mouth was dry. "Do you want food, Captain?"

I shook my head, "You boys eat. *'Jötnar'* and I are as one, I will eat when the storm abates." I could feel the seas weakening and I suspected the wind was too but I could not relinquish my hold on the steering board. It went from daylight to darkness without us even realising. The black clouds hid the sun from us. As the rain ceased and the wind lessened the motion of the ship became easier. I did not dare risk raising the sail for there were no stars to be seen. We were in the middle of the ocean. I had lost all sense of the direction of the wind. I would trust to the gods and let the wind take us where it would. When we saw the sun, we could begin to work out our position. I was just aware that the wind had not turned for some time as I had not had to move the steering board for hours. As the boys fell asleep, I stayed awake. I had to. Perhaps I dreamed with my eyes open or perhaps it was a trick of the Norns but I saw my father. His left arm was whole once more. He stood at the prow and pointed to steerboard. If our course was the same then that would be the west. He mouthed something but I could not hear. I rubbed my salt rimmed eyes and he was gone. The Norns were playing tricks with me.

When dawn broke it told me that east lay to larboard. We were still travelling south. "Wake! It is time to wake!" The seas were easier but the wind still blew strongly. When the four of them woke they touched and then kissed their Hammer of Thor. They made water and then Halsten came to me.

"Captain, you need to stand."

I nodded. "Keep her on this course." I stood and every joint and bone ached. I stretched. It was then I realised that I had to make water. With the wind behind me, I made water over the steerboard side. I had just finished and was pulling up my breeks when I heard and felt something scrape off the bow. I saw a piece of driftwood sliding down the side. Holding the backstay, I leaned over and picked it out. The wood was sodden. It had been in the sea for a long time. I felt a tingle as I picked it up. Turning I saw that there were some faded runes marked upon it. I ran my finger over them. It was the piece of wood I had seen when I had been a child on Orkneyjar. *Wyrd*!

Across the Seas

ᛒᛏᚱᛁᚱ

"What is it, Captain?"

"It is a message from the Allfather." I threw the wood into the sea and I watched. It began to drift west. It went in the direction my father had pointed. I was to travel to the west.

"Why did you throw it away, Captain?"

I took my place at the steering board and I told them the story of the wood and the dream. "I believe that there is land to the west and south of us. When I touched the sea, it was warmer. The gods or the Norns, I know not which, sent the storm. I know my destiny. Now we sail home." I pointed to larboard. "Our home lies in that direction. Take out the compass and hourglass. Fetch me the chart and food. I am hungry. Halsten you can steer until I am refreshed!"

We sailed north and east for two days. We sailed across empty seas and the sun only showed herself now and again. Had it not been for the smoke from the mountain we might have missed the island altogether but knowing that the mountain lay to the west of Maevesfjörður helped. I headed due north for the mountain. We had to tack back and forth for the wind came from the north and west but knowing that our home was close helped us. Our map was incomplete. We had no idea what lay between us and the drekar's stronghold. I had little idea of distance save that the smoky mountain looked down on us both. I would add a line when we landed but it would be pure conjecture.

When we spied the coast, we sailed north and east. The going was easier. The wind helped a little. Sven liked his food, "Captain I am looking forward to meat. I like fish but I have had enough."

I shook my head, "I fear that so long as we live on this island of ice and fire, we will have little meat. When the last of the salted meat is gone seal and whale will be the nearest food we have to meat."

"Could we not go home to the land we left? Larswick might have had enemies but we were well fed." Dreng also liked his food.

"I wish to go further west."

Halsten said, "The driftwood?"

"Aye, Halsten. It points us there. I will speak with Gytha. She is wise. I cannot believe that we left our home to find this barren rock. It is like Føroyar. It is a halt on our journey west. I feel it in my bones."

We spied the smoke from Maevesfjörður and I gave a silent prayer of thanks to Ran. He had watched over us. As we began to edge around the bay to the beach, I saw that the drekar was tied up in the first bay. There was a quay. It was crudely built but it would do. We would not have to ground the snekke. I never liked dragging a ship on to sand. There could be buried rocks just waiting to tear a hole in a hull. We had timber but not the right timber to build a ship.

Arne, Fótr, Siggi and Snorri Long Fingers strode down from the two halls to greet us. The relief on my brother's face was clear to all. Nudging towards the stern of *'Njörðr'* I said, "I thank the four of you. I would sail with you any time. You are a good crew."

Halsten nodded, "And I speak for us all. We would follow you beyond the Unending Sea."

Fótr caught the rope Dreng threw and wrapped it around one of the mooring posts. I smiled for he had to have practised that. He was trying to impress me. The boys let me land and the hug which Arne gave me showed me that he had feared he had seen me for the last time. "You had us worried."

I nodded, "We were tested. I have much to say but I would speak with Gytha too."

Snorri frowned, "Then there is more to tell than just a sea voyage."

"Aye uncle and I believe that your wife expected this."
Turning to the boys I said, "When the snekke is secured go and see your families. They will rejoice to see you and that is good."

As we walked to the halls, I could smell bread being baked. They had finished the oven. I saw women making cheese. There were fish drying and the fields had been sown with oat and barley. None of us yet knew if they would grow. I saw seal skins which were drying and there were small pieces of timber drying. They would be to keep us warm over the winter. Already there was a chill to the air and yet we had not reached Samhain.

Gytha was waiting for us at the knarr hall. I smelled ale. They had brewed beer. I could not help the smile which broke across my face. Gytha hugged me and kissed my cheek, "Although I knew you would return, for I dreamed it, I am overjoyed that you are here. Come, let us get in out of this wind." Inside there was a warm glow from the fire. Tostig appeared and handed her two horns of ale. She handed one to me and took the other, "Erik the Navigator!"

A crude table and benches had been made. The men had simply split logs and used wooden nails to bind them. I sat down and felt as though I was in a palace. This was luxury! I drank the ale and drained the horn. Arne shook his head, "Do not be so profligate, brother. We cannot produce great quantities until we have harvested a crop."

I nodded, "I am sorry but this tasted as though Odin himself had brewed it."

Gytha spread her hands, "Arne might be Jarl of this clan but you are the clan's hope for the future. Speak."

I left nothing out. I told them exactly what I had seen as I had circumnavigated the island. I spoke of the settlements I had seen and the drekar which had attacked us. When I told them of the wood I had found and how I had seen it before I saw that I surprised even Gytha. When I had finished my tale, she touched my hand, "I knew before you spoke that you had been chosen. The wood with the runes confirms it." She went to the fire and brought a piece of charcoal. "Write them here on the table."

When I had done so she studied them. "This time they were faded and I confess I am not sure if I have copied them aright. Perhaps this is how I remembered them."

She smiled, "It is a man's name although I have not heard of him. It could be Balik or Barik. It matters not. It is a message."

I was excited and I could see that Snorri was too. Arne just looked confused. "I do not understand this. What does it mean?" He looked at Gytha.

"It is simple and Erik knows the meaning better than any but the words from a volva may have more significance than that of a younger brother." It was criticism and I saw Arne flush.

Siggi grinned. "Cuz you cannot win an argument with a volva." His mother glared at her son. He might be a man grown but he was still her son. Abashed he sat back.

"What the words mean are that the clan has not yet finished its journey. We will, someday, head west."

Arne shook his head, "We have barely scratched the surface of this land. True it is not the home we hoped but we need to give the land a chance."

She smiled, "Of course but the Norns have yet to finish their web. Erik's thread and the piece of driftwood are combined."

"And there is one thing more. The spirit of our father came to me. His arm was whole and he pointed to the west."

Arne almost recoiled when I told him. He clutched his hammer. Gytha just smiled knowingly. To her that was confirmation of the direction we must take.

Arne sighed and nodded, "From what you say these settlements must be a couple of days west of us."

"That would be my estimate."

"They may not wish us harm and they might not know that we are here."

Siggi said, "You forget Leif Yellow Hair. If he did not sail east then he must have gone west. He would know. He tried to take animals. We now know that animals are more valuable than gold here. If Erik saw none on his travels then there are none on the island."

"My son is right. "If we cannot grow crops to make bread then we rely on that which our animals produce." Gytha's words were like a crack of thunder. They were ominous.

The weather began to change soon after I returned to the longhouses. There was frenetic activity. Men hunted or fished. After we had repaired it Aed and Padraig took the snekke out to catch the larger fish in the fjord. We made fish traps for the fjord too. Men went around the fjord to hunt the seals. They camped across from our home and rendered down the fat. The meat was salted and put into barrels. The snekke would be used as a ferry. We cursed Leif Yellow Hair for had we had the knarr we could have brought them all back in one trip. It was too difficult to use *'Njörðr'*. We still kept eight men at the longhouses. My news had been a warning that there could still be danger.

More babies were born. Maren gave birth to a girl, Ada. The clan was growing but that meant there were more who were vulnerable to both the climate and enemies. We thought we had escaped them but perhaps we were wrong.

It was Haustmánuður when the weather changed dramatically. We had had rain almost every day but it changed to sleet and then snow. Arne brought back the seal hunters and their booty. We had plenty of seal meat and shark meat. I hoped that we would be able to continue to be able to fish during winter. Gytha had organised a system of rationing. She had told Arne that it was better to have small quantities of beer and bread all through winter rather than enough to satisfy Butar and then none. The days became much shorter. In some ways, it was fortunate that Leif and the other families had left for there was just enough room for the clan in the two longhouses. We were cosy but the presence of so many people meant that the buildings soon warmed up and remained cosy. The difficulty was in living so close to our neighbours. Fótr slept on my sleeping platform. There were few single men now. Couples and their children shared beds. It meant they were warmer. Fótr was still young. Gytha did what she could but he was still lost. The memory of our mother's death so close to him had had an effect. It had made him younger than his years. I took to telling him stories to send him to sleep. I made some of them up. I remembered some of the stories my father and mother had told us. When I had stood watches on the drekar I had occupied my mind by making them up. Some were not necessarily made up. I told him the story of the Dragonheart and of Hrolfr the Horseman. He loved the tale of the sword which was touched by the gods and the story of Göngu-Hrólfr Rognvaldson falling to the bottom of the sea and surviving. It brought us closer together.

Arne, Siggi and I were still blood brothers. We had sworn an oath on the blade of Raedwulf but they had their own families now. Our brotherhood was for times of war. We shared secrets and we shared memories. We had all become warriors together. I trusted all of the warriors in the clan but the two with whom I would face certain death were Siggi and Arne. The three of us spoke each day. Arne had come around to the idea that we might have to sail west. As ever Siggi asked pertinent questions. At the end of each debate, we ended at the same place. Until the weather improved, we could do nothing and the change in weather might be many moons away.

By Gormánuður our land lay beneath a sea of snow. All was white. The mountain still spouted steam and Arne and I had told the men of the steaming geysers we had seen. Gytha and her volvas, guarded by warriors had gone there to see them. Gytha said they were sent by the Mother and were a good thing. I was not sure for one night in early Gormánuður, we felt the earth shake. It was enough to wake us. Gytha explained it away by saying it was the Mother stretching her limbs. The smoking mountain was a threat and no words of our volva could lessen that threat.

When we returned to our beds Fótr said, "Are we in danger, Erik?"

I was honest with my younger brother, "We may be, despite what Gytha says. I have put my hand in that water and it is hot enough to cook with. Something heats that water and this is not named the land of ice and fire for nothing."

"You wish to leave."

"Aye I do but I serve the clan and I bow to the will of the people. Gytha and I believe that there is a land to the west and it is not a land of ice and fire. It is a warm land which is fertile."

"Then I would go there for this land has brought us death and danger. I can never be happy here."

Fótr and I appeared to be the only ones who felt that way. We were warm and we had food. We were better off than in the land threatened by the Dane, Mercians and the Norse King. The hardship of no grain would be gone when the snow disappeared and the crops grew. We had not even heard wolves here. This land now pleased the clan. The life we had in winter was no different than it had been on Orkneyjar. But I was restless. That was ironical really for it had been my suggestion that we came here. Now I saw that the Norns had planted the idea of sailing west when I had found the driftwood all those years ago.

By Mörsugur we had almost no daylight and the great lumps of ice which had gathered along our coast and fjord began to increase and even join together. The sea did not freeze but ships could not move without fear of striking floating ice. We saw lights in the northern skies which terrified some. Gytha explained them as the gods giving us light. I was not convinced but I remained silent.

I had Fótr carve some fish hooks from seal bone. When we had been struck by the storm, we had lost most of the ones we had overboard. We had had other things to think about. I used the time to improve the charts I had. I could only estimate the distance we had travelled when the drekar pursued us but it gave me some idea of what lay to the south and west of the island. Nothing. There had been a storm and so we had seen no birds. The waves had been high and the troughs deep. That normally meant deeper water. I left enough space on my map to add more. The mark I made showed me that it was a day's sailing southwest of the island.

It was Þorri when we lost our first warrior. Marteinn Hunter decided to go and hunt seals. He took with him his son, Kalman. His son was just ten summers old. They chose a day when the snow was not falling and the air was cold. Kalman came back alone and his kyrtle was covered in blood. "My father has been attacked!"

Arne wasted no time. "Get your weapons! Attacked by who?"

"A great white bear. It rose from the ground and just swiped him with a paw. It took half his face with the one blow."

I had my boots and fur on already. I donned my fur hat and grabbed my spear. The sun had been up but an hour and yet it would soon begin to set. We had to hurry. Arne led ten of us from the longhouse. We followed Kalman but the footprints were clear to see. We were more than a mile from the hall when we heard the animal as it chewed on Kalman's father. We could not see it as there was a ridge of snow and the land dropped down to the frozen fjord. Arne said, "Stay here!" We all knew that Marteinn was dead and his son had seen enough already. "Spread out!"

I was on one side of Arne and Siggi the other. We were in the centre. As we crested the rise, we were greeted by a sight which still terrifies me at night. Twenty paces from us there was a huge white bear. I had never seen such a large creature. Marteinn was unrecognisable as a man. The white fur of the animal was covered in his blood. I had seen bears before but they had been the same size as a man. This one was more than twice the size of a man. It saw us. Turning, it rose onto its hind legs. It towered over us. Dropping to all fours, it began to run towards us. It moved so quickly that I was almost mesmerized. Luckily Arne was not. "Attack!"

We ran at the beast. I pulled back my arm. Arne reached it first and he rammed his spear into the animal's chest. The bear swiped it and Arne away dismissively. Siggi lunged at its neck and I struck at its eye. Butar on one side and Finn on the other rammed their spears into its side. Asbjorn had managed to get around its back and he stabbed it there. The rest of the warriors, emboldened by our success, also stabbed it. The beast flailed but blood was pouring from the animal and it was weakening. As it tumbled to the ground, I turned to see how Arne fared.

My brother was seated. His sealskin cape had been ripped and the fur beneath torn. He gave me a wry smile and shook his head, "That was foolish of me! Next time we meet such a beast, brother, remind me of this day!"

When we reached the animal, it was dead. Arne had recovered his composure. "It is getting on to dark. Siggi and Erik, wrap Marteinn's body in his cloak. We will take him home. The rest of you let us see if the rest of us can drag this beast back to the longhouse!"

The bear had made a mess of Marteinn. We collected the parts which had been torn off and wrapped them up. He was no weight at all. After ensuring that his son would see nothing, we carried him back over the rise. Kalman awaited us, "I am sorry, Kalman, but your father is dead. The animal which did this has been slain. He is avenged but you are now the warrior in the family."

He nodded, "I will help carry my father."

When we reached the longhouse Marteinn's wife and the rest of his family were waiting. The cloaked body told them all that there was to know. Gytha, wrapped in furs, took charge. "The ground is too hard to bury him and we would not have the foxes disturb the dead. We will burn him." It was the right thing to do but it was expensive. We would be using precious timber and seal oil to do so. None would disagree. We had to honour the dead. By the time the bear was brought back we had built a pyre and soaked his body in seal oil. We used less wood than we might normally have. When Gytha saw the beast she said, "Take the heart, liver, and kidneys from the animal. They can be burned with the hunter." It seemed right. The clan gathered as in the darkness, we lit the pyre and watched our first warrior die.

Even though the night was getting painfully cold we skinned and butchered the bear by the light of the funeral pyre. This was meat. It would be the first meat we had had in a long time. Sad though we were at the death this was not to be wasted. The Norns had spun their web and Marteinn's death might help us survive a little longer in this bleak land. When the fur was skinned, the men all made water on it. The process of preserving it had begun. I was one of the last to enter the longhouse as the fire died. For me, this was the final sign that this land was not for us. No matter what the others thought I would look for a new land as soon as I could.

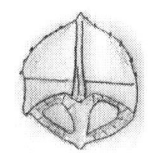

Chapter 5

The death of Marteinn hung over our people like a pall. His wife and family, not to mention the clan, had lost the best hunter in the settlement. We were confined to our halls and had to endure freezing winds and blizzards. There was no beer left and we had not been able to use the bread ovens for some time. A couple of the animals died. Although we ate them and were able to use their skins their loss was something the clan could not afford. We now had the bull and one cow left as well as two sheep, a boar, and a sow. It was not enough. Our cheese production would suffer. There were arguments and there were fights. Arne and Snorri prevented them from escalating but they were a warning. It was the end of Gói by the time the weather had improved enough for us to venture forth. The snow began to melt and the fjord was no longer frozen. Perhaps it had thawed some time ago but the weight of snow outside had prevented us from moving.

Arne decided to use some of the precious barley we had left to make bread and to brew a batch of beer. He and the farmers then went to examine the fields where we had planted the crops. The animals were let out to try to find grazing. There was precious little. I went with Fótr and the ship's boys to examine the drekar and the snekke. The drekar had fared better than the snekke. The snekke had suffered damage. Some of the strakes had sprung. We sailed her around to the beach and dragged her above the high-water mark. We had already taken her mast down and we turned her over. We had one barrel of pine tar. The bread ovens had been lit to begin the baking process. While it was still heating, we warmed the pine tar. While it heated, we took the opportunity of scraping the hull and removing the weed and creatures which had attached themselves to the wood. When darkness fell, we applied the pine tar. We would need to find more pine trees to make another batch. I recalled there being some on the lower slopes of the fire mountain. Finally, we pegged out an old sail to cover the snekke. Who knew what weather the night would bring?

A couple of weeks later and the snow had completely gone, the days and the nights were becoming the same length and we had seen signs of growth in the fields. I was desperate to collect pine tar but Arne forbade me. We had to hunt seals and we needed to fish. The clan had had a lean winter. We had to fill our larders.

This time we took the drekar to hunt. We rowed it the short distance across the fjord to the sands and rocks where the seals gathered. Arne was no fool. He knew that once we had decimated the colony then they would find another home. We would need to find another colony.

It was a good hunt. As we skinned the seals I spoke with my brother and Siggi, "I wish to sail to find another and better land."

"We have yet to give this one a chance, brother. We lost only one man over the winter."

"And that is why I would take the snekke. If I take Fótr and three of the ship's boys I leave enough here to protect the clan and to provide for the families."

Siggi nodded, "I think it is a good idea. We came here to escape our enemies and we have but there might be a better place. My mother is convinced that Erik is destined to find a new land. She has dreamed it."

Arne was a sceptic. He was more like my father than me. "No disrespect to the volva but she thought that coming here was a good idea too."

"Arne, so did I and Gytha never saw this as the end of the voyage. It was a stopping off point. Føroyar could have been our home but we moved on."

"The difference is that we knew there was a land here. We know not what lies to the west."

"Until someone sailed here then this was hidden. That is why I am happy to sail across the Unending Sea. I would be the one to find a new world."

His silence told me that he would let me go. He was stiff-necked and did not like to be seen to be defeated. When next I broached the subject, he would not refuse. First, we had seal oil to barrel and flesh to preserve. We had more trees to hew and fields to prepare. We planted a second, summer crop of barley and a crop of oats. The first crop was not as successful as we might have hoped but we would have enough for bread and some beer. All of this meant that it was some time before I was able to go with Fótr and Halsten to collect the pine tar. We took food with us as we would have to camp out. Halsten was a youth now and would soon be able to take an oar on the drekar. Fótr had his sling and the two of them, as we trekked up the lower slope of the mountain, were able to bring down a couple of birds. We would have hot food.

When we reached the trees, I walked to the edge of the woods. I could see across the bay. There was no sign of settlements there. I knew that the ones I had seen were further west. I spied no ships and so I had the other two light a fire. I had them light it on a flat rock which was at a slight angle. We would cook the birds and then we would render down the pine.

I chose a smallish pine tree and cut it down. Then the three of us began to dig the roots and the stump. I chopped it up into the smallest pieces I could. It took some time and the birds were cooked by the time we had cut half of the stump and some of the roots. I set the other two to collect as many rocks as they could. We were lucky. The mountain had many and they were hard. This was perfect for what we intended. I chopped at the roots. The ones we had removed I piled at the side. When they had the rocks, they gathered all the pine cones. I began to make the kiln. I piled the rocks around the fire. I packed soil in the gaps as I did so. When it was high enough, I finished chopping the stump and the roots. We put the pine cones in the bottom of the kiln and added kindling. When the fire took hold, we put the stump and roots on the top and then covered the top of the kiln with the larger, fatter stones. I used more soil and then we added a second layer of stones. That done we waited. It would take all day for the wood to be burned and the tar to be released. I had left a channel and lined it with a piece of leather. It led to the barrel we placed below it. As the tar was made it would trickle and settle in the bottom of the barrel. We ate.

"So Halsten, do you wish to be a sailor or a warrior?"

He smiled, "Are you reading my thoughts, Erik the Navigator?"

"No, but I saw that you brought your sword. That is a sign."

"I like sailing. I would happily steer but when Marteinn was killed I realized that if my father was killed, I would have to be the one to care for the family. I am no farmer. That means I would have to raid."

"And that means fighting those who are on this island. There are few of us. That would mean a blood feud."

"I do not think it will come to that yet and I have time to grow but I can see a day when this island has many more people and we will have to fight to keep what we have or to take what we need."

He was right and, for me, that was confirmation that I needed to find a better land. I did not sleep all the way through the night. I kept waking to check that the pine tar was flowing. I should have had the others help me but I did not mind. The last time I woke it was before dawn. The tar was down to a trickle and the barrel was three-quarters full. I was content, I had made enough to coat the whole of the drekar if I used it judiciously. As we had coated it before we left Larswick it would only need application if we sprung a strake. There were still bones and some flesh left from the birds. I put them and some water in the pot we had brought. The top of the kiln was hot and so I put the improvised stew there to warm. By the time dawn came, we would have a broth to sustain us for the journey the three miles or so to Maevesfjörður.

When the sun rose, the others woke and I saw that the tar had ceased to flow. I sealed the barrel. We would take the tree I had hewn down the mountain too. I had cut it in two and it was manageable. The smaller branches had been used for kindling. We ate and then I went to make water. I know not why I chose to go to the edge of the treeline but I did. As I was pulling up my breeks, I spied movement to the west. There should not have been movement. I stared at the spot I had seen the movement. Perhaps there were animals and this was a sign that we could hunt. Then I saw a ray of early morning sunlight glint off metal. It was men. There were warriors. They were heading for our halls. The pine tar and timber were forgotten. I ran back to the others. "Take your weapons and leave all else. There are warriors heading for Maevesfjörður."

I grabbed my bow and the wood axe and began to run. My mind was racing and calculating as I did so. We would be faster than the warriors for they had to climb up the slope through trees. We were running across open land heading downhill. We would get to Maevesfjörður before they did. As I saw the smoke from our bread oven rising in the sky, I wondered who these warriors were. The answer came before I had taken four more steps. Leif Yellow Hair. We had animals and we had women. Whoever lived on the other side of the island would need both of those and Leif wanted some sort of vengeance.

As we neared Maevesfjörður I shouted, "Alarm! Arm! Alarm! Arm!"

Men looked up from the fields and then ran back to the hall. The fact that three of us were running told them that this was urgent. I wondered if I would have the time to don my mail. I had not used my sword for such a long time that I was not even certain that it was still sharp. I stopped to speak with Arne, Snorri, and Siggi. The rest of the men were gathering weapons, donning helmets and mail while their families went to the drekar to get the shields.

"What is it, brother?"

I was out of breath and I pointed to the west, "Armed warriors are heading here. I know not the numbers!"

"Get your sword." He turned, "Enemies attack us. Men, we form a shield wall. Boys get your slings."

As I ran into the longhouse to find my chest, I saw Gytha, Helga and the other women who fought heading outside with swords and axes. Gefn took the wood axe I still carried, "I will take that, Erik!"

I donned my helmet and took out my sword. I was about to don Karl the Lame's byrnie when I heard a shout from Arne, "They come! Shield wall!"

I had no time for my mail. I still had my bow and ten arrows which could be used for war. As I emerged, I saw Fótr running towards me with my shield. We had fewer men than we would have liked. I think the attackers would outnumber us. There were eight youths such as Halsten. Eidel, Sven and Stig and then seven boys with slings. I saw that Arne had organized a shield wall as I approached, he shouted, "Those with bows skirmish line with the slingers."

There were seven archers amongst us. I dropped my shield behind Faramir and Folkman. They had no mail and were in the second rank. The front rank had our best warriors. Siggi and Snorri flanked my brother and they were flanked by Butar, Finn, and Asbjorn along with Dreng's father Ebbe, and Rek's father, Rether. Arne had picked the highest point in Maevesfjörður. The enemy were four hundred paces from us and racing across our newly sown fields. There were more than forty of them. I recognized Leif Yellow Hair and his son. The others looked like Danes. I had the best bow for mine was yew. I nocked an arrow. The other nine were in my belt. We would not release as one. That was not our way. We all knew our own weapons and our own ability. The same was true of the slingers. Fótr stood by me and he whirled his sling. I knew how good he was for he had brought down a bird with his first stone when we had collected the tar.

The enemy did not falter and that was a mistake. They did not form up and make a shield wall or a wedge. They would not only be tired but also lack protection from the shields of others. I saw that ten had mail. The rest had leather. Not all had helmets. Our front rank was made up of men who each had helmets and mail. I saw that they had archers. One stopped to send an arrow at us. It was wasted for it fell woefully short. I said, to the others, "The first flights are for their bowman but conserve your arrows and stones." We were vulnerable to their missiles and they only had six men with bows,

I tracked the archer who had released and saw that, as they had neither shield nor mail, they were faster and moved ahead of the spearmen. We had an advantage for we had height. I pulled back on the bow and sent it at the archer who also stopped to send an arrow. I watched his arrow. It landed thirty paces from me. He was looking up when my arrow hit his forehead and he fell dead. Those behind me cheered. On such tiny events are fates decided. Their archers began to release and they fell short. My next arrow hit another archer in the shoulder. As they moved up the slope, they had to endure the rain of seven arrows and the

Across the Seas

stones of our slingers. It was an uneven contest. The four enemy archers were struck. Three of them were wounded. One had been hit by a stone in the head and I saw him rise and start to stumble down the slope. As he did so an arrow hit him in the back.

Their spears and swords were now in range. We did not have the arrows to penetrate mail. We aimed at faces if we could, and those without mail byrnies. I aimed at one in the front rank. I sent my arrow towards his head. He brought up his shield and blocked the blow. I nocked another arrow and he moved a little closer. Peering over his shield he saw me aiming. As his shield came up, I sent my arrow into his thigh. He tumbled to the ground and I nocked another arrow.

They were now less than forty paces from us. I heard Arne shout, "Slingers and bowmen behind the rear rank!"

Fótr slung his stone and it struck the spearman I had hit in the leg. He went down as the stone hit his cheek and he stayed down. I saw a Dane with mail. He had a war axe and, seeing our archers and slingers fall back, he turned to encourage the others. I had an arrow nocked and, as he turned, sent it into his face. He was thrown back so hard that he knocked down the next two men.

Arne shouted, "Erik! Back!"

I ran. I saw that the women with weapons had left us space. The boy slingers were spread out along the side. I stood behind my shield, which lay on the ground, but nocked another arrow. I sent it into the air. It was a blind strike but I hoped it would fall into them. Dropping my bow, I slung my shield on my arm and drew my sword. I heard the rattle of stones on mail and helmets.

Arne shouted, "Now!" Our front two ranks leaned forward and I put my shield in the middle of Faramir's back. Arne had prepared well and we barely moved. I heard swords clashing. Then Folkman moved to his right. The enemy warriors were trying to outflank us. I stepped next to him and saw that I faced Leif Yellow Hair. His son, Wiglaf, was already engaged and he looked down in horror as Folkman sliced his sword across his middle. His guts spilt like a pail of red worms. Leif had mail and, when he saw his son die and me before him, I think he went berserk. He brought his sword from on high to take off my head. I held up my shield and felt my arm shiver as the mighty blow hit me. It was so hard that I had to take a step backward. He punched with his shield at my head. I saw it in time and although I moved my head out of the way he hit my shoulder and knocked me to the ground.

This was no longer an organized battle. There was no one to support me. Leif and I fought alone while the clan battled our foes. As I fell, I heard a cry of triumph. I hit the ground. Leif had mail on his body but not on his legs. I hacked sideways with my sword. He was moving forward and while my sword did not penetrate the seal skin it hurt him as it cracked into his shin and it tripped him. His movement accentuated his fall and he fell over me. I leapt to my feet and, as he lay prostrate on the ground, I rammed my sword under his arm. The tip came out of his neck.

Helga shouted, "Erik, behind you!"

My sword was stuck in the body of my enemy. I whirled as Sigismund the Sour, another who had left our clan, ran at me with an axe. I drew Raedwulf's dagger and all that I could do was to angle the shield. The blow caught the edge and the metal boss. It tore the shield from me. I grabbed Sigismund's sword hand and, as he fell, drove the dagger into his eye. When it struck his brain, he went stiff and fell. Throwing his body from me I looked up and saw that, although we were winning, we had men down. Butar Beer Belly was desperately trying to stem the flow of blood from his thigh. I saw my bow and picked it up. I still had arrows left. There was no honour in what I did but this was war! The clan was at stake. I walked close to where warriors fought and at a distance of two paces sent my last arrows into skulls. Each one caused death and that ended the battle. We outnumbered them and, as they tried to flee, two or three fell upon them and hacked and butchered them. Fótr and the slingers took their knives to slice and hack legs. Gytha and the women were like Valkyries as they slaughtered the wounded. In the distance, I saw two of their men as they hurried west. They would escape but the rest would not.

I ran to Leif and took my sword from his body. I hurried down the slope. I found one of the archers who had been hit by one of my arrows and then hit by a stone. I put my sword to his throat for I saw that, although groggy, he still lived. "You are a dead man but the choice of death lies in your own hands. I can give you a warrior's death with your dagger in your hand or we can give you the blood eagle!" The latter was a threat for I had never seen the blood eagle.

The threat worked, "A warrior's death!"

"Why did you risk all?"

"Our cattle died this winter and Leif Yellow Hair told us that you had animals and women."

"You are Danes?"

"Our jarl is Hakon Long Memory. His brother led this raid. You promised me a warrior's death!"

With my left hand, I took his dagger and handed it to him, "I will see you in Valhalla." As soon as his fingers gripped the blade, I sank my sword into his throat.

I stood and looked up the slope. The wives and daughters who had lost husbands were now kneeling next to their bodies. I saw that both Arne and Siggi, as well as his father, had survived but I did not see some other warriors who had fought with my father. I took off my helmet and sheathed my sword. As I walked up the slope Snorri and Arne came towards me.

"What did he say?"

"That our past has come back to haunt us. The leader who was slain…"

Arne smiled, "By you. Thank you, brother."

I nodded, "By me, was the brother of Hakon Long Memory."

Snorri frowned, "What are they doing here? Are they seeking us?"

"The archer told me all that he knew, uncle. Their animals died and Leif Yellow Hair told them of ours."

Arne knew our priorities, "We can debate all of that later. First, we have our own men to bury and then dispose of the enemy dead."

"Strip them of all their weapons and feed them to the sea. It is all that they deserve." He shook his head, "I have lost three shield brothers this day, Butar, Finn, and Asbjorn are in Valhalla."

I had known those three all of my life. Now only Snorri remained of those who had first followed my father. Our decision to come to the land of ice and fire now looked to be a bad one. Was my decision to find another home equally bad?

In all, we had lost ten warriors. One was Kalman Peacemaker. He had brought with him, good men. He had supported my brother. I feared that his death would weaken the resolve of the men who had followed him; men like Æimundr Loud Voice and Mikel the Follower. I saw Rek and Dreng. They were kneeling next to the bodies of their fathers. Ebbe and Rether had both died. My two crewmates were now the men of the family. Others were wounded but Gytha was able to help them all. We buried our dead for the ground was easier to work than it had been a month earlier. Arne used the last of the beer to celebrate their deaths for Butar would have appreciated the gesture. Then, while the women prepared food, the senior men discussed the battle and its implications. I was questioned by all for I was the one who had spoken with the enemy. "And he said that their jarl was Hakon Long Memory?"

I nodded.

"Then why did he not lead the men?"

None had an answer to that. "The coin we took is of little use to us. We cannot spend it. The mail and weapons are but we have fewer men now."

Snorri said, "Arne, I think that Erik's offer to sail and find a new land is a good one. If this is Hakon Long Memory then he has double reason to end our existence. We now have fewer warriors to fight our foes."

I saw resignation on my brother's face. I do not think he wanted me go and the reason was my safety. He feared I would not return. "Brother," I said, "I am a navigator. I can sail and I believe that the gods have pointed us in that direction. Gytha has said as much."

"I think you are right but you are my brother and, if you took Fótr with you, then I would be left without any other family."

I pointed to the families carrying their dead to the cemetery, "And others have lost their men. There are families who have suffered more than we."

Siggi said, "You have us and I believe that my cousin will come back."

Arne nodded. After we had buried our dead and while we drank beer to send them to the Otherworld, I spoke with my crew. The battle had shown my older ones, Eidel, Halsten, and

Stig, that the clan needed warriors. When I said I only needed three of them then they said they would protect the clan. Eidel smiled, "Besides, Captain, we three are the heaviest. You will need the lightest to reach this new world. I confess that I would love to see the land but I believe that you will find it and when we take the drekar will be my time."

I looked at Dreng and Rek. "And you two are the eldest in your families. If you need to stay with your mothers…"

Rek shook his head, "My father would not wish it. He was proud that I sailed with you. I would honour his memory. My mother has my sisters."

"And you, Dreng?"

"I have a brother, Ebbe. He can watch my mother." He looked over to where his mother was placing flowers on her husband's grave. "She will miss my father for she loved him but she is young. There are other men who might take her for a wife. I, too, wish to see this land in the west."

I spoke with both mothers. Rek's mother was older. She understood her son's need to travel. "His father was a wanderer. He will wander no more. Just bring him back, Erik."

Dreng's mother, Ada, was distracted. She was but a summer or two older than I was. She had birthed Dreng when she was young. When I asked her, she nodded absentmindedly, "Aye, Navigator, you are a good man and you will watch my son."

And so it was decided. I would take Fótr, Dreng, Rek, and Sven. My other three ship's boys would become warriors. We now had helmets, swords and even shields for them. We could not leave for many days. We needed to make the ship seaworthy and we needed supplies for three months. We would take three barrels with water in them and dried seal meat. With the fishing lines, we carried then we should be able to feed ourselves. We would sail for forty days. If we had found no sign then we would return east. My four companions were all happy to be on the voyage with me. Fótr would be the least experienced but the battle of Maevesfjörður had shown him the necessity of the voyage. We now had guards watching our herds and Arne had planted stakes as a palisade to slow down an attacker. Halsten and Stig chose to sleep aboard the drekar. If our enemies came then that was the most vulnerable asset we had.

Across the Seas

Gytha summoned me the night before I left. I say summoned for it felt like being taken into the presence of a queen. Yet when I was alone with her, she smiled and stroked my cheek, "I think that the fate of the clan rests with one who is so young and yet has the heart to carry the hopes of the Clan of the Fox."

I shook my head, "If you have dreamed of a future where I save the clan then I fear you have been eating strange mushrooms."

She shook her head, "My dream is of you, Erik. I see you in a verdant land. I see our people there but my dream was of you. Through your veins courses the blood of Lars and my husband. The threads which bind us have been woven by the Norns. When I die, I shall join the spirits. It will not be a death but a transformation. I do not fear death. I fear for my children and my husband for they are not volvas. There is no guarantee that I shall see them in the Otherworld. So long as you live then even if the rest of the clan perishes our blood will survive and our spirits will endure."

I nodded although I did not understand her words. I knew that I was speaking with a powerful witch and I was a mere mortal. She held my right hand in her two. Her skin felt soft and warm. Her eyes bored into me. "Erik, you will need to be strong. Before you leave, I will give you a stone. It is a blue stone. I found it in the river before we left Larswick. Ylva came to me in a dream and told me that it would guard and protect you. When you sail west and things look bleak and black; when you think that you will give up then hold the stone and think of me. I will come to you and I will counsel you. Do not give up."

I was being bewitched and I could do nothing about it, "I will. I swear."

She reached into her leather pouch and took out the blue stone. It was the size of the nail of my little finger and there was a metal chain. The chain was neither gold nor silver. "This chain is made from the mail of your father's byrnie. When we sailed west, I worked on it as did the other volvas. It has your father's spirit within and the spells of our clan. It will guard you."

I took it and hung it from my neck. I felt a warm glow and she smiled and nodded. "I thank you for the gift."

Across the Seas

"Do not return until you see land. Not land like this piece of ice-bound rock nor the land of Orkneyjar but land which is warm and green and fertile." She stared deep into my eyes and I felt myself falling deeper under her spell, "Swear!"

I had no choice, "I so swear."

Without her speaking I knew that I had just sworn the most sacred of oaths. If I broke it then I was doomed.

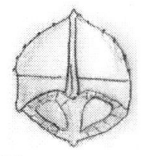

Chapter 6

We left on the day when the days and nights were exactly the same length. It was a propitious day for such a voyage as we intended. There was no mother to wave Fótr and I off. Arne and his wife came down to the quay, as did Gytha, Siggi and Snorri. Apart from Gytha, who smiled, their faces showed me their concern. The snekke was more laden than I had ever seen her. As we drank the water and ate the supplies, we would become lighter. I had my sword with me but not my shield and not my mail. I had my helmet. I had joked that I could. always use it for cooking!

Arne admonished me with his finger, "Three moons brother! Bring back Fótr and I care not if you find nothing! Just come back safely! Then we can rid your mind of this foolishness."

I nodded. I was not sure if I could trust myself to speak. I felt a lump in my throat which I could not explain. As the wind took us to the mouth of the fjord, I realized I was more worried about them for I knew that I would be safe. I did not know how I knew but I knew. Fótr was the least experienced of the crew and I saw that he stayed close to me. He would find his own feet as we sailed.

I had already decided on my course. I would sail south and west. It meant leaving sight of the island within a day and risked disaster if the sun did not shine but I had to believe that the gods and the Norns intended for me to take this voyage. The winds were against us from the outset and it took a whole day to tack out of sight of land. Dreng, Rek and Sven would have to steer and I began as I meant to go on. They each took a shift at the steering board. I watched them for a long day until I was sure they could manage it. The test would come when they sailed at night. I would be both teaching and sailing.

The days began to follow a pattern. The first thing I did when the sun rose in the east was to make a tally mark on the stick I had brought. I had forty-two days to find land. It was too easy to lose track of time at sea. I made certain that the hourglass began its march. I did this whether the sun shone or not. It meant we could manage the watches more equitably. Then I made water, drank some water and ate a little food. I would stand, while one of the others took the steering board, and take a turn around the tiny snekke. *'Jötnar'* spoke to me through the steering board and her sails but I needed to look at her each day. She was no longer young. Sighwarth was now the oldest man in the settlement and he had more ailments than younger men. He was more forgetful. My snekke was the same. Once I was happy with the snekke and the boys had been fed then if the sun was visible, we took a sight with the compass and marked our position on the white cloak we had cut up to make a map. The cloak had come from our dead enemies. It had been rent with sword cuts and, as a cloak, useless but as a blank canvas upon which to make marks, it was perfect. That done we headed south and west, always south and west.

After six days we noticed that the air was not quite as cold. That might have been the wind which turned from the northwest to the west. Our progress slowed. It was as we tacked once more that I worked out the wind pattern. The winds came largely from the west, sometimes a wind was from the south and sometimes from the north. That meant our journey east and home would be faster. Could I afford to sail west for fifty days? We had had no rain and were halfway through one barrel of water. We had caught fish regularly but the boys had not managed to bring down a sea bird. There were few of them and rarely came close. Sven had an idea about that.

"Captain, if we save the bones we do not eat until we have a sufficient quantity, we could use them as bait. We can wait until we see birds and then throw the bones over the stern. When the birds swoop, we might bring one down."

It was a good idea and it kept them occupied. The birds did not come. I had an idea of my own. We were making painful progress west and the wind was from the northwest. I took a chance and used the wind to sail due south for a day. We moved faster, the snekke flew through the water, and the gods smiled on us for we found rain. We rigged the spare sail and collected as much rainwater as we could. The change brightened all of our spirits and when the wind swung around to come from the north,

Across the Seas

we turned to head due west while we could. The wind was colder. We had to don our sealskin capes but we travelled faster. Then we had two days of the sun. It warmed us but, more importantly, it helped us to mark our position. I began to use the stars to teach the boys about sailing. I say boys but only Fótr had yet to grow a proper beard. The others were youths growing into men. When the next sailing season came then they would no longer sail my snekke. They would begin their own families. Even Fótr was just a year or so from taking a woman. I was the one who they gossiped about. I had seen more than twenty summers and I had yet to lie with a woman.

Each evening as the sun set ahead of us, a good marker for our progress, I would hold the blue stone and close my eyes. I hoped that Gytha would speak with me. She never did but that might have been because she did not need to. Our progress, although slower than I wished, was still progress. We had full barrels of water and while we caught less fish we still had salted seal meat to eat. We were not suffering. The only one who was not enjoying the voyage was Fótr and that was because he had stomach cramps. It was our diet. The boys and I were used to it and our bodies had adjusted. Gytha had anticipated such problems for all of us and she had given me a bag of berries. They had come from our home in Larswick. She had dried them before we left and kept them in leather bags. They were precious. I gave Fótr a handful each day from the fifteenth day of our voyage until the twentieth. He emptied his bowels on the twentieth day and from then on he improved. That was also the day when the air felt warmer. It felt as warm as the air in Larswick. My map showed me that we had travelled a long way south.

On the twenty-eighth day, the storm came. We had a warning for the clouds gathered to the northeast of us and I reefed the sail. We put the compass and hourglass in the chest. The skies were so black that we would not need them and I would not risk losing the hourglass. We tied everything down that we could and we removed the spare sail. The wind was freshening so much that I did not want to risk losing the spare sail. As the waves grew Sven joined me at the steering board while the other three lay close to the mast. They would be human ballast to keep us steady. When it hit us, I was sure that the snekke would be torn apart. I kept the wind behind us. I cared not which direction we took for this was about survival and not discovery. We climbed cliff like waves and then dived into what appeared to be bottomless troughs. *'Jötnar'* showed us just how tough she was. I had no opportunity to hold the blue stone for Sven and I had to hang on to the steering board. If we deviated from our course then we could broach the boat and that would be the end of us! The sky was so black that day and night were meaningless.

When I closed my eyes, I prayed to survive. Gytha's voice came into my head, *'Be strong! Your father's spirit watches over you!'*

Neither Sven nor I had the opportunity to drink. The only moisture we had was from the rain driving into us. It helped to wash the salt from us. Our seal skin capes proved to be our most valuable possessions. Our hair was soaked but our upper bodies were dry and that was a help.

When the motion of the snekke became easier and the waves lessened I croaked, "You three, drink some water. Eat some food."

Their faces showed concern as they looked at me. Fótr said, "Are we in the Otherworld, brother, for I am sure we must have died?"

I laughed, "Not yet but this may just be the eye of the storm."

In the event, it was not. The storm had passed us. I was able to allow Sven to fetch us some water and food. When he returned, he pointed behind us, "Captain, the sun appears."

I glanced behind and saw the faintest of glows from the east."

We knew our course. I drew the blue stone and touched it, "Thank you Gytha. Thank you, father. Your stone protected us."

When a grey dawn finally came, I saw the sorry state that was my snekke. The forestay had sheared in the storm. Before we could rig the sail, we would have to replace it. We had spare ropes and Sven and Dreng replaced the broken one. Fótr and Rek re-rigged the spare sail to collect water again. The storm had passed but I could still feel moisture in the air. None of us were able to work quickly and rain had come by the time I risked the sail. It was as though *'Jötnar'* was eager to be away from the place she had nearly perished. We knew which was east and west now. She ran west and south once more.

As I marked the tally stick Sven said, "Was that one day or two, Captain?"

"In truth, I know not. Let us say that we have, perhaps, ten or twelve more days and then we must decide if we turn or not."

He stood and peered ahead, "I see nothing on the horizon!"

"And I would not expect to. We have seen no sign of land. For the days before the storm, we saw few birds. When we see birds then I will look for land. We are alive. Our snekke is sound and we have not fallen from the edge of the world."

I sounded more confident than I actually was. I found myself fingering the blue stone more and more. Five days later we were rewarded. A flock of geese in their familiar arrow formation flew from the direction of the setting sun. There was land ahead. These were not seabirds. I wondered if they were heading for our island. The others did not seem to notice the birds. They were too high to hit with a stone. Our store of bones had been washed overboard in the storm and we could not entice birds down.

"Geese!" I pointed up to the sky. "There is land somewhere out there. Run out the fishing lines. We have hope once more."

The hope also brought ideas into my head. I knew not what we would find but the land would have to be better than the land of ice and fire. If we brought the drekar then when we found adverse winds we could row. We would have a faster crossing. I had hope before the storm and the geese, now I had belief.

We passed the day when we should have turned to return home. I saw my crew watching me as I marked the tally stick for the forty-first time. I smiled, "We will push on for another couple of days. We have enough water and there is one small barrel of seal meat."

None looked enthusiastic but I was the captain. It was the geese which kept me going. They were land birds and they had come from the west. Unless the gods were teasing me, they had to have left the land. It was out there.

Each dawn now saw me peering westwards seeking land. We had been travelling for, according to my tally stick, forty-four days when I saw gulls in the distance. I touched my blue stone and prayed that it was land in the distance and not a dead whale.

As we neared the birds, I saw that it was, indeed, land. We had found it! Some of the birds rose and I saw a smudge of darkness on the horizon. I spied trees and it looked green. There was no mountain wreathed in smoke and belching fire. My four crew turned and stared at me as though I was a galdramenn. I knew not how I had known but I had.

"We look for a beach. *'Jötnar'* has done well and I would not risk her hull on rocks. When we find one then keep a watch for people. If we find any we know not if they might be hostile. First, we land! We need a beach on which we can land. We dare not risk rocks."

As we closed with the land the birds dispersed. I saw fish in the water below us. They were feeding. Even as we edged towards the coast, our trailing hooks caught three fish and they were big ones. Sven had to use his knife to kill them. What we did not see was a beach, there were places I might have risked a landing if we were not so far from home but here, I was cautious. We sailed south and west along the coast. I would not head north. The sun was setting ahead of us when Sven spied a tiny sliver of sand and we headed in. We ground on the shingle and the four boys dragged us up above the high-water mark. I stepped ashore and thought that my legs would collapse beneath me. I dropped to my knees and kissed the blue stone, "Thank you Allfather, Gytha, and my father. I know that without you we would not have found this land."

I saw Fótr looking north and east. He shook his head, "Our home is so far away that I will be another summer older when next I see Arne."

I did not say that there was no certainty we would ever see our home again. "Sven, bring my bow and your sling. The rest of you gather firewood but do not light it yet. We will scout."

When my bow was strung and an arrow nocked, we headed up the small grassy slope. We kept low. The air felt warm. In Maevesfjörður the air always felt cool even in summer. I sniffed the air and I could smell animals. As I glanced down, I saw that we were on an animal trail and I saw the prints of hoofed animals. The trees were familiar too. I saw Ash, Rowan, and Beech. I observed that the trail twisted between trees and shrubs. There were buds on the bushes but no fruit. We walked for what seemed like a thousand paces. The sun was getting lower in the sky. I sniffed the air again. I could not smell smoke. I had seen no footprints on the ground. If there were men in this land then they were not close. Sometimes a warrior had to take a chance and I took one.

We turned and headed back. I heard animals racing from our path as we moved through the shrubs and bushes but I did not see any. We would eat hot food for the first time in over forty days and my mouth watered at the thought of it. The members of my crew had begun to offload the snekke. I had not ordered them to do so but it made sense. They had laid out our furs and the fire looked ready to light. As I unstrung my bow I said, "Sven, use the flint and light the fire. The rest of you, gut the fish."

I went to the snekke and took out my maps. I took a fresh piece of the cloak and used my charcoal to draw the coast. It was crude but drawing it gave me pleasure. I had done what I said I would. I walked around the snekke. The light was fading but the strakes looked to be sound. I had pine tar and I would give the hull a coating while we could. I was confident that we would find pine trees and we could make our own tar. We had a small axe with us. It would take time but we could bring down a pine tree.

I walked back to the fire. It was drawing well. The boys had found dry kindling. That, too, was an advantage. At Maevesfjörður we had had to dry wood out. Sven had put a small branch through each of the fishes and Dreng and Rek had put forked branches in the ground to support the cooking fish. Fótr was walking along the small beach scavenging more wood.

When he reached us and dropped the wood Fótr asked, "Do we sail home straight away, brother? This land looks better than the land of ice and fire. I did not think we would reach it but now that we have, I am keen to bring our people here."

I shook my head, "We will do a proper job of scouting. I do not intend to sail home for a month or so." The surprise was on all of their faces. I smiled, "We will get home faster for I believe that the winds are stronger in that direction. When we sailed here, I felt a current beneath our hull. It was warm and it slowed us. We will have that current to take us home. Besides, as pleasant as this land appears, we need to see what creatures and people live here. We are no longer a large clan. We cannot fight overwhelming numbers. We find a land where you can grow and become strong warriors such as those we buried at Maevesfjörður." I saw Dreng and Rek look at each other. They had both lost a father.

My words gave them thoughts to go with their fish. The white-fleshed fish was delicious. We sucked the meat from the bones and then returned the bones to Ran. There were creatures in the ocean who would devour them.

We should have kept watch but all of us were so weary and the furs so warm that we did not. The Allfather watched for us and we awoke refreshed. We ate some of the salted seal meat and drank water. As we ate, I gave instructions. "We will camp here for a few days. Fótr and Rek you will build shelters and forage for timber. I would have you make a salt pan so that we can make salt." I saw their faces fall. "Tomorrow I will take you two with me. We will all be walking maps when we get home. If anything happens to me then you four will take the message of this land to our people." With that sobering thought, I strapped on my sword and strung my bow. Sven and Dreng brought short spears and slings. We were prepared to hunt and, if needs be, to fight. I hoped that it would not come to a fight. We followed the trail I had taken the previous night. It was a better light for us and I saw that the trail went along a valley and there was a stream below us. I headed down the slope and found the water. Cupping my hand, I tasted it. The water was sweet and cold. "I am guessing it comes out near to our beach. Come let us resume our walk. We will find a piece of higher ground to see further."

We rejoined the path. I saw that we were heading along a ridge. The valley had not been deep and the ridge was not high. It was not a man-made trail. Men would have gone closer to the top. Animals sought shelter. The trail began to descend and I spied fresh animal droppings. They were not as big as those from a cow but bigger than from a deer. I picked one up and it was still warm. Looking around I saw tracks. I nocked an arrow and the other two nodded and held their spears in two hands. We began to descend. The wind was coming towards us. That was lucky. Through the trees, I spied water. There was a pond ahead. The animals we followed would likely gather there to graze. As we descended, I caught a glimpse of light brown fur. It was the animal and from its hoof prints, it was a type of deer. I did not recognize the colour and I could not see the head. I gestured for the other two to flank me.

The closer we came to the pond the more nervous I became. Deer used smell to detect danger but they would see us once we cleared the trees. I had a hunting arrow nocked. Barbed, it would tear a wound in the animal. I did not expect an instant kill but I would try to make it bleed to death and we would follow. I saw that it was a small herd of eight animals. They were curious looking deer. The ones I knew had a delicate mouth. These had a jaw which was square and they were much bigger. They looked to be as big as a cow in height yet not as broad. There was what looked like a male for I recognized the antlers although they were not like the antlers of the deer I had seen at Larswick. Sven's foot sent a stone skittering down the trail when we were twenty paces from them. They bolted and I snapped off an arrow. All thoughts of aiming scattered with the deer. I nocked another as we ran. The deer ran to the west, towards our camp although we were on the other side of the ridge.

The animals had disappeared by the time we reached the side of the pond. They had broken branches and their trail could be clearly seen. More importantly, I saw the blood on the leaves and the ground. The amount showed me that I had hurt the animal. "Come, let us run. Stay behind me. When we close with the wounded one I will send an arrow at it and then you two can finish it off with your spears."

We could hear them crashing through the undergrowth and they appeared to be climbing through the trees. The blood became more frequent. The animal had been hurt but it was a game one. We must have followed it for a mile or more before we saw it staggering just ahead of us. I would not need my arrow. It had no antlers. After giving my bow to Sven I drew my sword. The animal tried to move but failed and its hind legs collapsed. It had suffered enough. In two strides I ran up to it and hacked upwards into its throat. It shuddered and died. We were lucky that it was not a fully grown male or we would have struggled to carry it. As it was, I had Sven and Dreng ram their spears through the sides of the animal. They lifted the two spears

Across the Seas

on one side and I did the same on mine. We manhandled it up the slope to the top of the ridge. The ridge afforded a good view. We rested and I took in this potential home. I saw that just beyond our camp was a small bay and then a huge one. In the distance I could see what I took to be the other side of the bay but, equally, it could have been another island. As I turned around, I saw, many miles to the north, a tendril of smoke. There were people on what I took to be an island. We were not alone!

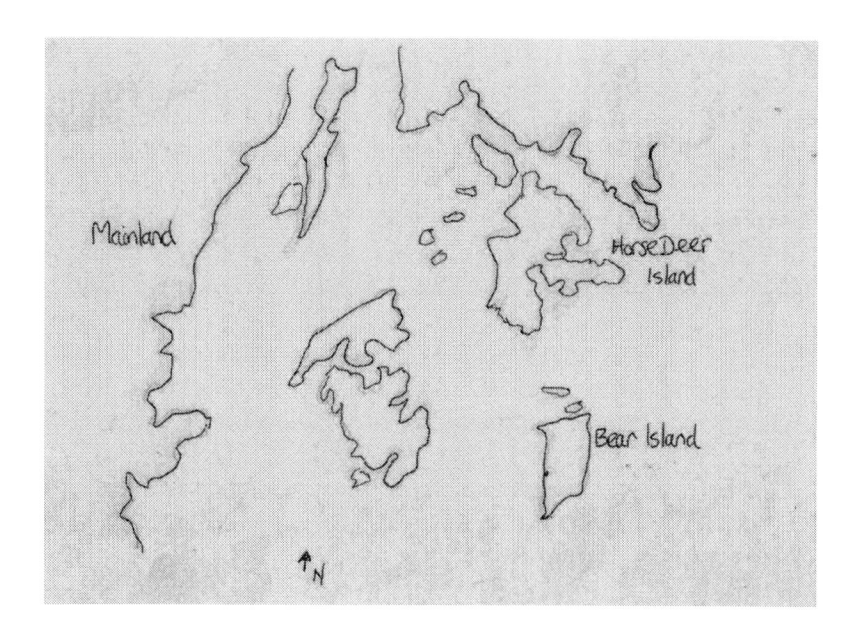

Chapter 7

It was after noon when we reached our camp. We had moved off the ridge as soon as we could. I did not want to be seen. Fótr and Rek looked up as we clattered through the bushes. "We eat."

The spears were removed and I skinned the animal. We would use its skin later. Then I began to butcher the beast. We would cook the offal first for that would go off. The stomach and guts we threw into the sea. Birds swooped down as fish rose to gorge on the bounty. Sven fetched the cooking pot we had carried from our home. While the heart, liver, and kidneys were cooked on the open fire the choice cuts were placed in seawater to be cooked. We would cook it all and then use salt to preserve it. The smell of the cooking meat made me stop my butchery so that we could eat. It was a treat and bloody juices ran down my chin.

"The smoke we saw tells me that there are people here. They may be friendly but let us assume they are not. We will need to make defences for the camp. We passed some vines which looked like brambles. We will cut them and make a palisade of them. They will not stop an intruder but they will slow him down and give us a warning. Tomorrow we will hunt again. I hope to have enough meat and salt in the next few days to enable us to leave and explore further south."

It took all afternoon to strip the meat from the animal. We cooked it in batches. I was not sure if they had rats or carrion in this part of the world but we took no chances. I had the boys build a platform to keep it in the air and we covered the cooked meat with the deer hide. It was not perfect but we had to conserve the meat in some way. While the fire was still hot, I heated some pine tar and coated the strakes close to the keel. I could see no damage but the storm had worried me.

The next day I took Fótr and Rek with me. I had not been able to save the shaft or the feathers from the arrow. They had been broken when the deer fled. When we had butchered it, I had managed to salvage the tip. I had no spare feathers but there were ash trees and I planned on collecting some as we passed. We could always find feathers.

I counselled the two of them. "When we find these deer then I will use an arrow. You try your slings first. You might get lucky. Then we have to trail them. These animals, I call them deer but they are nothing like any deer I have ever seen, might be dangerous. If you have to strike with your spears do so forcefully but be ready to drop your spears. Fótr, you are really too inexperienced to hunt but..." He gave me a serious look. I had been in more danger when I had been his age. He would have to learn. "When we are close then watch your feet. Do not frighten the animals."

They both nodded. I had already decided that I would use the deer hide to make the boys jerkins. If we killed enough then I would have one too. Already the kyrtle I wore had become torn when we had run through the woods. This time I headed up the beach to find the river. I needed to explore it and who knew what animals we might find. I led the way with an arrow nocked. The wind was from the east. I did not know how sensitive were the deers' sense of smell. I saw, as we went, signs of animals which lived by the river. None were big animals. I saw the tracks of what appeared to be a weasel as well as the tracks of what looked like an enormous fat rat! None were worth hunting. We walked a long way up the river which became another pond. We stopped and I examined the ground. There were deer prints but we saw no deer nor any deer dung. They had visited here but not for some time. I was loath to expose myself. The deer did not use this pond and I wondered why.

I headed for the first pond. I knew that I could not use the same animal trail for our smell would carry. I carried on north and east. The ridge began to descend. I was about to turn when I saw prints which were not animal. They were human and they were heading for the second pond. Perhaps that was why the deer did not use it. They had been hunted. The fire I had seen in the distance told me there were people. Now I knew that they ventured to this part of the land. We could not stay in this land! We approached the pond, I now called the deer pond, from the north. There was a trail and it looked to be man-made. I saw the deer. They were grazing the saplings which were on the western side of the pond. I headed into the woods so that we could approach from the west and our smell would be hidden. This time it was not a slip by one of us which startled the deer but a grey fox. We must have surprised it and it ran from cover. The deer were forty paces from us but they ran towards us when the fox broke cover. I barely had time to send an arrow at the leading deer. This one was a big male. My arrow hit it in the chest. I dropped the bow and drew my sword. The enraged animal came for me. Two stones whirled and one struck the deer in the head. It made it turn its head and I swept my sword almost blindly before me. I connected with the deer but its shoulder hit me in the chest. I fell backward and all went black. I saw my father. Was I dead?

"Erik!"

The voice seemed to be coming from far away. I opened my eyes and saw my younger brother staring down at me. I tried to smile but my face hurt. "I am well."

Rek shook his head, "You are not, Erik the Navigator. Your head is bleeding. The antler caught your face and there is blood at the back of your head."

"Help me up." I think they might have refused but the command in my voice brooked no objection. They pulled me to my feet. I felt a little light headed. That was the loss of blood. I turned and saw that my sword still lay in the stag's shoulder. He was dead. I retrieved my sword. "Where is my bow?"

Rek handed it to me. I said, "Rek, take your seax and gut the deer. Take the stomach and the guts out. Then we will head back to the camp."

As Rek began to gut the animal he asked, "We will leave the stag here?"

"This one is far bigger than the one we killed yesterday. We cannot carry it. You two do not know the way back to our camp. I should have brought Sven and Dreng. This is my mistake. I was trying to be fair. Instead, I should have been a leader. Do not worry. We will soon return." Rek took the guts from the animal. "Carry them and we will drop them away from the animal. The carrion will be drawn to the guts." I smiled, "When I have eaten some food and drunk some water then I will be fine.

Across the Seas

We had less than a mile to walk but I was suffering. I could not let them see that I was not yet right. I needed a drink and I needed to eat something. I used my bow as a staff. Rek ran ahead as soon as we saw the sea. By the time I reached the camp Dreng and Rek had brought the water skin and some food. I saw that Sven had the cooking pot and he was filling it with sea water.

Sven was the eldest. He had seen almost fifteen summers. He said, "Sit, Captain. Let me look at this wound. Your face will be scarred."

I took the skin from Dreng and took a long swallow. I put it down and Sven began to wash the blood from the back of my head. I heard Fótr gasp, "I can see bone!"

"Be silent!" Sven continued to bathe it. "Dreng, fetch the vinegar and honey. It is bad, Captain. It is a deep cut. I have stemmed the bleeding but I cannot stitch it."

I took a piece of seal meat. It was more to occupy my hands than anything. How would the four of them get home if I was dead?

Dreng came back. When Sven used the vinegar, I felt such pain as I had rarely had to endure but it passed. Then I felt him smear on honey. "Rek, keep the cloth pressed against the wound." He came around to the front and began to wash the blood from my face. He shook his head, "You have been lucky. This is just a scratch. It is deep but I can staunch the bleeding." He repeated the washing with the vinegar. This time it did not hurt so badly and then he used the honey. He took one of the bloodied pieces of cloak. "I am sorry, Captain, but this needs to be your bandage." He used his knife to cut it into strips and then began to bind my head. He left just one eye to enable me to see When he had done, he nodded. "Lie on your fur, Captain."

I tried to get to my feet but they buckled. Sven shook his head, "You are in no condition. You lie down and we will fetch the deer."

I was in no position to argue and I lay on the fur. I had no sooner laid my head on the ground then all went black.

I dreamed.

I heard Gytha's voice and she seemed to be inside my head. You have done well, navigator but your work is not yet done.

This is not the land. You need to sail on. Trust your instincts for they are good. Believe in your crew for they are your future.

I sailed the seas. I saw the sun rising to my left. We passed through islands and I saw a forest. I was alone and I climbed a trail passing strange and wondrous animals.

Then I saw a waterfall and I saw a maid. I was standing on top of the waterfall. The maid was not of our clan. She was dark skinned with jet black hair and eyes which were like deep purple pools. She stared at me. Then she dived into the water. She rose, like a fish from the depths and her hand beckoned me. I realized that I was on the waterfall now. I could not help myself. I dived from the top. I seemed to fall forever but I did not reach the bottom.

"Captain, it is morning. Captain."

I opened my eyes and saw the thin grey light of dawn. Sven stared down at me. He looked relieved, "You are alive. We thought you dead."

"I slept all night?"

"Aye, Captain. When we returned with the deer you had not moved. We skinned and butchered it. We ate the heart but you did not wake. We took it in turns to watch over you." He stood. "Wake! Erik the Navigator lives!"

I sat up. I did not feel dizzy but I was ravenously hungry.

Fótr ran to me, "We can go home now?"

I was going to shake my head but thought better of it, "No, little brother. I dreamed and I saw Gytha. This is not the land she saw. We will sail on but you will be pleased to know that we have finished hunting. You cooked all the meat?"

Sven said, "Aye."

Then give me some and we will begin to put the rest in barrels with the salt."

Dreng said, "We do not have enough."

"Then we top up the barrels with salt water. It will have to do. Today we prepare for sea. I spied some greens yesterday along the river bank. They look to be edible. Collect them. When you pass the ash trees bring back thin branches that I can turn into arrows. Make them straight ones. Find shellfish. We leave tomorrow." I pointed south. "We sail in that direction."

Across the Seas

I forced myself to my feet. I felt a little dizzy when I stood. The stag had been a warrior. Even though mortally wounded he had protected his herd and tried to kill me. I would be as the stag. I helped to take the barrels from the snekke. We had brought small barrels which could be easily filled. The meat filled the two small ones and there was some left over. "We use that on the voyage! We will eat better than we did coming here." When my scavengers returned from the river, the greens were washed and put in a hessian bag. Finally, we collected the shellfish and added that to a pot of water.

"Fetch me the two hides." I took out my seax. It had a very sharp edge and I cut each of the two hides in two. I then cut holes for the arms and heads. They were rough but, while at sea, the four of them could make them fit. It would occupy them and produce something useful. Once that was done, we loaded the snekke so that we could leave in the morning. I had planned on staying here longer but my dream and the human footprints had made me change my mind. We had three full barrels of water. We had two barrels filled with venison and one and a half with seal meat. Those, along with the fish we would catch, would see us back home. My bow, the arrows, and my sword were in the snekke.

It was dark by the time we had finished. I had taken the opportunity of checking the ropes and the sail. All were in good condition. The steering board withy was replaced and the snekke tied so that she floated. I would see if the pine tar had worked. We lay on our furs around a good fire and ate our stew of shellfish, venison and seal meat. The greens we added were necessary. They added little flavour but my mother had always added greens when she cooked and we had grown up healthy.

The greens had an effect. Dreng woke and had to empty his bowels. The speed with which he ran into the woods told me that it was the greens which had worked. I loaded the cooking pot in the snekke and checked the hull. She had not leaked. We placed the furs on the deck. I was about to shout for Dreng, for the others were already in the boat when I heard a shout of alarm from the woods. I grabbed my bow, strung it and nocked an arrow.

Dreng appeared. He had his breeks in his hand. He shouted, "We are under attack!"

I saw, emerging from the woods, warriors. They had long black hair and wore animal skins. In their hands, they carried fire-hardened spears and bows. This was why Gytha had told us to leave. I pulled back the bow and released the arrow. It hit the leading warrior in the chest. The force of the arrow was such that he flew backward and the others stopped. The ones with bows sent arrows at us. I was already moving for Dreng had passed me and was clambering aboard the snekke.

"Raise the sail!" An arrow struck the sand next to my foot. Another hit my jerkin. It stuck there. Fótr and Rek whirled their slings. I did not see if they hit any of the skraelring. The snekke was three paces from the shore and, as the sail was lowered, began to move away. I threw my bow aboard as Sven hauled over the stern. As I tumbled aboard, I saw that the warriors were at the beach and forcing their way through the sea to get at us. "Keep your heads down." Two arrows struck the stern. "Sven, take the steering board." As he did so I drew my sword and turning, swept it across the water. One warrior had closed to within a pace of the stern. My sword ripped through his skin jacket and scored a red line across his chest. He looked at me in surprise. The wind caught the sail and we leapt away. Arrows came at us but I saw that they had stone tips. They were not as good as mine. I counted, there were ten warriors. One lay with my arrow in his chest. Two were tending his wound and I saw that one had been hit by a stone and his face bled. We had been lucky. Had Dreng not needed to go into the woods we might have been surprised.

I sheathed my sword, "Is anyone hurt?"

They shook their heads. Sven reached over and took the arrow from my leather jerkin. He handed it to me. "This is as close as they came, Captain." There was the tiniest spot of blood on the stone end. I had barely felt it.

I took out the blue stone and kissed it, "Thank you, Gytha!"

It was as I looked back that I realized the maid I had seen at the waterfall in my dream had the same look as the warriors. I wondered what that meant. While Sven took out the hourglass and compass, I stood to look south. I could see nothing ahead.

There was no land to be seen. I could see the sun and I put the steering board to go south by west. When the lid on the chest was closed and I sat down, I saw that the land we had just left continued to the west and north. It looked like a huge island. I would have liked to sail along the coast but the warriors we had seen had made me wary. I should have taken heed when we spied their footprints.

I saw that Sven apart, the others were almost terrified. I smiled, "Dreng I would put your breeks on. That is not the place to get a splinter."

Rek and Sven laughed but Fótr shook his head, "Were they men or aelfes?"

"They were men. I cut one with my sword and one of you made one bleed with a stone. I have heard of men that colour who live far to the south of the land of the Saxons. Some have black skin. They are just different types of men."

I realized then just how much less experienced was my brother than the rest of my crew. They looked calmer than he was.

"Will we meet more men like that?"

"We might." I would not lie to him. I saw him pondering that.

We sailed all day. The boys spent the time scraping the deer hide. They would make their own jerkins. It kept them occupied and was a useful activity. As night fell, we shortened sail. I risked Sven and Dreng having a watch while I had a little sleep. I dozed but, when I woke, I felt refreshed. The sun came up and we had an empty sea before us. I used the compass and the hourglass while we sailed through empty seas. Except that they were not as empty as the ones after we had left the land of ice and fire. We saw seabirds. We saw more geese. There was land and it was close. The land was elusive. It hid from us. I began to wonder if I had taken the right direction. What would have happened if I had sailed due west? Speculation was idle. We had plenty of food and water. All was good. As the sun set to steerboard I saw a dark line ahead. There was more land. Gytha had been right. I wondered if we would reach the land before the sun had completely set. We did not and I would not risk a night landing. The attack at our last camp had been a warning.

"Shorten sail. We will edge along the coast. Fótr you can have the first watch with me. For the rest, get what sleep you can. Tomorrow we find a new land."

It was when Dreng watched with me that we smelled the woodsmoke. There were men and they were close to the shore. A short while later, not long before dawn, we spied a flash of light. Someone had walked before a fire. There had to be men camped on the beach. This land had a bigger population than the one we had left. Why had Gytha sent me here? I had to trust her and the spirits. I was now in the hands of others and I found it uncomfortable.

When dawn broke, I saw the coast was still to our steerboard. We were still sailing south. I had kept the steering board central and the wind had not veered. We had to have steered a straight course and yet the coast looked to be further away. While Sven woke the others, I turned the board and headed west. The wind was a little stronger from that quarter. I saw that this was a huge bay we had entered. Had we continued to sail south then we would have closed with the coast. As the others readied themselves, I let Sven have the steering board and I went to the prow. I shaded my eyes. I had lived for many years on Orkneyjar. I recognized features. As we closed with the coast, I saw that we were heading for a channel. To steerboard was an island. When I saw the tendril of smoke rising from the island then I made my decision.

"Prepare to come about!"

I walked back to the board and took over from Sven. I headed south and east. I wanted somewhere without people. If I managed to persuade the clan to come back then we might be able to fight to hold on to land. Five of us could do little and if we were killed then those at home would never know of this land. As we resumed our course, I drank some water and ate some of the salted deer meat. The people I had seen had used crude bows with little power. Their arrowheads were stone. I closed my eyes as I pictured the warrior I had slashed with my sword. The tip of his spear had been fire-hardened. If it had been Vikings who chased off an intruder then we would have used our best warriors armed with our finest weapons. We could take this land. I just had to find this place which lay hidden from us. I guessed I would know it when I spied it.

Our voyage down the coast was a revelation. There were isolated communities which were marked by smoke. We normally saw them on beaches or at the mouths of rivers. They looked to have crude boats which were little better than floating logs. They were not sailors. Then we might see nothing for many miles.

"Why do we not land, Captain? We have seen no smoke for many miles."

Sven was right and I put the steering board over to close with the coast. Out of the corner of my eye, I saw clouds to the north of us. They were grey tinged with black. Sven had been right to counsel me. We could land for I had seen nothing for the last hour. We had just turned the hourglass. Then the wind began to turn. Normally this was a gentle process. I had simply been able to adjust our course. This time the wind almost swung. It felt as though we had run into a cliff. We had not used them yet but, as we were just a thousand paces from the coast, we would use oars.

"Down with the sail and run out the oars. You can bend your backs."

In the time it took to take down the sail and seat my four rowers the wind had begun to push us out to sea. We were not in deep water. These would not be walls of water and deep troughs but the rowers struggled to keep us heading to the coast. Fótr was not strong enough. We were crabbing around.

"Fótr take an oar with Sven. Rek, join Dreng!" It worked and we no longer crabbed but we were just managing to hold our way. The seas were getting stronger. I slipped the compass inside my kyrtle and jammed the hourglass between my feet. If I lost either then I knew not how we would return home. The Norns were spinning. The rain followed the wind. We had no spare sail rigged and none of us wore our capes. The storm had come from nowhere. My crew were tough but the rain had an effect on them. It seemed to suck the power from their arms. Sven looked at me, his eyes pleading. It was not for him but Fótr and the others.

I nodded. I had to shout above the noise of the wind and the rain, "In oars. You have done all that you can. This is the work of the Norns. Take shelter. We will run with the wind." I put the steering board over and we began to turn. We almost broached for Dreng was standing when the wave hit us. Mercifully we righted ourselves. *'Jötnar'* was a survivor. It became much easier with the wind behind us. Glancing over my shoulder I saw the coast disappear in a cloud of murk and rain. We headed into the open ocean.

The storm blew most of the morning and into the afternoon. The rain ceased but I had no idea when it did so. When our passage became easier, I called to Sven. He took the board and I put the hourglass and compass in the chest. There was little prospect of sun. I knew it was getting toward evening when the sky to larboard began to darken. I decided to risk the sail. The wind had abated and I wanted to head west while there was still light.

"Hoist the sail!" With the sail billowing, I headed first south and then tacked to head west. The wind was from the north and we zig-zagged our way southwest. We saw the light disappear in the west and I reefed the sail a little. I needed to sleep but not yet. I let Sven take the oar while I made water. I drank and ate. Standing helped me to think. The Norns had sent the storm to stop our landing. Gytha had told me in the dream that I had to continue to search for a new home. I would land the next time I saw a beach. Even if there were men already there we would land. From what I had seen we had better weapons. I had a helmet and a sword. The boys had spears with metal tips. They had daggers. We were Vikings and we could fight.

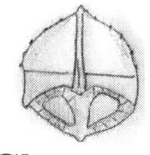

Chapter 8

I had the four crew take it in turns to sit with me. It was just to keep me awake. When I shared the watch with Fótr I found him snuggling into me. This was hard for him. I knew that this experience would make him a man. I felt guilty for I had ignored him. "Are you sorry you came, Fótr?" I kept my eyes ahead, looking for land.

"No, brother. I did not think it would be like this but each time, before now, that you sailed away I thought that you were having a grand adventure and I envied you. Now I see that it is not easy and takes as much courage as facing enemies in a shield wall."

"Fear not, little brother, I think we will return home. I fear we will be away longer than those in Maevesfjörður expect. I think that Gytha apart, they will think we have perished and they will be sad. We can do nothing about that. I believe that ahead lies a land on which we can build a home. As soon as we do then we sail back. The wind which drove us away from land will take us home just as quickly." I heard him sigh. "Have your arms recovered from the rowing?"

"They still ache and my hands are red raw and blistered."

"There is a salve in my chest. We will apply it when daylight comes. Over time they will harden and your arms will become like young oaks. It is part of your journey to becoming a man."

He fell asleep next to me and I did not have the heart to wake him. Dawn crept up on us and I saw, in the distance a thin line. It was land. I woke Fótr, "Rouse the others. Let the sail fly. I am keen to feel the earth beneath my boots once more."

Once more the wind had veered during the night and now came from the south and east. The Norns were spinning and I went with it. I had not filled in my map for two days. There would be large gaps in it. When we landed then I would use the time ashore to fill in as many of the gaps as I could. Much would be conjecture but I had an idea in my head of what this land

Across the Seas

looked like. This was more like Orkneyjar than the land of the Saxons. We had been an island people. Perhaps we were being directed to a land similar to the one we knew. As we headed towards the coast, I saw that my theory about the land looked to be correct. I saw a mass of islands. Some were little more than rocks but I saw islands as big as Orkneyjar and Hrossey.

I ignored the smaller ones. I was looking for one with a beach and, if possible, no warriors! I spied one which looked to be more than a mile across. "I intend to sail around this island. Look for men and look for a beach."

We sailed towards the east coast of the island. I saw that it was about four miles long and was completely forested. I headed north until we reached one end. We turned west and sailed through a narrow channel between the main island and a tiny one. Ahead I saw another small island to the west. We had been sent here for there was no smoke and no sign of people. It was as we headed south that Rek spied the inlet, "Captain, there is a small bay and I can see sand."

I now trusted my crew. They were not the ship's boys who had come to me years earlier. I turned the steering board and headed into the bay. I saw that it had beaches on two sides. I headed to the end and we ground on sand and shingle. We had made landfall. Even as I stepped ashore, I felt the heat from this land hit me. The breeze, while we had sailed, had tricked me. This land was warm. While we dragged the snekke on to the beach I heard the sounds of strange birds in the trees. The sand showed the tracks of animals and birds. This would be our home until we returned to Maevesfjörður.

Although we had not seen a sign of men, I was wary. I left Fótr and Dreng to tie up the snekke and make a camp. We needed a fire and we needed food. We had clothes to dry. "Peg out your hides and we will begin to tan them." They nodded. Fótr had changed since he had come on this journey. He obeyed instructions immediately. "Sven and Rek, fetch your spears and slings."

As they retrieved them Sven said, "I seek a sword, Captain. If you had not had a sword then the deer would have killed you."

I smiled, "Then you have taken another step on your way to be a warrior."

Across the Seas

I saw a tiny beck emptying into the bay. We would have fresh water. Next to it was an animal trail. There were the prints of deer. They looked to be the same kind as we had seen on the warrior island. As we headed up the trail I spied bushes and this time they had berries on them. I did not recognize them and I would not eat them until I had seen some creature devouring them. I also heard the buzz of bees near to the bush and I saw them fly off to a hive which hung in the trees. We would have honey. This land was getting better and better. This time I was not hunting. I was looking for signs of man. I knew the island was not a large one. The island seemed to be fairly flat. There was a slight rise which we soon crossed and then the ground dipped once more. In the distance, I could see above the trees, a rocky knoll which suggested a high point. We crossed small streams and then the path headed north.

We emerged at a pond. What I noticed immediately were the swarms of insects which bit us. They had been annoying as we had walked through the trees but once we reached the water it became truly terrifying. The air near the pond was black with them. As we reached it, a small herd of the same deer we had seen on the warrior island fled. I saw otters diving beneath the water. There were also large rat-like creatures and they were on fallen trees close to the outlet of the water. They dived beneath the water as we approached. We did not linger. It was too painful. I smelled the sea and after passing through a scrubby patch of thin trees we reached the sea. We had passed this place earlier when we had circumnavigated the island. There was a beach but not a large one and I led my crew north. We kept to the tree line. We passed the tracks and trails of many animals. We would be able to hunt. The north of the island had beaches. There were two islands there. Both were tiny ones. A third smaller one lay further west and further south was another island. This was, indeed, like Orkneyjar. We headed back through the woods. It was as we crossed another animal trail that I saw prints in the mud. It had rained here too and an animal had passed this way. It was the tracks of a bear. This was a much smaller bear than the one which had killed Marteinn but it was a dangerous animal.

I pointed to the tracks, "There may not be men here but there is danger."

It was after noon when we reached our camp. The boys had prepared a fire but not yet lit it. The camp was organised; the furs were laid out and the wet clothes were drying. Fótr was showing that he had learned from the others.

"There is no one on the island. Fetch the chests from the drekar and we will dry them. There is wood aplenty, we will boil up sea water to make salt. You can light the fire now."

I sat on a rock while they scurried around the camp. I took out my map and I drew the lines of what I had seen. There were gaps, huge ones, but if we persuaded the clan to come then I would have markers to guide me back here. There were more lands to the west and I would explore them but this place would house the clan. We had better land to clear. There were green vegetables growing by the beck and there were bushes. We could be safe here. We could grow here. I now needed to get back home and take them persuasive evidence to convince them. I would dig up some plants and take them with their soil back to Maevesfjörður. This was a major undertaking. What I had yet to see were pigs, cattle and sheep. I had seen birds which looked similar to the hens and ducks we had at home. We could domesticate those I was certain.

The sun had warmed the land and I took off my top clothes and sat in my breeks. The damp clothes I wore would soon dry. Sven came to me as I sat back on my rock. "How long do we stay here, Captain?"

"Until we have explored the land to the west and found just what this land has to offer. We keep close to the camp this day. If there is one bear then there may be more. No one leaves sight of the rest of us. I need sleep. I leave it to you to organise a watch. The water looks fertile. See what shellfish you can find."

I lay on my fur and the warm sun soon made me fall asleep. I had a dream free sleep and woke refreshed. The sun was setting. I looked up and saw the boys around the fire. Fótr grinned, "Good sleep, brother?"

"Call it a nap but I feel refreshed." I donned my tunic again. It was still warm from the sun. "That smells good, what it is?"

"We found some lobsters. Rek dived into the water to catch them. He was rewarded by a nip but he caught three."

"We make traps. They are easy enough to make and we can catch bigger ones."

Sven nodded, "We added some river greens and herbs. This is a better home than Maevesfjörður."

I was pleased that he agreed with me. The sun on our skin and the warmth made us all feel better. The food in our bellies added to that but I missed beer. We still had no cereal to make beer. If we had it then this would be a perfect place to live.

My sleep in the afternoon meant that I was not as sleepy as I might have been. I took a watch despite Sven's objections. I think the Norns were at work for I heard noises in the night. Had I been exhausted I would not have heard them. I roused the others. Better they lose an hour or so of sleep than be killed while they slept. The fire had died to a low glow. Something was approaching in the dark. My bow would be of no use. I drew my sword. "Fótr and Rek, stay by the fire. Put some brands in to heat them. If this is a wolf or a bear, we might frighten it away. Find your slings. Sven and Dreng, spears. Stand behind me."

I heard them murmur their assent.

I saw in the dark two glowing eyes. It was an animal. The wind sent a whiff of its scent towards us. It was a bear. "It is a bear. When I give the command all shout at once and we will see if we can scare it away."

I heard a growl. It was a bear for I saw the eyes rise as it rose on its hind legs. It had been attracted by the smell of our food. From the position of its eyes, it was bigger than me. "Now, make a noise and we will try to frighten it."

I shouted and roared. The others did so. One of them banged a dagger against the cooking pot. It did not work. In fact, it roused the animal. I heard a roar from the dark and flash of teeth in the firelight as it lurched at us. One swipe from its claws could take out my face. I held my sword before me. My only chance to save my crew was to hurt it. Stones struck it as it raced towards me. Sven and Dreng held their spears before them. Rek boldly and bravely took his spear and rammed it at the bear's leg. The spear was batted away and flew into the bushes. I had to stand firm. I had a sword and I was the largest of us. If I ran it would kill us all for a bear was fast. It was the stones from Fótr which aided me the most. The bear, I saw now that it was a black one, flailed its paws at the stones which were striking its head. Rek must have picked up his sling to join in for the number of stones increased. The two spears had a greater range than my sword and both were rammed into the bear's side. It roared even louder and batted one from Dreng's hands. I swung at what I hoped was its throat. My sword tore through fur and I felt it grate against bone. More stones hit it and I pulled out my sword. The bear's blood spattered over me but still, it came on. I stepped in to close with it and rammed my sword upwards. The bear's claws wrapped around my back. They tore into my flesh. I had to endure the pain. If I died then the others would too. I felt its breath as its teeth came towards me and I pushed up. My sword drove through the hole I had made in the animal's throat and into its brain. I was released and the bear fell backward.

Fótr and Dreng ran up with torches. The bear was dead. It lay in a pool of blackening blood. It was not a fully-grown bear and looked young. It was a male. Perhaps it had thought I was another male. Sven said, "Fetch another brand."

Fótr asked, "Why?"

"Because the bear has raked your brother's back and I would see to his wounds. I need the honey and vinegar too."

I wiped my sword on the pelt of the bear. "It did not hurt much." It was a lie but they would be worried enough as it was.

Sven wiped his hand across my back and I saw, by Fótr's brand that it was bloody. "You have been lucky, Erik the Navigator."

As Sven tended to my wound, I spoke to the other three. "We will need to build warnings along this trail."

Dreng said, "Leave it with us, Captain. These animals of this new world do not seem to like you."

"Aye, we may have escaped their warriors but their animals are fierce. Even their insects have teeth." I slapped another of the biting insects. It was not quite the perfect world I had thought.

When dawn broke, we skinned the bear. The fur was a good one for our weapons had done little damage to it. We butchered the animal and began to cook the meat. We did not want other predators and carrion seeking the raw meat. The bear delayed us.

I had planned on sailing west to view the land there. Sven insisted upon me resting for the scratches were deeper than he had first thought. The water from the stream was good and we did not need to venture further upstream and risk the biting insects.

It was painful to don my tunic and jerkin but I did so. The next day we boarded the snekke and headed west. I saw other islands. Some looked bigger than the one we were on but I sought either an island as big as the land of the Saxons or a mainland. We saw no smoke on the islands we passed but, as we neared a coastline which stretched north and south as far as we could see, I did spy, in the distance, smoke. I said nothing to the crew but that meant men. There would be warriors here. Possibly they would be in greater numbers. It took until noon to reach the shore. I headed north and edged my way along it. We had not travelled far when I spied what looked like tiny skin huts. I had found a settlement. Drawn up on the beach were what appeared to be boats except they had no sails. They looked like the log boats we had seen before. We continued north. We were sailing into the wind and our progress was slow but our slow progress enabled us to see the land more clearly. We found, just two miles further north, another group of men and their boats. They appeared to be fishing in the rocks. We were seen and this time, as the boats were already manned, they began to paddle out to us.

Dreng said, "They are coming for us, captain!"

I nodded, "Prepare your slings. Sven, use my bow. I will turn around and sail south again."

Sven asked as he strung my bow, "You will not sail across the water directly to our camp?"

I shook my head, "I would hide the island where we are camped. They cannot see the island from the shore." I pointed east. All that could be seen were the islands which lay closer to the coast.

By the time we had turned the boats, I could now see that they were either a hollowed log or made of skin, had closed with us. There were four of them and each one held five warriors. They moved quickly as the paddles were raised and lowered efficiently. They were, however, inshore vessels. They could not navigate the open sea. Perhaps that was why the islands were devoid of habitation. As the wind caught us, we began to lose them but, as we headed south, I saw more boats putting off from the shore. They came from the village we had first seen and they were heading to cut us off.

There was a large group of islands to larboard. I decided to head to the west of them. I put the steering board over. We began to lose the first four boats but they still pursued us. There were six boats coming from the other village and they would get close to us. Glancing over I saw that all the men in the boats were paddling. They would find it hard to send arrows, stones or spears in our direction.

"Do not loose stones unless I say so. Let us try to avoid making enemies." Our snekke was made for waters like this. She could turn quickly and without chests and the barrels of food and water she fairly flew over the waves. The sheltered bay meant that the waves were small and inconsequential. If these warriors followed us into the open sea they would broach. I saw that they had to steer them so that they hit the waves square on. I was confident that they would not catch us but if they looked like they were then I would sail parallel to the waves. We could do that but they could not. Gradually we opened up a lead and I saw that they were tiring. When we reached the islands, I put the steering board hard over and headed north and east. I sailed us through a channel between two long low islands. Then I spied a gap between two more islands to the east of us. I would head for that if we were not being followed.

"Sven, watch astern and see if they follow us."

He joined me at the stern and peered south. After a while, he said, "No, Captain."

"Good, lower the sail and run out the oars. We will head due east. If they cannot see the sail then they might believe that we have landed on this island." As soon as the sail came down, I turned and headed for the gap. The wind was with us and the four crew found it easy to move us. I told them to keep a regular pace. I headed for the large island which lay to the north of our camp. I turned to look astern as we neared the large island. I saw deer on one of the headlands. In my head, I then thought of it as Deer Island. I saw that Rek and Fótr were tiring. We were too far from the coast and the group of islands for us to be seen. "In oars and raise the sail."

It was late afternoon when we reached our camp. I had sailed beyond our island and approached from the east. The waves were bigger there. They gave us security from that direction. My worry was that they might see our fires if they occupied one of the islands to the west of us.

We landed and I said, "Drag the snekke on to the beach. We will make a fire but hide it from the land. Use only dry kindling. I want no smoke. Sven, make traps from the path and the rest of you prepare food." They had prepared some already but I wanted Sven to ensure that they worked.

I sat and added to my map. I now had a better picture of the islands which lay between us and what I was calling the mainland. When that was done, I went back to the bear pelt. I took a sharpened piece of rock and began to scrape it. I had arrows to make but I could do that when darkness had fallen. Arrows were best made by touch. I needed the light to prepare the pelt.

We were all occupied in silence. Our stew bubbled away and the boys had hide jerkins to make. If we were attacked then they would provide better protection against stone arrows and knives.

"And tomorrow, brother?"

"More of the same. We head south. There is a headland there. I would know if it is an island or attached to the other land. Then we hunt and gather food for the journey home."

Sven said, "When I was preparing our defences, I saw birds eating the berries. They did not die."

"Then tomorrow I will try one. If birds can eat them then so can we. I would take plants back to show the rest of the clan. They will know about the potential of these plants. We have to persuade the clan to come here."

Rek said, "It is a long way."

"And in that distance lies hope for our enemies will not find us. Hakon Long Memory knows where we live. The King of Norway does. We have upset both men and they may well seek vengeance. An ocean between us gives us security."

We had a night free from disturbance. I had made six more arrows. I had used flint tips and gulls' feathers. They were not the best of arrows but they might work against the warriors we had seen. I was loath to lose a metal-tipped arrow.

The next day we headed south and approached the coast from the open sea. We knew where the village with huts lay. It was beyond the horizon. I headed for what I took to be an island. As we neared it, I saw that there were two tiny islands with a good channel between them. What I had taken for an island was attached to the land and so I sailed down the coast. We saw smoke in the distance but no boats. Trees came all the way to the beach. We saw many birds flying. They had hunting hawks here. Once again, I saw deer. As the sun passed its zenith we turned and headed back to the camp. I had seen enough of the coast and I would not risk a confrontation with the warriors.

That evening I told my crew of my plans. "Tomorrow we hunt the deer. I would slay two if we can. Their hide is thick. This time we render down their hooves too for that makes a good glue and can be used as a sealant for the drekar. We try the berries and then collect as much food as we can. We have no more than three days here and then we sail home. I estimate that it will take less than fifty days to get home. We should reach it by the middle of Skerpla when the days are the longest and the weather is at its best. If we can persuade the clan then we can be back here before the days and nights are the same length."

The Norns were spinning. Even as I spoke the words they were plotting and laughing.

I tried the berries. They were a deep red and they had a tart taste but that was good. We collected a pail of them. That evening we would try them with meats and fishes. We also found wild garlic and wild onions. We collected those too. Sven and I ate some of the wild garlic as we prepared our weapons. Then we went hunting. I suspected that the deer would be close to water for the day was hot. That meant we would be eaten alive by the biting insects. My sword was sharp and I had eight good arrows. We had four spears but only Sven and Dreng would use them. Fótr and Rek would use stones. It had been some days since I had walked around the island but I had a picture of it in my head. I was a navigator and I had learned to keep a map in my mind. There was a breeze and it blew from our camp. I decided to walk around the island and approach the pond from the west.

As we walked, I saw clouds gathering over the mainland. A storm was coming. That would keep the warriors we had seen from bothering about us. I daresay that they had gathered around their campfires and spoken of us. Our clan would have done the same. If they were Vikings then I could predict what they would do but I could not begin to predict what these primitive people would do.

We found the animal trail which led to the pond. We walked in single file and I had an arrow nocked. Another was held next to the bow in my left hand. As we entered the forest, I closed my eyes and asked the Allfather to guide my aim. A deer and a bear had tried to kill me. My face still itched from the first and the second's claws had made my back ache. The ground had no leaves and it was dry. We were able to place our feet where they would not make a sound. Sven was especially careful of putting his feet on a skittering rock.

The day was still. The birds had stopped their noise at our approach and that would alert the deer but when I heard them munching the leaves, I knew that they had yet to sense us. I took a chance and gestured for Sven and Dreng to flank me. Fótr and Rek moved behind them. The deer were not at the pond. They were in a small clearing where a lightning struck tree had fallen. Their tails swished away the flies. Already the insects made their way towards us. However, they did not seem as bad as they had been. They annoyed me but I found that I could live with it. I saw an older stag with a broken antler. He had had some fights. Close by him was an older cow. The other females were all suckling their young. I saw the old stag's head come up. I was twenty paces from him and I could not risk waiting. I sent an arrow into his body, just behind his head. He leapt away. Sven and Dreng threw their spears. They did not hit the male but struck the old female. The heads on the spears were sharp and they drove deep within the old cow.

As the stones of Fótr and Rek struck I shouted, "Take the other two spears and follow me." I nocked my second arrow and ran. The older cow was mortally wounded. She was staggering already and I ignored her. I ran after the stag. I saw the blood trail and it headed north through the trees and on to the game trail which led to our camp. I spied the stag. It was standing on the trail. Its head turned to me. I remembered the other stag and I would take no chances. Beyond the stag, the rest of the herd just fled. He was dying and he would take out his killer. He suddenly launched himself at me. I pulled back the bowstring and my arrow hit him in the chest. I dived into the undergrowth. The dying animal crashed to the ground. By the time I had stood he was dead. I saw that our camp lay less than a hundred paces from where he had fallen. One of the arrows had broken. I would have to retrieve the head when we butchered the beast but the other was whole and I used Raedwulf's dagger to work it free. I nocked it and headed back to the pond.

I was a hundred paces from it when Fótr, Dreng, and Rek ran towards me. "What is amiss?" I saw that their faces, especially Dreng's, were covered in red bite marks.

"These insects are eating us alive! Brother, you and Sven must have some sort of charm for they do not eat you."

I pointed to the wild garlic which grew in clumps all around us. "Eat some of those or rub them on your face. They have not bothered me as much."

Leaving them to try my tip I headed back to Sven. He had already rammed two spears through the mouth and rear of the deer. He looked up, "The others?"

"They are eating garlic. Come, we will try to move this closer. The other is almost at the camp and there are few insects nearby."

We managed two hundred paces before it became too much. This was a fine animal and had plenty of meat. The other three appeared and between us, we manhandled the two carcasses back to the camp. We now had food for the voyage home and also for our people. I was content.

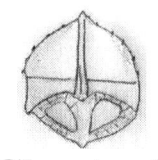

Chapter 9

The next two days were spent in slicing the deer meat as thinly as possible and preparing it to be dried and salted. The thinner the meat the longer it would stay preserved. We covered it with salt. We had managed to make plenty and then we left it to dry. In a perfect world, we would have left it longer. We did not have that luxury. The heat would help us to dry it. When I saw the rain clouds forming, I had the boys rig the hides over the meat to stop it becoming wet. While they did that I went through the barrels of salted meat. Some had begun to turn and I put that to one side. We had seen some large fish off the shore and meat that had gone off would be good bait for them. In this way, I emptied one barrel. I washed it in seawater and then put it close to the fire. We would put the dried meat in that barrel. The surplus we would carry with us. Then I began to render down the hooves of the two animals to make glue.

The storm hit hard. There was not as much wind as I had expected and Odin was there for his hammer smashed into his anvil and his thunder and lighting rang around the bay. I saw one of his bolt's strike a tree on the island I called Deer Island. Flames leapt into the air. I touched the blue stone. "Allfather watch over us!"

It was night by the time the storm passed. I began to carve some of the deer bones into larger hooks. If we were going to catch larger fish then we needed larger hooks. The next day passed much in the same way. We all worked with urgency for we were going home. Just as we knew that our families would worry about us so we fretted over them. We were well fed. Would they be? Here we had no enemies to threaten us but were the Danes or the Norwegians hunting them? My only worry was Dreng. The other two had recovered from the insect bites but Dreng appeared to be unwell. When I asked him, he just said that he was tired. The others did much of the work he should have done. They were now oar brothers.

Across the Seas

Two days later and the last remnants of the storm had passed. It was heading out to sea. I saw black clouds scudding away. I took it as a sign that we should head east. "Tomorrow we leave. Tonight, we pack the chests on the snekke and load the barrels. We will leave the deer meat as long as possible to dry. Our last task will be to collect greens, wild garlic, and the berries." The storm heading east dragged west winds behind it. They would take us home quickly.

I went with my seax while there was still light and the ground was moist. I dug up some of the berry plants and their soil. I did the same with the greens and the garlic. We had an old pail which had sprung a leak and I would use that to transport the plants to our home.

It was as I headed back to the camp that I spied, on the large island which was the closest to us, a fire and it burned on the beach. Our fire could not be seen from the sea as it was hidden by the barrels we would use for the last of the fresh water and the dried deer meat. Were the warriors in the paddled boats searching for us or was this just a coincidence?

I put the pail in the boat and gathered the others around me. "We douse the fire and take it in turns to watch. There is a fire on the nearest island. I do not wish to be surprised. We load the snekke this night. Fótr, you and Rek will sleep aboard the snekke. One sleeps and one wakes. We three will watch on the beach. Keep a weapon close to hand if you hear anything then shout. I would rather lose sleep than lose one of you."

"Aye, Captain, but why not leave tonight?"

"Because the storm is at sea. I would rather the storm stay to the east of us. I would not wish to catch it up."

The Norns were spinning. Whatever decision I made I knew there were dangers. I took the middle watch. It was the hardest. When Dreng woke me, I rose and went to make water at the beach. Rek was in the prow of *'Jötnar'* and he was alert. I nodded to him, "Is all quiet?"

"Aye Captain."

"Then sleep and I will wake Fótr later. I can watch here from the shallows."

I strapped on my sword. My other weapons were already in the snekke. I had my sealskin cape about my shoulders for there was a chill in the air. If we had to board quickly then there was nothing which would be left on the shore. Our snekke was our home. We each had our own space aboard and we were comfortable. I walked along the shore. There were rocks there. I saw little point in wetting my boots. I walked eight hundred paces and sat on a large rock. I looked across the bay. The water hissed on the sand as each wave broke. The tide was at its lowest and would soon come rushing in. Our snekke was so small that we could launch her on any tide. I stared at the white caps at the top of each wave. The waves here seemed different from those at home. I knew not why. I licked my finger and held it up. The wind was coming from the west. We would have a speedy start to our journey. We were getting towards the longest days of the year. I glanced behind me and saw that the sky was just a shade lighter than black. Dawn would be here soon.

It was as I looked back that I caught the movement. I saw boats approaching. Even as I ran back to the snekke I was shouting, "Awake!"

Dreng had barely managed to get to sleep and I saw him untie the last rope which tied us to the shore. Rek was standing by the sail and I shouted, "Raise the sail!"

Sven awoke and I saw him run with his spear to push the snekke into the waves. I ran through the water and grabbed hold of a rope to pull myself aboard. As the sail was lowered the snekke backed off a little for the wind was against. The shapes of the boats were closing with us. "Throw stones at them. Sven use my bow!" I soon heard an arrow fly and the sound of stones striking wood. I pushed the steering board hard over. Rek, tighten the forestay.". As soon as he did so the snekke moved quicker. The nearest boat full of warriors was less than twenty paces from us. I drew my sword and sat so that I steered with my left hand. Fótr whirled his sling and a stone smacked into the forehead of the warrior at the front of the nearest boat. "Get the steersman!"

Sven released an arrow. The distance was just fifteen paces and he could not miss. The arrow hit the skraeling steering the boat in the shoulder. He dropped his paddle. Having lost two of the paddles the boat slewed around and I straightened the steering board to hit his prow. They were an unstable vessel and it turned over. I then reversed the steering board. We began to move quicker than the other boats which followed us. We had been followed before and I knew that this would not end quickly. As soon as we reached the end of the island, I put the steering board hard over to take us east. The wind whipped along behind us and pushed us. The waves were already higher. One of the boats was less than twenty paces from us. Arrows and stones flew at them but the boat had a high prow and we caused no casualties. The warriors were strong and their arms powered the boat as quickly as our sail for we were laden. The wind behind helped them as much as us. It was when I turned the board to sail northwest that the gods came to our aid. The warriors were no longer bow on to the waves and a large one hit them hard and spilt them. I saw a hand come out of the water and then disappear. I would not relax until daylight came.

    We had left in a hurry and my hourglass and compass, not to mention my charts, were in my chest. As dawn broke, I saw that we were moving towards the coast of what I believed was the mainland. There were people there and we did not need to stop. It was noon when I noticed that the snekke was not moving as quickly as it should. "Sven, go and check the prow. We seem to be dipping more than we should."

    When he came back his face told me all. "We are taking on water. It must have been when we hit their boat."

    I could see the land. It was some twenty miles away to the north east. In the back of my mind, I vaguely remembered a rock we had seen south of it. "Start bailing. Use the cooking pots, the cauldron, my helmet, anything which will hold water."

    My memory had not been playing tricks. I saw two tiny rocks. When I first spied them, I thought that they were too small to land but, as we neared them I saw that the closest looked to be a mile long. There were seals basking on the beach. If seals basked then we could land. The wind saved us. We reached the beach, scattering the seals before too much water filled our bows and dragged us beneath the waves. As I slipped over the side I peered across the narrow neck of the island to the mainland beyond. I saw no immediate danger.

    We pulled her out of the water. We had not broken any of the strakes but the collision had sprung them. We had nails but we would need to seal them. "Find driftwood and light a fire." I spied a couple of spindly trees. "Sven go and cut them down. I want planks making and then we can strengthen the bows."

"I just have an axe. We need an adze to shape them."

"I do not care how it looks. Just so long as it is stronger. Dreng, empty the bows." I took the glue and the pine tar. We had two small clay cooking pots. We had not used them yet. I intended to use them to melt the glue and the pine tar. We would never use them again.

When the fire was going, I placed the two pots close to the fire to gently heat them through. I saw the thin tree fall and hurried over to Sven. "Give me the axe." I took the axe from him and hacked a triangular piece from the stump of the trunk. I then brought the axe over my head and struck the trunk in the centre along its length. I put the wedge in the split and hammered it in. The tree was small enough that it first creaked and then began to split. "Strip the bark from it while I make a second wedge."

The rest of the crew joined in and I took a second wedge. I put the second wedge higher up the split and I hammered it in. The trunk split. We repeated the same action with the two halves. We had two rounded pieces of wood and two crude planks. We took the four planks back to the snekke. They were slightly too long for the damaged part but they would add to the buoyancy. They would slow us but a little. We had not discarded the bandages I had worn on my head and my back. They were already soaked for they lay in the bows.

"Rek and Fótr, I want you to place the bloody bandages next to the bows where the planks are split. Dreng, hold the first plank in place and press against it. Sven put the glue and the tar on to heat." When he had gone, I said, "Now I am going to hammer a nail in by the bow. It is a long one so make certain your hands are not near it. I have twelve nails. I will put five in each strake."

"Aye, Captain."

I reversed the axe and drove the first nail into the strake. The strake was soft and it went through that easily. It snagged on the bloody bandage but I drove it harder and it began to bite into the plank. That was harder.

"It is through."

I gave one last bang and then moved to the other end. I repeated the process. It was easier there, for there was no bloody cloth and the strake was not sprung there. By the time I had finished nailing on both planks in place the glue was hot. We had some fur from one of the skulls of the deer we had hunted. I had intended making a hat. This was more important. I used the hide as a brush to spread the glue over the sprung strakes and those around them. While that dried, I went to the other side and hammered two nails into the two rounded pieces of timber to hold them against the side of the drekar. "Jam barrels against the repairs on both sides."

"Brother, why do we need planks on the larboard side? The strakes there are not sprung."

"True, Fótr, but we need the snekke to be balanced. Use the fire to cook some food and I will paint the hull with pine tar. We will have to wait here until it is dried."

Sven pointed to the northeast, "Do not make it too long, Captain."

I followed his finger and saw a huddle of people on the cliff tops of the land to the north west. I knew not if it was an island or the mainland. I had yet to fully explore the land. We had been seen. We could not hurry the drying. I smiled, "Let us eat and then prepare to do battle again in case they are foolish enough to take on the cubs of the fox!" It was little enough but it made them smile.

Night had fallen by the time I was satisfied that the tar had dried. We still had some left and I was prepared to land again if we had to. The question was where? Wherever we landed now the locals knew we were coming.

I had Sven in the bows when we set sail. I did not use full sail as we headed east. I wanted the bows to ease into the sea. We sailed for some hours and Sven came astern. "It is dry, Captain. I think the repair will hold."

I nodded, "I will not risk full sail yet. Get some rest. Come the dawn we will use full sail and trim the cargo."

I knew from Ulf North Star that a slight adjustment in the way a ship was laden could add speed and make life easier. We had the larger barrels around the mainmast. As we sailed north and east, I debated leaving the smaller barrels at the bows and using the humans aboard to balance us. If I had Rek and Fótr at the bows we would ride slightly higher there and damage the repair less. Sven and Dreng could sit by the mast. One thing was certain, I had had my last full night's sleep until we reached our home.

I would not have a moment free from worry for the whole voyage back to our home. *'Jötnar'* was hurt. I hoped it was not a mortal wound. If she succumbed while we were close to land then one of us might make land but once we had passed the first landfall then we had an empty ocean for forty days.

The sun shone for eight days. The wind blew for eight days. It meant I was able to add more detail to the map of the first landfall and to keep a more accurate record of our course. I determined to teach the others how to sail the snekke and read the compass. My encounter with the bear and deer had shown me that my thread could be cut in an instant. Even Fótr had lessons and he proved adept. I suppose he was like I was when Ulf North Star and my father had taught and trusted me. I never slept at night. I could use the stars but they could not. However, I was happy for them to steer during the day. Then Dreng became increasingly unwell. He first began to vomit and then had a fever. It was good that they had little to do for Rek and Fótr tended to him while Sven aided me. As I look back, I think I should have done more but I was not a healer. I tried to make amends later.

We had enough rain to keep the plants I had brought watered. There were green berries on the plant as well as riper ones. We ate the ones which were about to become overripe. They prospered and new shoots appeared. We had not had the opportunity to fish for the larger fish. I saw a shoal of them. They leapt from the water close to the snekke one day. I remembered Gytha's words of food leaping towards us. I now saw it. Sven shook his head, "See the size of them, captain! Imagine cooking one of those. It could feed five families."

"And out here, in the ocean, who could catch one? We have seen a few sharks. They must eat well but you can see why they are grown so big and so bold."

His words set me to thinking. There was a new land to the west of us and none had heard of it. There were people there but they were like none I had ever seen before. What else lay beyond the western sea? I suppose it was the open ocean. Few men liked to sail beyond the sight of land. If we had a better way of recording our position then who knew what was possible? My crude maps could only be read by me. Or perhaps my crew. We knew what each squiggle meant. We knew what the marks meant. If we perished on the way home then they would be lost. The five of us were now the most valuable thing the clan possessed. We were the key to a safer future and a better life.

The only dark cloud was Dreng. He had the shits. We had all had them but Dreng seemed to suffer worse than any of us. They were so bad that Sven and Rek had to hold him as he hung over the side of the snekke. I told him to drink as much as possible. He seemed to improve albeit briefly. I watched the others. They seemed healthy enough.

We were twenty days into our voyage when the weather changed. It was not just that we lost the sun and the sky above became a sea of white, then grey and finally black clouds. It was also the fact that the seas became rougher and rain fell. So much began to fall that we had to rig the spare sail and, instead of saving the water, we directed it over the side for within half a day we had full barrels and the snekke was in danger of becoming swamped. The rain fell for three days off and on. The winds blew us south and east instead of north and east. We reefed the sail but I knew that I now had less information about our true position.

When the sun returned and we began to dry out I spoke with Sven. "I am unsure of our position. We have sailed east and north for twenty days. I think we were more than halfway home. The three days of storm has taken us south and east."

He looked at my maps. I had one with Larswick still there. The now burned town was marked with the cross of the church we had used as our home. "If we head north and east and miss Maevesfjörður then we might strike Hibernia or Føroyar. We would know where we were then."

I looked at the sky and then the tally stick, "According to my stick it will be the longest day in ten days' time. We know that in Maevesfjörður that meant that there was barely any night. At Larswick we had some hours of darkness. When we reach that day, we will have an idea of how far north we are. If we barely have a night then we have sailed far enough north. If we have some hours of darkness then we still have some way to go."

Sven nodded, "You are a navigator!"

We sailed north and east. When we reached the longest day, I used the hourglass to measure the length of the night. It was almost three hours. We were still south of our home. We had seen no land birds and few seabirds. The land lay many days away It was two days later that Dreng became far worse. He had had problems since we had set sail. He had had loose bowels ever since. Fótr and Rek waved for me to come forward after he had failed to wake up.

"Brother, he has had the shits for days. This morning he has not woken up."

"Why did you not tell me it was so serious?"

"He thought it would pass. He seemed to get better when we went to the second island but, since before the storm he has become worse."

Sven was steering and I looked at the two of them, "You are both well? You do not have Dreng's symptoms?"

They shook their heads. "No, Erik. We are the same now as when we sailed here. Dreng was the one who became ill when we were on the island."

I nodded. That was normal. "Has he eaten anything which is different?"

"No, but, on the island, he liked to go off and forage. He ate different things from us. Perhaps you should ask Sven. He ate with Dreng."

We had become three small crews. In my eagerness to balance the boat I had made a situation where we all ate separately. "Keep him warm and give him as much water as you can. If either of you notices anything different in your own bodies then tell me!" They nodded. I went back to the steering board. "Dreng does not look well. Does he eat the same as you?"

"No, Captain. He used to keep little pieces of food which he would nibble. He ate the deer and the seal. He ate the fish but he did not eat the garlic as we did. The insects bit him more than any of us."

I remembered that. When we had hunted the deer Fótr and Rek had eaten the wild garlic and they had not suffered as many bites. Dreng's face had puffed up red and angry. I suddenly remembered that he had been bitten by biting insects on the first island. Had they poisoned him? I needed Gytha. I resumed my place at the steering board and, clutching the blue stone, asked Gytha and the Allfather for help. None came.

Later that day Fótr waved me to the mast where we had laid Dreng, "Brother he is barely breathing and look," he pointed to his breeks. Dreng had emptied his bowels.

"Fetch my sword. I fear Dreng is dying." As he went, I leaned close and spoke in Dreng's ear. "You have sailed far with me Dreng son of Ebbe. I fear you are slipping into the Otherworld." Fótr returned and I took the sword hilt and placed it in his hands. "Here is my sword. If you do pass then this will be your path to Valhalla. I pray to the Allfather that you live but I fear your eyes have seen the sun for the last time." I turned to the other two, "Watch him." Returning to the stern I said, "Sven, go and watch your friend. I fear he is dying."

The sun was setting behind us when Sven stood and called, "Captain, Dreng is dead. He breathes no longer."

I had been expecting it but that made it no easier. "Lower the sail. We will bury him and send him to the Otherworld. I pray my sword has granted him entry to Valhalla and he can speak with our father, Lars, there. He will be reunited with his own father, Ebbe."

When the snekke was still and bobbed respectfully in the sea we took my sword from his fingers and wrapped them around his own dagger. We took some of the ballast and we put the stones in his boots. We wanted him to sink. Ran would watch over him at the bottom of the ocean. That done I spoke, "Dreng you came to me as a child and found a new world with me. You became a man and I was honoured to sail with you. I swear that your mother and your brother and sister shall be watched over by me. Go to the Allfather." I nodded to Sven. The two had been friends.

"Dreng we had hopes. We shared dreams. You died too soon but I swear that my life will be one in which you can share. When you watch from the Otherworld know that all that I do will be in your memory. I will sire a son and he will be Dreng Svensson. I will teach him about you, the friend who sailed to the edge of the world." I saw that Fótr was weeping. I nodded to Sven and we lifted Dreng's body and slipped it over the side. His sealskin boots, made from the seals we had hunted together, dragged his body beneath the waves. Even as we hoisted the sail a single gull swooped over and called to us. Dreng was in the Otherworld.

Dreng's death cast a pall over the snekke. Everyone's spirits plummeted. We knew we were close to home. All of us had hoped that he would recover but whatever it was inside him had been deadly. In addition to the loss of the person we had lost his weight and we had to rebalance the snekke. Sven was the most affected. He became more silent. He was grieving. I had lost a mother but this was different. Dreng had been just a little younger than Sven and they had shared hopes and dreams. It made Sven look at his own life. As we swapped positions so that he could sail he spoke to me three days after we had buried Dreng.

"Captain, when we set sail, I wished to be a navigator like you. Now that Dreng is dead I wish to take a wife and to learn how to farm. Does that disappoint you?"

"No, Sven, for I chose this life and I am happy. There may come a time when I am ready to take a wife and leave the sea but not yet. The land we spied I would like to explore."

"The land with the fierce warriors?"

"The skræling?" I nodded, "I saw nothing in the way they fight to frighten me. In the hall at Maevesfjörður, I have a mail byrnie. Their weapons could not penetrate it. When we fought the Danes at Larswick we fought many enemies and they were armed as we were. We won. I believe we can carve out a home in the west. Who knows we might be able to civilize these skrælings?"

As I settled down in my bear fur to sleep, I dreamed of a home in the new land.

The wind had been consistently with us all the way east. I noticed as I made my mark on the tally stick that the days were not getting any longer yet we were still travelling north and east. I also noticed that the air felt colder. I made a decision. I would

Across the Seas

sail further east than north. The wind took us quicker. I was aware that we might miss Maevesfjörður to the north of us and so I had Fótr and Rek watch the larboard side for signs of land. The sea bird which had appeared when Dreng had died had told me that land was within bird flight. The question was, where?

It was the middle of Sólmánuður when Fótr shouted, "Brother! I see a cloud due north of us. It does not move like the others."

"You think it is the island of ice and fire?"

Fótr had grown. Since Dreng's death, he had gone about his work differently. He was now more confident, "I believe it is worth investigating. If it is the land of ice and fire then our present course will make us miss it. If I am wrong then I will apologize."

"There will be no need for that. Prepare to come about!"

I put the steering board over and we headed due north. I saw the cloud he meant. The wind from the west meant that the cloud should have moved east. There were clouds moving east but this one cloud, which looked different from the rest did not change. I realized that it was to the northwest of us. I kept heading north for had we turned west then we would have slowed and if this was our home I wanted to get there as soon as possible. It soon became clear that we would not reach it before dark but, as darkness fell, I saw the sign which told me that this was our home. There was a flash of light. The mountain was belching smoke.

"It is our home! We have crossed the sea!" I clutched the blue stone, "Thank you Allfather. Thank you, Gytha!"

Chapter 10

Knowing where the mountain lay helped me. We crabbed our way north and west. Now the wind brought us the smell of brimstone. It slowed our progress but the smells of the land guided me to our fjord. Rek suddenly shouted for he spied a fire and that meant our hall. I reefed the sail and Sven manned one oar and Rek and Fótr the other. I kept the glow from the hall and the mountain to my left, the larboard side, and headed for the dark patch of water. The light flickered as though people were walking in front of it. I was curious because it was the middle of the night. Why were people not abed? With just three of them on the two oars, our progress was slow for we were fighting the current. I did not wish to risk the rocks. When we finally entered the fjord, my caution had taken us the eastern side. I put the steering board over and we crawled our way to the drekar which I could now see as a dark shadow. I saw figures close to the halls. The light from the fire showed that there were many who were standing around the fire. They did not see us. We bumped next to the wooden quay. Sven was on the steerboard side and he had raised his oar when he saw the quay. He leapt ashore and stumbled. We had been at sea for a long time. I threw him the stern rope and he secured us to the bollard. Rek and Fótr were well practised now and they had the second rope tied even as I stood.

"We leave the snekke for now. I would know what is amiss."

I strapped on my sword and led my crew along the quay towards the path which led to the halls. As we crested it, I saw that most of the clan were gathered around the fire. Mothers had their arms around their children and there was little conversation. What had happened?

It was Gytha who saw me and she shouted, "They are back! The wanderers return!"

All faces turned towards us. Arne saw me and he ran up to Fótr and myself. He threw his arms around us. "We thought you dead!"

We hugged him back. I saw Sven and Rek heading for their families. I would have to find Dreng's. "What is amiss brother? Is there war?"

He shook his head and stepped away. Pointing to the mountain he said, "Two nights' since the ground shook and shivered. Rocks fell from the mountain. There was a large bang and a river of fiery stone made its way down the mountain. Gytha said to stay outside. We wished to be close to the drekar but you are back! We celebrate!"

Gytha came towards us, "You found it." It was not a question and I nodded. "I dreamed I saw you." She ran her finger down the scar on my face. "I saw the stag!"

Ada came towards me. "My son?"

I shook my head, "We found the new world but he took ill on the voyage back. He went to the Otherworld with his hand on the hilt of my sword." She did not need to know the rest of her son's death. I saw her eyes widen. Her two children were close to her and she hugged them. I saw her fighting back the tears. Her husband had died before we left and now her son had been taken from her. Life was not fair.

She nodded, "Thank you for that, Erik the Navigator. It is a good land? It is a land worth my son's death?"

There was no criticism in her voice. It was curiosity. Her son would, hopefully, be in Valhalla. He had not died a warrior's death but he had died a warrior. I had to hope that Odin had allowed him in.

I took her hand, "Know that I will be as a father to your children. You will want for nothing. I swear it."

She kissed my hand, "I know it for you are a good man, Erik. Dreng felt as though you were like a big brother. He would have followed you..." She realized what she was about to say and she began to weep. "Come, children, let us go to your father's grave and tell him of your brother's death."

I would have followed her but Arne shouted, "We have lived in fear. Now we celebrate. Let us broach the barrel of beer we had saved!"

I pointed to the water, "We have a snekke to unload. We have salted deer and bear meat. Let us feast on it.!"

We celebrated our return, Dreng's death and the end of the threat from the mountain with a feast which lasted until the middle of the morning. I discovered that the ground had not shaken for one whole day and Gytha determined that our return had appeased whatever god controlled the mountain. People could return to their halls. We showed off all that we had brought. I showed the plants. Two had died but enough remained of the others to give an indication of the potential. There was even a little fruit left and Arne, Gytha, Snorri, and Siggi tasted it. They were intrigued with the deer hide.

"These are bigger than our deer."

Fótr laughed, "Tell my brother about that. He was hit by one and we thought him dead and if he takes off his tunic you will see the scars from the bear which raked him."

Rek nodded, "And they are the ugliest deer you have ever seen!"

Arne shook his head, "You have risked so much for the clan. You have done more than any of us expected."

I nodded towards Gytha, "Our volva knew. She came to me in a dream!"

She shook her head, "I dreamed the same dream. The spirits sent my face for that reassured you. It was *wyrd*."

"And is the fiery mountain a sign that we should leave? Should we return to the new world?"

Siggi said, "You would return straight away?"

I laughed, "I have just done the voyage in a snekke. *'Njörðr'* will be far more comfortable. My little brother has stood a watch. How much easier when I have the men of the clan to do so. We would go back on the morrow."

Arne looked at Siggi and Snorri. There had been a debate about this already. Snorri spoke. "We all decided that we would wait until your return before we took a decision. This is not just for us to decide. We need to hold a Thing. We have fewer men now to row the drekar. If we do not have enough then how can we row the drekar?"

"The same way I took the snekke, slowly. There is rain for drinking and fish in the sea. We take enough food for fifty days and I know we will make landfall by then."

"And these warriors, these skrælings, what of them?"

"They use stone. They do not use metal weapons. Their boats do not have sails. At least six perished when they fought us and that was with three boys!"

Fótr nodded, "I killed one!"

I was becoming angry with the men of the clan. Had Dreng died for nothing? "Do not take my word for it. Ask my crew. Fótr would you go back?"

He nodded, "I would not even have to think about it."

Gytha put her hand on my arm. She knew I was becoming angry and she said, "The men are right, Erik, navigator, bear killer, stag wrestler, we need a Thing. We should speak with the men before we hold the Thing and persuade them. Some are fearful."

"But I have returned!"

"And Dreng did not. This home we have made is safer to some."

Arne was trying to be reasonable. I was in no mood for reason. I stood, "Safer? When you have not enough barley to make beer? When you have to sleep outside for fear of your homes being buried in rocks or fire? And what of the Danes? Have you forgotten Hakon Long Memory? He will return!"

They all looked at me as though I was a petulant child. The exception was Gytha. "I promise you that your efforts will not be in vain. We will hold a Thing but the drekar has not been maintained. She will need work. You would not wish to sail west in a ship which might sink."

I smiled, Gytha was wise. "You are right. The snekke will need repairs too."

"But not today. You have done well but I can see that you are weary. Arne, take your brother to bathe in the pool we found."

"Pool?"

"Aye, we found a pool close to the shore. It lies to the west of us. It is not almost boiling like the pool we found, it is comfortable enough to sit in. Come, I will take my two brothers and they can tell me all."

We took our cloaks to dry ourselves with. As we walked, he asked, "Dreng's death was not a good one?"

I shook my head and told him. "When we sail to the new land, we need to think about the food we take. If we had had a volva then Dreng might have lived. It was my fault for I did not notice how quickly he deteriorated."

Fótr shook his head, "You did more than anyone. You know, Arne, that he went without sleep many nights. He was the one made the voyage possible."

We reached the steaming pool and to change the subject I said, "Has this land become so attractive that people do not wish to travel?"

He shook his head, "The opposite." He sank into the water and Fótr and I joined him. It was pleasantly warm. There was the smell of brimstone but I could live with that for it was in the air around our halls all the time. "Many are disappointed in this land and wish to return to Larswick. They see the King of Norway as a small price to pay for beer and bread. There are only a few of them but when you did not return at the time you said you would then their numbers grew. It will be interesting to see the effect of your words. The problem is that we have now lost the knarr to Leif Yellow Hair's people. The drekar is the only ship."

Fótr sank beneath the water and then rose up. I saw lice fall from his hair. The water and the brimstone were killing them. I had no doubt that my body and hair were being cleansed too. Fótr shook his head and said, "But the drekar is ours. Our father built it."

"He took on the responsibility of the clan and I inherited it. The drekar belongs to the clan." He looked at me, "Could the drekar hold all of the clan?"

"With the snekke, I believe it could." I frowned as my mind worked out the problems. "However, we would have to travel when I did. That would be in Harpa or Skerpla."

Arne smiled. He had already worked that out. "Then that gives us half a year to prepare the minds of the people and the two ships. If you saw no cows nor sheep and pigs then they become even more vital. The cow is with calf."

I was disheartened but he was right. "They have animals. We saw many but none were domesticated." I brightened, "Our ancestors must have domesticated wild animals. We could do that with these strange deer. They give milk as do our cattle. Perhaps we could domesticate them."

We spent a pleasant time working out what life would be like in this new land. I knew then that we would return. It was a matter of when. And I had a task. I had a snekke to repair and, in light of my experience, a drekar to prepare.

I slept the sleep of the dead that night. I had eaten well and drunk for the first time in many moons. I slept in a hall and there were others to watch over me. When I woke, I went outside and found the settlement a hive of activity. Gytha was waiting for me. She linked my arm, "Come and tell me all."

We began to walk, "I thought you had seen it all for I felt your presence."

"That was the stone. The spirits told me you were alive. I saw Dreng as he passed over to the Otherworld. You say there is honey there?"

"I saw honeybees and I saw hives."

"Then we do not need barley to grow cereal for beer, we can brew mead."

"But what of bread?"

"You saw grass growing?"

I had to think and then I remembered that I had. When we had sailed down the coast, I had seen clear fields and what looked like grass was growing there. I nodded.

"Then if grass can grow so can cereal. Here we have short turf but it is not grazing. Once we clear the forests then the Mother will come and seed the land. There will be cereal. We will be able to grow it and from that make bread. And the people you saw?"

"I only saw warriors but they looked primitive folk. They did not look to have metal."

"But they live from the land and wear the skins of animals and make boats from logs?" I nodded. "Then they worship the same gods as we do. We can civilize them. You have done well. Do not let your brother's words dishearten you. He wishes everyone to be as enthusiastic as he is. That never happens. Our natures make us all different. You have proved what can be done." She looked to the west. "We now have to brace ourselves for the storm before we leave."

"The storm?"

"I know your thoughts, Erik. You fear Hakon and his Danes."

I nodded, "I can't believe that they followed us all the way here just for vengeance."

"That may be a coincidence. There were others who fled to this island because they had been driven from their homes. Hakon might be just such a one." We had reached my drekar. "Take me around the drekar and tell me what we shall need to do when we sail across to this new land."

I was in more comfortable territory now. As we walked the deck and I pointed out features I gave her my thoughts. I told her of the storms we had endured. I thought that the more seal skin capes we had the better. I spoke of the diet we had endured. She was pleased that rain would give us our water. "We also need to give families space. We were lucky. There were just five of us. This will take forty days or more and there will be fights and arguments. Having their own areas will help. Apart from the times, we need to row, we can do that. Then there will be the animals. It is a long journey. We will have to work out some way to store their dung for we can use it in the new world We need to keep them tethered and calm. We saw no metal. We should use metal for our ballast. There are stones aplenty on Bear Island."

She laughed, "You are the only one who would have thought of such a thing!"

"The snekke will be useful. We carried just five but she could carry chickens and sheep as well as a couple of families."

"You are thinking of Padraig and Aed."

"They know the ship and are good sailors. They can read a map and I can give them directions. I thought to ask Rek to sail with them or Sven. Had he been alive then Dreng would have been perfect."

"You did nothing wrong, Erik, and you are the only one who has thought this through." She brought herself close to me. She smelled of rosemary. "I will be with you through all of this. If there is opposition then Snorri and I will quell it. Whatever you need from me then ask."

I nodded, "You will need salve and medicine. We discovered that garlic kept away the biting insects but had I been more alert I might have found some way to stop Dreng's death. You and the volvas of the village can save lives."

"Then we shall brew and conjure from now until we sail!"

She left me to walk the deck. I thought of improvements we could make. I had helped to build this ship and I knew her well. We had taken weapons after the battles we had fought. They were now stored in the halls. If we were to use them as ballast then they would need to be oiled and placed in sand-filled sacks. That was an easy task but time-consuming. If we were going to fish as we sailed then we needed nets rather than lines. They could be made. We would need pots and barrels and rope! We had to make rope as often as we could. It was as I began to check off the list that I realized we could not sail in less than four moons and that would take us to the end of Haustmánuður. That was too close to winter for us to risk. I looked astern. I had forgotten *'Jötnar'*. She would need rebuilding. My repair would have to be undone and proper strakes made to replace the ones which had sprung. By noon I knew what was needed and I headed to Arne and Siggi to speak with them.

Sven and Rek approached me as I neared the halls. Sven said, "We should have thanked you, Captain."

"Thanked me? Why?"

"We would all have perished but for you. You took on a bear to save our lives and we are in your debt."

I nodded, "When I sail to the new world, I would have one of you on the drekar and the other on the snekke but I will not command. If you wish to say no then I will understand."

They shook their heads. Rek said, "For myself, I would be more comfortable on *'Jötnar'*."

"Then we will make it so. You have your own lives to lead. Sven, you need a sword and, I have no doubt, a helmet but it would help the clan if the two of you would help me and Fótr to repair the ships. You know them better than any."

Sven gave a slight bow. "We will be honoured."

Arne and Siggi were by the fields looking at the crops we had sown months earlier. "You have missed this joy, brother. Each day we come and see how little the crops have grown." His voice was heavy with sarcasm.

"The seeds will help us in the new world. Even if we cannot eat them, we can plant them."

Siggi laughed, "The sailor is telling the farmers what to do!"

"And in this, I will take his advice. We saw you leave with Gytha."

"I now know what we need," I told them.

Arne nodded, "Much of the metal is poor quality and scrap but even scrap is better than nothing. You have come up with a good idea and the clan needs something to do in winter. Making ropes and nets will keep them occupied. We can make barrels and fish traps too. There are ash trees up the fjord, we will use them and the feathers from the seabirds to make arrows. We can make heads in the new world. You are right. This will take months." He looked west, "And, like you, I fear our neighbours."

"Who is it does not wish to leave here?"

"Æimundr Loud Voice and Mikel the Follower but since your return, Uddi Long Face has joined them. When Butar, Finn, and Asbjorn were killed we lost the sage voices of the clan. Sighwarth sometimes supports the idea of a new world and then, at another time is the most vehement opponent."

Siggi laughed, "Aye and then Arne mentions Pridbjørn's knarr and he supports us once more. Pridbjørn was his friend."

"If we went to the new world, the land of the bear and deer, we could easily build a new knarr for him. There I saw trees which were bigger than any I saw in the lands of the Picts. And the trees are like an ocean. I saw no breaks. It may be the people who live there farm but they do not do so close to the coast for we saw no clearances."

Arne pointed to the women who were gathered outside the boat hall. Some were making cheese while others were making capes. "We have more women and children now than men. If we have to fight then we have fewer men."

"Arne, even our little brother had the skill to lay low their warriors."

"He said he killed one."

"He may have done but we did not stay to check!"

"So, we hunt the seal first and make salt. The crops will grow or they will not. Standing and watching will not encourage them to rise!" It was as we turned, I noticed a black line in the distance. It had not been there when we had left. "What is that?"

"That is what happens to the fire which flows from the mountain. It turns to black rock. It is as hard as the edge of a good sword."

"And it has stopped spewing?"

"It seems so. The ground shook first and then it burst forth. We had two such eruptions in the time you were away. The last one was bigger. Some of the rivers of fire reached the sea. The tiny piece of sand which lay to the west of us is now rock. This island is growing and changing its shape!"

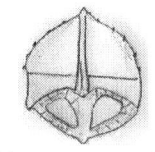

Chapter 11

Over the next month, we hunted seals. Their skins could be made into something which would protect us when we went to the land of the bear and the deer. Dreng might have died but the experiences we had shared would now help all of the clan to benefit. The four of us who had sailed were consulted by all. Halsten, Stig and Eidel were envious of Rek and that helped him to get over the loss of a shipmate.

I spoke with Padraig and Aed on those seal hunts and told them of our plan. They were as enthusiastic as I was. Both had children now and their wives were hardy women. Helga was my cousin and she was also a warrior. I told them of my charts and of Rek's offer to sail with them.

"He was a boy when last we sailed with him."

I nodded, "And in the years since then he has become almost a man. He may not be a giant like Sven is becoming but he knows how to steer. It means there will be three of you to take the steering board. It may be that we become separated on the voyage. I hope not but Rek knows how to sail."

"But we have no hourglass."

"And there were many days when we sailed beneath black clouds with neither sun nor stars. I kept a record and the winds were, generally, from the west. At dawn and dusk each day you will know the direction in which you sail. So long as it is south and west then you will be heading in the right direction. And I will hang a light from my stern for the few hours of darkness we will have to endure."

It was Tvímánuður when we saw the knarr approaching from the west. It was not Sighwarth's knarr. This one looked to be slightly bigger. We were working on the drekar. We had her drawn up on the beach and were coating the hull with pine tar. We had almost exhausted the pine trees. Some had been lost when the river of fire had burned them. There might have been others but they would be far from our home. We would not trek for them. Although not a warship, we were wary of the knarr and Arne, when he was told of the approach, ordered the women and children into the halls and the men to gather their arms. It was at that moment I saw how few we were in numbers.

The knarr approached our quay. Our snekke was tied there and I went to stand on its deck with Fótr, Rek and Sven. We did not recognize the captain. The knarr was laden. There looked to be at least seven families aboard her. The knarr bumped into the quay and two boys tied them up. The captain, who looked to be of an age with Arne, stepped on to the planking. Arne did not have his weapon drawn. There was no danger from just eight men.

"I would say welcome to our land but that you have come from the west and we have endured attacks from there."

The man nodded, "Aye, I know. I am Leif Eriksson." He held out his arm for Arne to clasp. My brother did so. "We lived on the west coast of this island but we have had enough. A man cannot make a farm work here. We are heading to Hibernia. Some of our folk lived there and we think that we could farm there at least."

I saw the relief on Arne's face, "Aye this land is not an easy one. Why did you come here?"

"The King of Norway left us little choice but he has no power in Hibernia. We would stay the night here. We know there is nothing east of here until Føroyar. We have supplies but one more night ashore would please the women."

Arne hesitated until a voice came from behind us. It was Gytha, "Make them welcome Arne Larsson. It is the right thing to do."

She was a woman but she was a volva and there was command in her voice. Arne nodded, "Forgive me, the volva is right. The attack last year has made me forget my manners."

Leif turned and said, "We can land." He looked at Arne, "Can we camp near to your hall?"

"Aye."

"Camp close to the halls on the headland."

Arne said, "Back to work." He put his arm around Leif. The visitor was smaller than my brother. "There is more to your leaving than just the land. No man risks the savages of Hibernia without good reason."

"It is Hakon Long Memory; since he came, we have had more outlaws than families. He rules the west of the island as though he is king. They seek women."

"They do not farm?"

We reached our fire and Arne gestured to the flat, black rock we used as a seat. It was amazingly smooth. Our breeks had polished it until it almost shone. "They have farms but they use thralls to work them. They raid."

Siggi shook his head, "Where do they raid? There is nothing around here."

"He has two drekar. Neither are particularly big but he sails east and raids the land of the Saxons. You have done the voyage. It is not as frightening as they say. The winds west make it easy. They are away just forty days and come back with grain and more slaves. There are rules in the lands of the Saxon and the Frank. There is justice. Here is the frontier. They want your women."

He just blurted it out and it shocked me. I spoke for the first time. "Why, if they have slaves?"

He smiled but it was a sad smile. "Hakon Long Memory is a strange man. He wants Norse or Danish blood coursing through the veins of his warriors. He believes that Saxons and Hibernians are weak. He has this idea to breed a clan of warriors who can return to the land of the Saxons and wrest it from King Harald!"

"But that will take years!"

"I told you he was strange. I came here for shelter and to warn you. He is coming for you. He sailed to raid the lands of Wessex fourteen nights' since and that is how we were able to leave. He will return and this will be his last voyage before winter sets in. He will bring back grain for beer and bread. He will bring back slaves and he will have warriors who will come and exact the vengeance for his dead brother and other slights he says he has endured. He now has a pair of sons who believe as he does. They have seen but twelve summers and they are as bad as their father. I fear to think what they will do when they lead their father's men."

"Thank you for the warning but you had no need to tell us. You owe us nothing."

"But I do. My son and the daughter of Leif Yellow Hair, Hilda, were married. It was she told us of the feud which led to their departure. She liked your clan and argued with her father. When he died one of Hakon Long Memory's sons, Harold, took a fancy to Helga. When my son tried to stop him, he was slain. I could do nothing about it for the Danes were all at home and we would have been massacred. The Dane took Helga. Two days' later we found her at the foot of a cliff. She had killed herself. I come to you in memory of Hilda."

I remembered Hilda. She had been pretty and, at thirteen summers, she had her whole life to live. Leif Eriksson had two reason to mourn for he had also lost a son.

Arne nodded and stood, "Then we thank you. We have a drekar to repair."

"And they want that too. Each time they sail east they return with more men such as they. I think they visit Dyflin and other wild ports to seek other outlaws. Three ships would give him a fleet."

Arne said, grimly, "We will fight them!"

"I beg you to leave this place. The last time Hakon came you had parity of numbers and prevailed but since then he has doubled his fighters. You cannot win."

Arne looked at me, "Erik, tell him of our plan. I believe this argument may sway the last of the doubters."

"Your plan?"

I nodded, "I sailed west in a snekke and found a land."

"The Green Land?"

"Perhaps." I was confused. I had seen no sign of others when we had landed. "A land filled with bears and deer?"

Leif shook his head and laughed, "Eirik the Red said it was a land full of green but the ones who went there found just snow and a land even more inhospitable than this one."

"And that is west of here?"

"Aye, due west. Ten days' sailing."

I shook my head and smiled, "Then that is not the land I found. I sailed for more than forty days and we sailed south and west. We found a land with deer and bear." I tapped my jerkin.

"I made this jerkin from the skin of one and these, "I picked up the pot with the plants we had taken, "are the sorts of plants which grow there."

He touched the plant. The last fruits had dried on the plant. We had left them to see if we could propagate from the seeds. "They look like grapes. So this land can grow vines?"

"Perhaps. We stayed there for just eighteen or so nights and returned to tell the clan."

I saw him look west, "Then this Vine Land might be a place we could live?"

"I do not lie. There are warriors there, skræling, they are fierce. When we go, we expect to fight for land."

"And how big is this land?"

"We sailed along it for seven days and nights. We saw no end to it." I stood, "And now I must go to my ship. If you would speak with me more then I will answer your questions when we eat."

I had piqued his curiosity and interest. That evening as we shared our food with them, he questioned me at length. When I stood to retire, he said, "It is *wyrd* our meeting. The Norns are spinning Erik the Navigator. I spoke with your young brother and he confirmed all that you said. If you could do that in a snekke then I believe you will succeed with the drekar. When you and your brother have your home watch for my ship. It will not be for some time but I would live in this land of the vines."

They left the next day and I never saw Leif or his people again. I often wondered if they had made the voyage. I realized that it would be easier for one to follow. They were not sailing into the unknown. He had seen the berry plant and knew I spoke the truth. Adventure was easier under those conditions.

After they had gone Arne convened a Thing. We held it two days later. Sven and Rek were both old enough to attend. Eidel, Halsten, and Stig were men grown. The five of them stood with me. Fótr looked unhappy. He was with the other young boys and they could only watch. He was half a year from being able to attend. In six moons he would be a man. He stood with Dreng's brother, Ebbe.

Everyone knew what Leif Eriksson had told us but Arne explained again. "We know that our neighbours cannot raid yet.

They are in the lands to the east of us. That will give us a month to prepare. The ice freezes at Gormánuðr and they would not risk the sea to attack us. If they have not attacked by Gormánuðr then the earliest they could do so would be the end of Gói." He allowed that to sink in. This was the task of a jarl. He had to plan and think for the clan. Arne had consulted with Gytha and Snorri before he had spoken. "I still plan on leaving. Gói would be the earliest that we could go. My brother told me that the journey will take more than forty days. As harsh as life is here, it would be harder at sea, in winter, on a drekar. The question is, who would wish to come with me?"

That began a debate. All those who supported the idea remained silent at first. It was important to allow the opposition to speak. Æimundr Loud Voice and Mikel the Follower, as we expected, began the debate.

"Jarl, you are right. This land is not the land we thought it to be but why risk this unknown land that a young navigator claims to have found? We could sail home. Leif Eriksson and his people had the right idea. We could sail to Hibernia. If we merely flee the King of the Norwegians then we will be safe there."

I was going to speak but Sven stepped forward. He was brave for he faced the entire clan. "Æimundr Loud Voice, I resent your choice of words. Erik does not claim anything. We did find a new world and the plants we brought back are proof. This is my first Thing and I will follow the rules but if you suggest that we lied about our journey again then when this is over you and I will have words."

"I fear no boy!"

"And I am no boy!"

I could see that this was getting heated. Sven had been wrong to speak thus. A Thing was time for reflective debate. I stepped forward, "I realize that it may seem incredible to some of the clan that we managed to do what we did." I looked over to Ada, "It cost Dreng his life. I do not say that life will be easy in the land of the bear and the deer but it will be better than here."

With the heat taken from the argument, it became a cut and thrust of argument and counter-argument. When a natural silence fell then Arne said, "We have spoken enough. Those who agree with me and think the clan should make a new home in the land my brother found then stand with me."

Four warriors remained alone, Æimundr Loud Voice, Mikel the Follower, Uddi and Sighwarth. When Sighwarth joined us then we knew the clan was with us. "You and your families can have these halls and we will leave food with you but at the end of Gói we will set sail to the west."

I hoped we did not have another Leif Yellow Hair who might try something untoward. I saw Gytha approaching the three men to speak with them. I said, "Sven, you almost began a war with your words."

"I am sorry, Captain, but I could not stand idly by while you were insulted."

"I thank you but I can fight my own battles." I turned to Arne, "And speaking of battles, how do we defeat Hakon for he will come and we both know that it will be before the winter bites?"

He and Siggi smiled, "We know and we have made plans. Snorri and Gytha applied their minds to this. We cut down the thin saplings which are of no use at the moment. We sharpen the tips and we bury them, while the sea is yet to freeze, beneath the surface to protect the beach and the quay. We can remove them before we leave but when they bring their drekar to attack then they might well impale themselves on the stakes."

Sven had not moved and he pointed west, "And what if they come over land the way they did the last time?"

Snorri smiled, "The Norns spun and the gods aided us. When the river of fire flooded down to the sea it built a wall of stone. It would have taken us years to do that which the mountain did in one day. They either come by sea or they do not come at all."

Gytha joined us and I waved Sven away. This was family. She smiled, "I promised the three of them that I would curse their families if they did as Leif Yellow Hair had done. I told them that we would help them to lay down the keel of a knarr to take them home. They were happy about that. All is well."

Gytha was the heart of the clan. I think she always had been. The longer we had been here the more powerful she had become. I wondered if she took power from the fire in the mountain.

I still had the snekke to repair. She was drawn up on the beach and we had stripped her back to the undamaged strakes.

The sprung ones and the wood we had cut in the land of the deer and the bear would be used for firewood. Before we put the spare and scrap metal into the hull, I had Siggi and Sven make more nails. We had seen the value of them. Fótr, Rek and I painstakingly rebuilt *'Jötnar'*. We had a quantity of pine tar but not as much as I would have liked and so we used wool and fur to pack between the strakes. It made the tar go further and made a better seal. We left the boat to dry on the beach and then went to see to the drekar. By the time we had finished the snekke the rest of the men, with the exception of Mikel the Follower, Uddi and Æimundr Loud Voice had hewn the timber and sharpened it. We had fire hardened the tips in the fire.

The three of us took the decking out of the drekar and put it under the sail. Then we began to remove the stones. We placed them at the side of the trail which led to the halls. If Æimundr Loud Voice and the others wished to use them then they could move them further. It was as we removed the last ones that a family of mice fled our hull. I was not sure if they would return. If they bred on the island then the foxes would enjoy the change of diet. *Wyrd.*

With the stones removed we were able to examine the hull. Arne and I had built this with my father and Snorri. I saw the rune I had put in the bottom. I had remembered the piece of wood I had seen floating and I had decided to leave my mark too. We let the hull dry for a day or two and we helped the others to drive the stakes beneath the surface of the sea. We stripped off and worked in teams of four. Half an hour was the most that a team could manage in the icy waters. We used my hourglass to measure the time. The stakes were rammed in so that they were at an angle. The point was just the length of a leg below the surface. It would not be seen, especially at night, but it would drive into the hull of a drekar trying to enter the harbour. We only had two shifts to do but the others were in the water each day.

When we had let the air get to the hull, we examined it a little more closely. The timbers looked sound but, as a precaution, we packed them with pieces of fur and wool before painting the inside with pine tar. We had the luxury of allowing it to dry for another two days before we began to load the scrap metal. The women had woven rough sacks. First, we half-filled each one with scrap metal. These were the swords and daggers we had recovered which had bent and the badly damaged byrnies. Then we filled the sacks with the black sand from the beach and laid them in the bottom of the drekar. We took our time for I wanted a balanced drekar. When we came to the damaged helmets, we flattened them with hammers. In this way we had a layer of sand and metal filled sacks which ran the length of the hold. We rode a little lower in the water but we still had more to load. That would have to wait until we had decided what weapons we needed. We would also load barrels for the voyage.

By the time we had finished so had the other men and we were defensible. Our ships were protected. It was now Haustmánuður and the weather was changing. We had harvested all of the barley and oats. We had given two sacks to Mikel the Follower, Uddi and Æimundr Loud Voice. The two sacks were all that we could spare and their voyage would be shorter than ours. They would need them and then we set about building their knarr. We built it on the beach. We were limited in its length by the size of the trees. My advice was sought, for I had built two ships and was a navigator. Some of our men were angry that Mikel the Follower, Uddi and Æimundr Loud Voice had not helped us and yet they expected us to help build their knarr. I silenced them, "My crew and I will help Mikel the Follower, Uddi and Æimundr Loud Voice build their knarr. We would have no men working against their will that is bad luck and would offend Ran."

In the end, ten men helped us and Æimundr Loud Voice was grateful to me, "I am sorry if I offended you, Erik. I meant no harm."

I nodded, "I know. You are well named!"

He laughed, "Aye you have the right of it."

By the middle of Haustmánuður, we had the skeleton built. She would be just twelve paces long and eight paces wide. That was more than big enough for the three families. We then began the harder part. We made the strakes. It meant hewing wood and splitting it. Already we had exhausted the trees which were close to our halls and we had to have men chopping timber further up the fjord. We did not carry the logs down to the beach. We tied

Across the Seas

them together and towed them down the fjord. It saved time and kept the timber from drying out.

The nearest pine was on the other side of the fjord. To test the snekke we replaced the ballast and the deck. I sailed across with Fótr and Rek to bring down the tree we would need for the mast. It had to be tall and straight. Pine was best. I had an ulterior motive. I wanted pine tar and I told Arne that the three of us would camp out. We cut down the tree and while Fótr stripped the branches and leaves Rek and I began to dig up the stump and roots. This was the best time of year to collect the resin. In spring it rose up the tree but, as winter approached, it gathered in the roots. We had made rough clay pots to hold it. None of us were good potters but the vessels just had to be able to hold a hot liquid and be stoppered. They would do.

The nights were getting longer now and so we worked after dark. We managed to get the stump and roots out. Fótr, when he had finished cutting the branches, built a kiln. We had brought some of the hard, black fire rocks. We could create a hotter fire and make more tar. We had found a rock with a natural channel and we placed the bowl beneath it. Then we lit the kindling and when the fire was going well put in the chopped stump and roots. We covered the top and then ate.

Rek said as he chewed on the seal meat, "I will not miss this place. I have seen somewhere better. I have told my mother and my sisters. They do not like this land. I would sail now, Captain."

"As would I but we are not quite ready. We still have things to make and we owe it to the three families to do as much on the knarr as we can. We will not finish it before the snows come." Already we could smell the snow in the air. We had experienced one winter and this time we knew what to expect.

I sat up all night feeding the fire and the tar trickled out until not long before dawn. I stood and walked next to the water. The settlement was shrouded in darkness but I knew that men watched for our enemies. We knew that an attack was coming and we watched. I agreed with Rek. I would be glad to leave. I knew that my mother and my grandfather lay here but my father lay in the land of the Saxons. Their spirits lay in my head. Gytha had told me that she had used the dead to speak with me and that gave me comfort. I had not known that it was my mother and her father but now I would listen to the thoughts in my head. I would know that the dream I had when I awoke, came from them. It was a comforting thought.

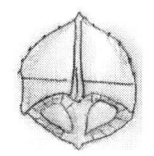

Chapter 12

We managed to have half of the knarr's strakes fitted and the mast step fitted before the snows came. We had even shaped the mast. The three families who would use the knarr were grateful to me. We stopped work and, before the ground and the snow froze, we hunted the seal. They had become wary of us and we had to climb over the ridge to the next bay to find them. We slew many. We needed their meat, their oil, their bones, and their skins. When we returned to our halls the snow was so deep that we struggled to get through it. Some thought it meant that our foes would not come but Arne and I knew differently. The sea was free of ice. The wind came from the west and Hakon Long Memory would be angry. Leif Eriksson had left him. That would hurt his pride and he still needed revenge for his brother. He would come. He would come because he would think that we would not expect him. We would watch because it just cost us a little sleep and that was easier than risking the great sleep. We began to use two men to watch each night. I had told Arne that when we had returned from our voyage, we had been guided by the fire and it had made us invisible. We watched without a fire. The men who watched used furs.

It was my turn to be sentry and I watched with Gandálfr. We had the middle watch. I was warm for I had a hat made of deerskin and lined with duck down. Bear Island had yielded us great treasure. The duck down made my head feel warm, despite the freezing air. Around my shoulders, I wore my bear fur. Gandálfr had a fur but it was not made of one animal. He had pieces of stoat and weasel as well as squirrel and hare. Where the skins were stitched the wind whistled in. We had our swords but wore no helmets. We sat by the pile of ballast we had unloaded from the drekar. It gave us some protection from the wind. They would use most of it for the knarr but it provided a handy windbreak for us.

"Was it warmer in this new world of yours, Erik?"

Across the Seas

I heard the doubt in his voice. Gandálfr had never been further south than the Maeresea. "You have heard men talk of the land of the Moors and Miklagård?"

"Aye, they sound like magical places."

I had never been to the lands of the Moor but where we had been was the hottest place I had ever experienced. "I dare say they are like the land which we visited. It is hot. We needed no shelter at night and during the day we were sweating just sitting around. We used fire for the flames and not for the heat. Here we wait for the crops to peer, fearfully, from the ground. There, I think that they will leap out." He cast me a sideways glance, "I swear it. Ask the others and they will tell you."

"Yet I still fear to cross the Unending Sea."

"And in that, it is well named. I can understand the fear of those who never crossed it but we did. We saw the land and who knows if there is another sea beyond the land we saw."

I saw him thinking about that. Ideas such as mine needed absorption. I looked out into the fjord. It was a still night and our breath froze before us. My bear fur kept me as warm as though I was before a fire. My feet could have been warmer but I could live with that. We were not using the hourglass. When Gandálfr and I felt we were ready to sleep we would wake the next pair. The night was so silent I could hear Gandálfr breathing. I swear that I could see the fjord start to freeze. Then I heard, in the distance, a man-made sound. It was too regular to be natural. It was the sound of oars slicing through water. I nudged Gandálfr and pointed to the sea. I slipped my hat from my head. The cold hit me like a slap but my hearing sharpened. There was an oared ship out to sea and that meant one thing; a drekar. I pointed to the hall and slipped off my bear fur. I could not fight in a fur. I drew my sword. The enemy warriors were coming. I could not see them which meant they were still around the headland. There were warriors who had been with Leif Yellow Hair and joined this other clan. We had not killed them for we had not seen their bodies. They would know the entrance was tricky and would edge the drekar in. There might be two of them. Siggi, Arne, and Fótr appeared. Fótr gave me my bow and my arrow sack.

I smiled, "As before, Fótr, you watch your brother's back!"

He was bigger now. He was almost as big as Halsten. He had a seax in his belt but it would be his sling which he used first. He whirled his sling, "Always!"

We stood where the path began to climb. It would give us a wall of men and we could make it bristle with spears. The quay was covered in snow. We had not walked upon it since the last snow had fallen. The snow would slow down an enemy. It was slippery. Men would risk slipping and falling between our ships and the quay. More men appeared behind us. Some wore helmets and some wore mail. If this was two drekar which came we would be outnumbered and our deaths, although glorious, would be inevitable. I sheathed my sword and took an arrow. I had twenty arrows and all of them had a good tip. If I struck then they would kill.

I saw the prow as it edged around the headland. It was a dragon. It appeared to stop and then turn. I could hear no voices. This was a well-drilled crew. I saw the prow turn and then the oars bit and it came towards us. We now had the clan all ready. Every warrior and boy were ready to fight. Helga and the women warriors were ready. Gytha and the volvas conjured. I heard the oars but that was all. The prow came towards us. I knew that we would be invisible for we did not move. Suddenly, I heard the sound of wood being torn apart. The drekar drove on to the stakes. Although moving slowly they had enough way to tear the wooden stakes into the heart of the dragon ship and kill it. As the water flooded in the bows dipped. The drekar came on and the stakes drove deeper into its heart. I heard voices from the steering board and watched the second drekar sail up the fjord. They would land at the beach. Men shouted as the water filled the ship. Those in mail tried, in vain, to shed their mail and they sank beneath the water. Others threw off helmets and swam towards us. Most would sink beneath the waves for the icy water would kill. I sent my arrows towards the white faces I saw in the dark. I saw a warrior with a leather byrnie raise his sword and shout, "Charge!" He was forty paces from me and my yew bow drove the arrow into his chest and he fell face down in the water. The boat then began to sink from the stern and men tried to clamber over the bow to reach the safety of the rocks at the end of our quay.

Arne shouted, "Siggi! Take half the men and go to the other beach. Slingers. Kill them!"

Stones were hurled at men who had thrown away armour to avoid drowning. My next arrow hit a warrior in the shoulder and threw him around to land on the quay. I saw warriors felled with stones. The men on the drekar just wanted to live. The water meant certain death! The ship had begun to sink but the water would be too shallow for it to completely disappear. It became a half-submerged bridge. Warriors made it to the rocks at the end of the quay. When we had built the quay, we had made it long enough for just a drekar, a knarr, and a snekke. Now I was happy we had made that decision. We faced roughly the same number of men as we had but we also had boys like Fótr whose stones could break arms and crack skulls. It enraged the wet warriors with waterlogged boots as they tried to run down the snow-covered quay.

Arne and Snorri stood together with Galmr and Gandálfr. The quay was not wide enough for more. They had shields and spears. I nocked another of my arrows and sent it down the quay. The light was not good but the men who advanced had packed together. Four, at the front, had shields. My first arrow gouged into the cheek of a Dane. He still came on. They were moving more quickly now for the stones thrown by the half dozen boys had felled one warrior at the rear. Soon I would have to discard my bow and defend myself with my sword. I had an arrow nocked and ready when one of those at the front misplaced his foot. The snow went from drekar to quay. He stepped on to snow without wood beneath it. His foot slipped and his shield lowered. He was ten paces from me and my arrow caught him in the chest. He slid between *'Njörðr'* and the quay. I nocked a second arrow and hit the warrior behind him in the stomach. I dropped my bow and drew my sword. I stepped behind Gandálfr for I had no shield.

The sodden men struck our line but we had eight men to their four as the rising path enabled those of us in the second rank to strike at the heads of the enemy. Arne, Snorri, and Galmr were encased in mail. The men who came at them wore tunics. I brought my sword over from on high as Gandálfr and the Dane below me sparred with spears. I hit his helmet so hard that it was dented and Gandálfr's spear took him in the stomach when he faltered. Fótr and the boys continued with their rain of stones. The cold began to get to the men who had waded across their doomed drekar in kyrtles and tunics. Their movements and reactions were slower. They died and it was not a glorious death. They were butchered. Some were barely able to raise their weapons.

When Arne had slain the last one, he said, "Fótr, go and see how Siggi fares. If he needs our help then we will come. For the rest let us ensure that these men are all dead. Collect their weapons!"

I retrieved my bow and slung it. I only had a few arrows left to me. I picked the arrows from the dead as we passed. If I left them until later then the air would freeze the bodies and they would be broken. I also took any metal they carried. We took their coins even though they were of no use to us. They were metal. We could use the metal. None had to be sent to Valhalla for all were dead. We reached the drekar bridge. The moon had come from behind clouds as the battle had progressed. I could see that the drekar had managed to demolish all of the stakes. Our trap had worked better than we would have thought. We had the winter to work out how to remove the wreck and let us leave. I saw a couple of bodies floating and they bore my arrows. I would have to find a way to retrieve them. Bodies floated in the water. Even as we watched I saw one body tugged beneath the black fjord. There were predators there who would feast on the dead.

Fótr came running back. He slipped, slid and then fell in a heap. It made me smile, "Careful brother." I held out my hand to help him up.

"The other drekar did not land. It sailed up the fjord. Siggi and the others are watching it."

I turned to Arne and Snorri. Arne nodded, "Then this is not over. Back to the hall. Light a fire and have the women fetch food. If we are to fight a battle when dawn comes then we will be warmer than our foes."

Galmr said, "Do we not march to meet them?"

Arne shook his head, "Why? What lies to the north of us that you would wish to defend? We wait for daylight and meet them with full bellies and feet which are not frozen by the snow."

We went back to the hall. Galmr had a wound in his leg and Gandálfr's arm was cut. Gytha and her volvas tended to them. Her smile told me that she was unworried. I went into the hall to fetch my helmet and shield. I would not need my mail. There were others who would be in the front rank of our shield wall. My bow made me special not my skill with a sword. I had my deer hide jerkin and that would suffice. I picked up the last of my arrows. I had twelve left. With the four in my belt that was sixteen arrows, I could use before I took up my sword. Once outside I retrieved my bear fur and hat. I saw the wisdom of my brother's plan for as soon as I donned them, I felt heat coursing through my body. I had been cold and not known it. Siggi had left men to watch the fjord and Mikel the Follower was guarding his knarr skeleton. With a fire going a pot of seawater was put on and seal meat dropped into it.

We watched the sun rise in the east. The lack of clouds brought more ice with the dawn. I could see the sheen of ice beginning to form on the fjord. The Danish drekar would be able to sail down it and return to the sea but Siggi's men said that there was no sign of it. When the light became strong enough, I saw that they had landed just a mile up the fjord. I smiled to myself for they had landed on what looked like a beach. I knew it was not. There were rocks beneath the waterline. They had been disguised by the snow. They did not know it but their ship would be damaged. They would assume the grating they heard as they landed was shingle. I was the navigator. I knew my fjord. They had landed on rocks!

Siggi and two others, Faramir and Folkman, went with him. They had two short planks tied to their boots. We had found this was an easier way to walk across the snow. It was not quick but it prevented feet from sinking into the snow. When they returned Siggi was in good humour, "There are just forty men there. I think I recognized Hakon Long Memory. The sun from the east shone on eight men with mail byrnies. They were debating."

Arne rubbed his beard. He looked at the sky which was a clear blue without a cloud in sight. It would be a cold day. The air was making our breath crystallize as we spoke. "We wait. Let them make the decision."

Æimundr Loud Voice asked, "But what if they just leave? The threat will still be there."

"The threat will always be there. Do you not remember Leif Eriksson's words? There are two sons. I have not seen any youths with these bearded warriors. Did you, Siggi?"

Siggi shook his head, "They were all warriors. My cuz is right, Æimundr Loud Voice, even if we kill all of these warriors then, in the fullness of time the sons of Hakon Long Memory will come for us. Your hope is that you finish your knarr before that happens."

He nodded, "Then with the Allfather's help we will kill these men and we will continue to build the knarr in the winter!"

All looked at Æimundr Loud Voice as though he was mad. Soon there would be no daylight to build the knarr and the falling snow would mean they would have to dig out the knarr each day but we said nothing. He, Uddi, and Mikel the Follower had made their decision. They could change their mind and come with us but I suspected that he had objected too much to change his mind, His stiff neck might doom him.

It was an hour after the sun had risen when the Danes and the others who followed Hakon Long Memory began to march towards us. We had time to organize and Arne shouted, "Shield wall! Men with mail byrnies in the front rank. Brother, you and your bow have done good work this day. Continue to do so. Take the boys with slings and climb to yonder knoll. You can harass their right flank. They cannot hold their shields before them and protect their right. Weaken them."

I wondered if I was sent thither because I was not a warrior on whom my brother could rely. I served the clan and I swallowed my pride and said, "Aye, Jarl! Come, boys. Let us win this battle for the Clan of the Fox!"

The knoll lay ahead of our shield wall which was on the rising ground that led from the beach to the halls. Arne would not allow them to cause mischief with the half-built knarr. There was a risk that Hakon Long Memory might bring his men to attack us. If he did so we were fleet of foot and he would invite a wedge of spears into his side. When we reached the knoll, I laid down my shield. I had ten boys with me. Rek had a bow and ten arrows. His arrows were not as good as mine but if he found flesh then he could slow up a warrior and help one of ours to prevail. I saw Fótr looking enviously at his friend. If we survived this battle then I would help him to make his own bow. He would need it in the land of the deer and the bear. The two of them had become friends. They were shield brothers as Siggi, Arne and I were. They were close in age but Fótr was now taller than Rek.

I took off my bear fur. I would not need it. "Our task is to hurt the enemy. No one sends a stone or arrow at them until I give the command. Let them wonder why we wait here. Listen for my words and ignore all others. When I say release then send your missiles towards them. When I say stop you cease and when I say run then you head back to the halls!"

Gal Faramirson said, "Will that not be cowardly?"

Rek turned on him, "Hold your tongue and do as the Captain says! He is a warrior and knows what he is doing! I could not see you facing a charging black bear without fleeing with filled breeks!"

I smiled. I had created, without knowing it, my own oathsworn.

The Danes had formed a wedge. I saw that Hakon Long Memory led them. I knew why he did it. He intended to break our line and that was the most effective formation, but that would only work on dry ground and not when you were struggling through the snow. The ones behind could defend those in front but their boots would have no purchase to push their comrades into the wall of spears. I saw that they would pass within forty paces of us. That would be the time to unleash our weapons. It would be just before they struck. We would be able to keep up our attack while our spears held them off.

I nocked an arrow and drew. Rek emulated me. The boys began to whirl their slings above their heads. I was close enough to see the faces of those in the ranks behind the Dane. They glanced towards us. Their right arms carried their weapons. Their shields were to their fore. The men knew what was coming and I guessed they were anticipating the shower which was coming their way.

"Now!" I sent my arrow at the third warrior. His byrnie did not cover his arms and my arrow drove into his right arm. Rek's arrow hit a leg and our stones clattered off helmets, legs, and arms. I saw one man stumble. Another dropped his sword as a stone hit his hand. Even as I sent my second arrow into the back of the Dane behind Hakon, the two lines clashed with the sound of metal on wood and the shouts of warriors invoking the gods to help them. It was as I was nocking my next arrow that I saw Arne bring his sword down towards Hakon Long Memory's shoulder. I suspect had he not been cold and tired then the Dane might have been able to bring his shield up to block the blow. Arne was fresh and had been fed. He was quick and he was fighting for his clan. I believed he was better too although when my father had been badly wounded his skill and strength had not seemed to matter. He had been better than his opponent but still suffered. Arne's sword hit the Danish mail. I am positive he broke the bone there for I saw the Danish shield droop. I sent an arrow into the shoulder of the man behind the Dane. I saw Arne's shield smash into the Dane's face and then my brother swept across to hack into his enemy's neck. The blood splashed high and then stained the snow beyond the battle.

The death had a dual effect. Those at the rear, most of those who survived, turned and fled. They were the ones who had joined Hakon for gain. His four remaining oathsworn, including the man I had just wounded, sought vengeance. The one I had wounded turned and ran towards me.

I shouted, "Run!"

My boys would stand no chance against him. I sent my last arrow towards him but it was hurried and it hit his shield. I dropped the bow and grabbed my shield and drew my sword. It was just in time. The warrior might have an arrow in his right shoulder but he was a Viking. I barely blocked his sword with my shield. The force of it knocked me to the snow. I landed on the bear fur. He sensed his victory and brought the sword down. I rolled to my left and as I scrambled to my feet held up my shield to block the blow I knew was coming. My arm shivered with the shock but I also saw spatters of blood coming from his wound. That gave me hope and sometimes that is all that a warrior needs. Instead of backing off I roared and ran at him. I pushed my shield at his sword hand while I swept my sword from behind me. I caught his thigh. I was wearing my helmet and as our heads closed, I brought mine back to head butt him. He reeled and I lunged at his chest. He wore mail but my tip broke two of the links. I pulled my arm back and rammed it at the hole I had made. My sword sank through the leather and his tunic. I felt it grate off a bone. He was a strong man and he batted the sword away with his hand. My sword was torn from my hand. Whipping out Raedwulf's dagger I rammed it into his throat. He gurgled his life away.

I turned around and saw Rek and Fótr were standing behind me. Rek had an arrow nocked and Fótr had a dagger. I stood and smiled, "There are swords to be had and you deserve them. Take your weapons."

Arne had taken the Danish leader's head and he flourished it in the air. The survivors had reached their drekar and were hoisting the sail. I walked with Sven to my brother. I said, "They are doomed!"

We reached my brother as Sven said, "Why, Captain?"

"She hit the rocks when she grounded." Men on the oars were backing her into the fjord. I saw the gash below the waterline. "As soon as she moves forward the pressure of the water will fill her. The best that they can hope is that they reach the far side of the fjord. If they make the open sea they are doomed."

We all walked back to the halls to watch the voyage of the doomed drekar. It was clear to all except, perhaps, those on board that she was sinking. The wind from the north and the oars on each side which drove her towards the sea were making it more certain that they would sink in the fjord. The drekar, which was already low in the water, suddenly lurched to one side and water spilt over the gunwale. The men must have moved to the other side for the whole ship began to sink beneath the icy water. I saw the steersman run to the sails to hack through the back stays to slow down the water. It was too late. The sail flapped, loosened as it was. It made it look as though the drekar was waving for help. The water filled the drekar. The helmsman raised his fist at us and them jumped over to try to swim to the other shore. One by one we watched them drown. They were wet and exhausted already. Some tried to swim away from danger and head to the other shore. None made it. The drekar's mast and yard stood above the water.

I turned to Fótr and Rek. "Get to the snekke. We can save the sail."

Arne said, "You have no need. It will be easier to get the one from the first drekar."

"The Norns have spun. They have given us two sails. Æimundr Loud Voice will need a sail and a spare is always useful. There will be no danger."

I was proved correct. By the time the short day ended we had two sails. We were frozen to the bone but our enemies were dead and we were safe.

Chapter 13

The families making the knarr were given one of the sails. The other would be a spare for the drekar. Mikel came up with the idea of using it to cover the knarr so that they could continue to work on it. They did not think it would be finished by Einmánuður but now that the threat of the Danes was diminished, they had a chance.

All of our men and, indeed, most of the boys had a sword and a dagger. They had been taken from the two scenes of battle. Many had helmets but there were more lying in the fjord. There were mail byrnies which would rust in the icy waters there. I gave away the byrnie I had captured. I let Sven have it. I had Karl the Lame's but I was so convinced that I would not need it I put it in a sack with sand and added it to the ballast in the drekar. Even though icy winds blew each and every day I made sure that, no matter how little light we had, I would still examine the snekke and the drekar. The bear fur kept me warm, as I looked for damage.

For the rest of the time I copied my charts for Rek, Padraig and Aed would need them. The cloak maps I had made were added to and then I made an identical version for the snekke. We had a spare compass but the hourglass would remain in my care. I resurrected the pot lantern for the stern. That might be the snekke's only lifeline. Gytha and the volvas wove and they spun. It was not all spells. They wove clothes. I had told them that I had seen neither sheep nor goats but that did not mean they did not exist. I had not even set foot on the mainland. The skrælings we had seen had worn animal hides and so the clan prepared for a land without wool.

When the light was not good enough to copy maps or to carve bone tools I sat and talked with Siggi, Snorri and my brother. Fótr was my shadow. He would be close enough to fetch me food or some of the watered beer we were reduced to drinking.

He wanted to be a navigator and now that he was almost a man, he joined us.

"This empty island, the bear island, could you find it again?"

I nodded. "I think so. The trick will be to find the first piece of land. That will be the closest landfall. I think that was an island but there were people living upon it."

Snorri was carving a spear to hunt fish. He was carving a seal bone. The timber we had taken for the knarr had yielded many branches. Some could be used to make the hafts of spears. We wasted nothing. "I spoke with Gytha. She has had many dreams lately." He looked at me, "Dreng's spirit came to her."

I looked up, "He is not in Valhalla?"

Snorri shook his head, "His spirit wanders the waters where he died. He is alone. There are no other spirits with whom he can talk. He has spoken to Gytha. My wife believes that we should spend the first year making our new island home strong. If you are right about the size then it can support the clan. Until our children have grown and the clan becomes larger, we must look within."

Arne said, "That is a great deal of responsibility on my brother."

"He can handle it, nephew."

I had been paid a great compliment by Gytha and her husband. "Arne, the sea is where I am comfortable. I think Ran guides me. He sent me the piece of wood upon which were written the runes, twice. He wishes us to go to this new world. My fear is losing touch with the snekke."

Siggi smiled, "That sounds a little arrogant, cuz. You sailed the snekke and you reached the land of the deer and the bear. Even if we are separated there is no reason why Padraig and the others should not."

"I will remind you of your words when are deep into the ocean and great cliffs of water tower over us."

We sat and stared at the fire in silence. Arne spoke quietly, "I fear my worry is the diet. Salt meat and fish. No beer and no hot food; it fills my heart with dread."

"And until we can plant and harvest cereal then there will be none."

Fótr suddenly piped up, "What if they have no winter there?"

"What?"

"Well, brother, you said the people we saw were dark of skin. I have heard from others in the clan that the Moors are dark of skin and in their land, they have no winter. If this land is the same and there is neither snow nor frost then animals can graze outside all year. The crops will not take as long to grow and will be ready for harvest sooner. This is a new world. The Allfather has given us the chance to make it ours. You and Arne seem to be seeing the land as a horn of ale; half empty. I see it as being half full. Save for the biting insects I saw nothing when we were there which made me fearful."

Fótr was the same age as his cousin Tostig but Fótr had a little more knowledge of the world. It had been the right decision to take him with us.

Winter passed slowly. On quiet days we heard the sound of hammering as men worked on the knarr. More often than not we heard nothing save the whining of the wind as storms and blizzards wrapped around us. And then some of the animals became weaker. We had no grazing for them and they had been on reduced grain rations. Gytha advised Arne and we stopped brewing beer. As she told us the animals were more important than beer. The lack of beer made everyone's spirits plummet. When we passed the shortest day, which, thanks to the black storm clouds appeared to last less than an hour, I started to count down the days until we left.

At the start of Gói, we had a brief thaw. We knew it was not the end of winter but some of the snow melted and the days were marginally warmer. We took advantage. We cleared snow from the fields and allowed the animals to graze on last year's stubble. Half of the men worked on the knarr. The rest of us fitted new ropes to the snekke and drekar. The old ones were not wasted. We would keep them as spares. We lit the fire and melted metal to make spearheads and arrowheads. We made a new plough and scythe. The damaged mail we had taken after the battle was put to good use. We chopped more wood. There was none nearby but the slight thaw enabled us to walk to the nearest copse and clear it of the saplings. The thaw lasted seven nights but in that time our spirits were raised and the knarr's hull was almost completed. The three families saw hope. Then the freeze returned. There was a scattering of snow and we were enveloped once more in a world of white. The animals were brought back inside and we lost the sun.

Arne asked any others if they wished to go to the land of the Saxons. Thanks to Gytha none did. She had the women of the clan thinking the way she did. We had lost men and there were families whose head was a woman. I was asked over and over why I did not father a son. There were many women of thirteen summers who could bear children. Eidel, Halsten, and Sven were already casting their eyes over potential brides. I did wonder if Æimundr Loud Voice, Uddi and Mikel the Follower would change their minds and come with us but they did not relent. I was sad.

The sail over the knarr enabled the three families to work even on the coldest days and the hull was finished. The mast was ready to be fitted into the mast step but that would have to wait until the sail was removed. Soon they would coat the hull with pine tar. In a perfect world, we would let it dry for a month and then soak it in the sea. The Norns were spinning and they would not have the time with the knarr that they wished.

At Einmánuður the ground shook. I had not been there the last time and I was truly terrified. It felt as though a giant had grabbed our hall and shaken it. I confess I ran outside with just my bear fur to cover me. I looked at the mountain but did not see any fire. There had been fire the last time. A fissure had opened and a beck of fiery rock had flowed down the mountain's sides. This time it was just a shaking of the rock. Even as I stared at the mountain, I saw boulders bouncing down. Luckily, they came not towards our hall but the wall of stone which was the result of the last fiery river. The largest stones punched a hole in the wall. If they had hit my ship then it would have been destroyed. Now I understood the power which had made the village sleep out of doors. This was winter. There was no possibility of sleeping out of doors.

Gytha, wrapped in a fur cape, came out to get me, "Come, Erik. This is a gentle shaking. You will know when the mountain begins to burn for there will be a crack like the sound of Thor's hammer."

I would not have returned for any other than the volva. I did not sleep any more that night even though the earth ceased to shake. For the next eight nights, we had more shaking. It was not always the same time of day and the strength seemed to increase. We had more sunlight and the true thaw began. We had had a warning and we heeded it. Our ballast was in place and so we loaded that which the people would take. The anvil was placed in the hold by the steering board. The smaller barrels of salted meat were placed in the hold. Each day more was added. The knarr, which would be named *'Mountain Dragon'* in honour of the mountain which towered over us, was painted with pine tar. We had just one pot left for the voyage west. Within a few days, we could launch the knarr.

Then we were woken by the crack which Gytha had told me of. This time the whole of the clan raced outside. We looked to the mountain and the smell of sulphur was overpowering. Worse, we could not see the top of the mountain. It was wreathed in smoke. When we saw the red river flowing down the mountainside, we knew that our days on the island were numbered. I had never seen this river and it moved so slowly as to appear harmless. I knew from the others that it was not. I saw it reach a single tree. Suddenly the tree flared into flame and was destroyed.

Arne said, "We have time. Let us not panic but we load the ships. I looked at Mikel the Follower. They would not have the luxury of letting the tar dry thoroughly. They would have to launch her immediately. I could not help them. I had two ships to load and their decks to lay.

"Come Fótr, Rek, Padraig. Our work begins."

I had hoped to have clement weather and time to load the drekar carefully. The mountain and the Norns had determined otherwise. I had already packed my chest and that was in the knarr hall. What we had to place in the hold were the items we would need when we reached our new home. With so many people on board, we would not be able to lift the deck. We would be packed from gunwale to gunwale. If we had to row, we would only be able to use the middle oars. Rek, Fótr, and Aed worked on the snekke. Eidel, Stig, Halsten and Sven joined Fótr and me on the drekar. All the time we were working we felt the earth move and rumble like an old man's belly. When we glanced up at the mountain, we saw the red snake slithering slowly down to the sea. It looked, each time we spied it, as though it would miss our halls. Gytha had urged us to hurry and so we did not take that as a certainty. As we had built the knarr on the beach it was not easy to shift it to the sea. I heard the men grunting and groaning. By the time night fell we had loaded all that we could load into the holds of the snekke and drekar. Normally we would have ceased work but we could not afford to and so we laid the deck. That took time. It only fitted one way. If a piece of the deck was set in the wrong place we would have to start again. I thanked my dead father as we worked for we had used runes to mark the wood and help us. Even so, we were exhausted by the time we were called to food.

Helga came for us, "My mother said there is little point in killing yourselves. Eat then sleep. The fire snake is still slipping down the mountain."

Helga was like her mother and forceful. We obeyed her. Once we had eaten, I went into the hall. I fetched out my bear fur and hat and then my chest. Arne asked, "Are you so fearful, brother?"

I shook my head, "I have had my last night under a roof for many months. When we reach our new home and we have built our hall then I will sleep with a roof over me. Until then I will get used to this. I do not mind."

He saw Fótr dragging his own chest outside. Arne gave me a wry smile, "It is not hard to see which brother Fótr favours."

He sounded disappointed but he was not. He had his own son, Lars. Fótr needed a father and I would be his foster father.

I had spent the short days in the heart of winter packing my chest. I had made the voyage and knew what I needed. Since my return, I had made a second pair of sealskin boots. I had those at the bottom of my chest. I now had two sealskin capes including one with a hood. I had given away my blankets. I had my bear fur and would not need them. I had made more clothes. My cousin Helga had helped me as well as my brother's wife, Freja. Raedwulf's dagger and my sword were also in the chest along with my helmet. They would not be needed. I had made ten arrowheads from metal. They were at the bottom of the chest too.

My arrows would be close to the top. My bow had a place made for it by the steering board. I was captain and such luxuries were reserved for me. Finally, I had, at the top of the chest, all the things I would need for the voyage. I had made a spare compass and my older one now had a leather lanyard so that I could keep it around my neck.

We had kept a fire burning all night. We did not worry about wasting wood for we were leaving. The fire kept me warm. I slept but I slept fitfully for the mountain rumbled and belched all night. I was awoken, just before dawn, by a second almighty crack. I stood and saw stones landing on the mountainside. Ash began to fall and I saw a second fire snake. This one was faster and, alarmingly, it had taken a different course. Arne and Snorri came from the hall and their faces told me that this was worse than the last time the mountain had spewed forth fire.

When Gytha came out she took charge of the women. "Cook all the food that we have. This may well be our last hot meal." Women nodded and hurried to obey. They dropped salted meat into the cauldron on the fire. She came to me and said, "And today we will see your true worth to the clan. Take this opportunity and grasp it in both hands."

"Come Fótr. It is still dark but we have enough light from the mountain to do that which we need." We carried first my chest and then his, down to the drekar. Ours would be the first aboard. There was no rush for the clan was waking to the news that we were leaving. They were gathering all that they would take with them. We had just secured my chest with ropes to the metal rings at the stern when there was a huge explosion. It knocked me from my feet. I watch as a fiery stone plummeted down and crashed into the knarr hall. The wood began to burn. Arne and the men ran to rescue those who were within. Siggi shouted, "Get out of the buildings!"

We hurried back and were in time to see a black-faced Arne shake his head and say, "Those that were within are dead."

Gytha asked, "Who was it?

"Pridbjørn's widow and her daughters. Her sons were helping to move the knarr."

We had no time to mourn for a second burning stone hit the other hall and that ignited. All had left that hall. Siggi's cry had saved them. Arne said, "Move your chests to the quay. Erik, we need to load now."

I pointed behind him, "It may be too late."

The second fire snake which had raced down had found the gap where the boulder had smashed through the wall of rock. It was heading for the halls and from there it would race down to the drekar and the snekke."

We grabbed Fótr's chest and ran to the drekar. Leaving my brother to fasten it I shouted, "Load the barrels of water and food! Fetch the cauldron of food!" I dared not panic. An ill loaded boat could doom us all. The men who had been helping Æimundr Loud Voice and his people came racing back. The three families would have to cope on their own.

Padraig and Aed came to me. "We have loaded the snekke!"

"Good for I need your help. I want the larger barrels by the mast then spread the rest out around the outside. When that is done fetch and tether the animals."

Gradually families made it to the drekar and stood, nervously, waiting on the quay. We could not let them load until the barrels were secured. My men knew the drekar well and they worked efficiently. Aed shouted, "All fastened Captain!"

"Then get back to your snekke. Cast off and wait for us in the fjord." I folded the bear fur and lifted the lid of my chest. I took the compass and the hourglass. I put the compass around my neck and laid the hourglass on the fur. Then I closed the lid. We were going to sea.

I turned to Sven. He had boarded and his chest was already fastened, "Load them, Sven. Smile and put them at their ease. I will go and tell my brother."

As I made my way through the throng of people waiting to board, I saw that the red snake had spread and was racing towards the halls. It was less than forty paces away. I saw that the men had dug a channel to try to divert it away. I thought it a vain attempt but even a few moments might help us.

"Brother, we need to go. The people are boarding."

He nodded, "You are right. The Norns are spinning. They do not wish us to live here. Had we left when you said then those who died in the hall would still be alive."

Gytha's voice was like ice, "Arne, you are the jarl! You did all that you could. It is *wyrd*. Come! Your brother is right and now he leads!" She turned to Helga and Maren, "Come let us take the cauldron. We will eat the stew on the drekar."

"Get to the ship. I will tell Mikel that we leave."

I thought it foolish but I admired him for trying. I waited until the others were running towards the drekar. The fire snake was less than ten paces from me. I was mesmerized. I saw it strike the channel that had been dug. It slowed it as it flowed, briefly, away from the quay, and I ran. Arne's efforts might just save us. Gytha and Snorri were waiting to board. I had never seen such a crowded drekar. Would we all fit?

"Fótr and Sven stand by the sail. Eidel, Halsten, and Stig let us loose from the land. Get aboard or burn!"

The fire snake was racing down the path towards the wooden quay. The quay would doom us all. Gytha and Snorri jumped aboard as I shouted, "Loose the sail!" Eidel and Stig leapt over the side. I ran and hurled myself. There was a gap of two paces for the wind had caught the sail. I saw Siggi grab the steering board and head us away from the quay. *'Njörðr'* waited for me. I caught the gunwale and clambered up the side.

Siggi said, "Where is Arne?"

"He went to warn the knarr. It was foolish but he is honourable."

I grabbed the steering board and headed out to the snekke. I saw the river snake hit the quay and it flared up. A wall of heat hit us. Although we were not heading for war we had the shields along the side. They blocked the wall of fire. They would afford protection from the waves and they were out of the way. The heat caught them and helped to push us to safety. The fire drove us away from danger. The Allfather was watching us. The river snake struck the sea and it hissed. A wall of steam rose and then the red snake turned black and died as it hit the water. Ran had saved us too. The gods wanted us to prevail. I watched as more fire snakes poured down. They buried the quay and the drekar which lay, still, beneath the waters. There would be no trace of our home in the fjord. The island was wiping us from the face of the earth.

Across the Seas

As we reached the fjord, I saw the snekke under reefed sails and to my great relief, the knarr putting off. Arne stood at the prow of the knarr. The settlement was destroyed. It lay covered by the fire snakes. The quay burned and was turning black as the red fire turned to stone. Maevesfjörður had lasted less than a couple of years. It would be buried beneath black stone. It was a monument to our people. My mother and grandfather lay beneath along with other members of the clan. We had not made a home in the land of ice and fire. Would the land of the deer and the bear be any different?

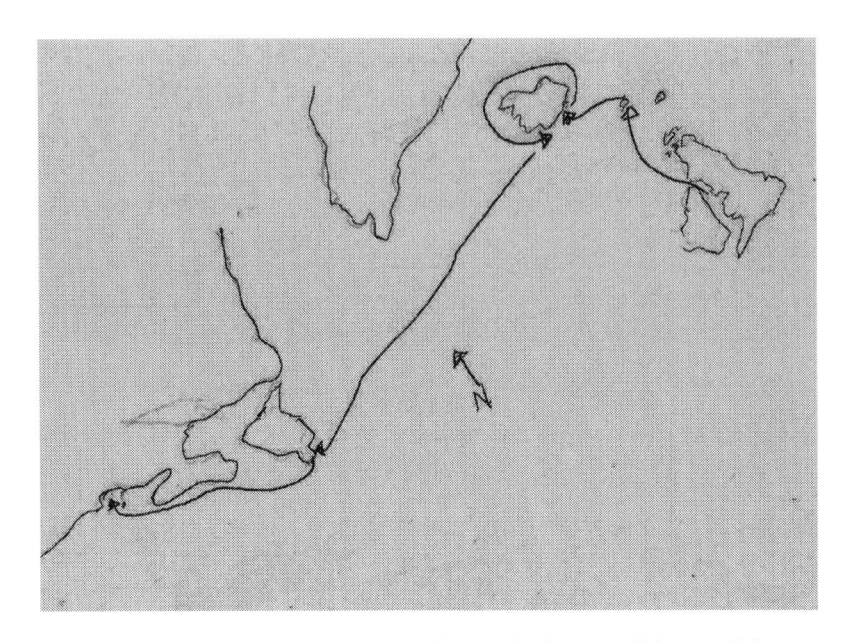

Erik's Voyages from Larswick to the land of ice and fire and the Island of the Bear.

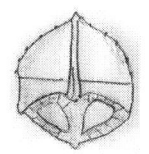

Chapter 14

We transferred Arne to our drekar and I led the three ships from the fjord. Dawn was breaking as we did so. The mountain was still spewing fire. Ash was falling like snow and the air smelled of brimstone and sulphur. When we reached the mouth of the fjord we turned south and west and the knarr south and east. We would never see our friends again but we had both fought the mountain. We shared that as a memory. As we turned, we saw the full effect of the eruption. It was not just the fire snake on our side of the mountain. There were others and they flowed down towards the sea and us. We were just two hundred paces from the shoreline and we heard the hiss and saw the steam as the fire snake died in the sea. Ran could defeat the fire snake but the beast which came from the bowels of the earth had no enemy on land who could defeat it.

The fire snake poured into the sea. The island was growing. This was the part of the coast I had not explored. With the sun from the east, I saw the houses on the settlements which dotted the coastline. One of them would belong to the sons of Hakon Long Memory. If they saw us departing it would not help them. The sea was wide and I doubted that they would find our new home. Part of me knew that if they did then we would defeat them. We had fought them twice and hurt them. The Allfather was on our side. We could put Vikings behind us. If we had enemies other than nature then it would be the savages we had already met. The deck was covered in ash. We were covered in ash. I saw the women clearing it but it was a useless gesture. Even as it was cleared more fell.

Snorri tried to make light of it, "It is a pity we cannot store this. If we had it when we plant our fields then it would help the soil."

"All I know, uncle, is that it dirties my deck and we shall have to clear it." He nodded, "I leave it to you and my brother to organize the families. I have enough to do sailing the drekar without worrying about who sleeps where."

He smiled, "I can hear in your words that you are worried, nephew. Fear not. You and your brother have the best of your father in both of you. You will get us to this new land. We may have trials and tribulations along the way and not all of us will reach it but we will get there. My wife has dreamed it."

I nodded. Tostig had asked to help us sail the ship. Although the same age as Fótr he had no experience. I smiled as my brother became exasperated when everything had to be explained. What was second nature to Fótr was a foreign language to Tostig. We had two other boys, Folki and Fal who helped Fótr. I had Sven, Halsten and Eidel who could help me to steer. They would not need to work the sails. We had enough men aboard to make the raising and the lowering of the sail the work of moments. Fótr took the others around the drekar. He was showing them what was the purpose and function of each stay and sheet while also checking that everything was well. His time on the snekke had been vital. I fingered my compass. I would need neither the compass nor the hourglass until we had cleared the wreath of smoke which covered the island.

This first part of the journey was important. *'Njörðr'* and I had to get to know each other again. I had sailed the lively snekke. My drekar took longer to turn. She had less exaggerated movements. I had many people on board. On the snekke, we rarely moved. Here there was constant motion from those on board. I wanted them all to be still but I knew that the excitement and trauma of leaving our home made that impossible. For that reason, I kept the wind behind us so that we struck the waves head-on. We had less chance of broaching. The winds and the fiery mountain helped us to move away from the land quicker than I had expected. I glanced astern and saw that Padraig was having no difficulty in keeping close to us. *'Jötnar'* could sail beyond us any time he chose. I felt *'Njörðr'* judder. My ship was reading my mind. "I do not wish to be back in the snekke. You need not be jealous. I am happy to have your hull beneath my feet." I turned the board slightly. The motion became easier.

We did not lose sight of our temporary island home all day. The island itself disappeared but we saw its wreath of smoke to the north of us. Gradually the women's efforts to cleanse the deck began to succeed. We could see the wood. Despite the cold, I saw women take clothes from their children to shake them over the side. It was as though the drekar was throwing off ash herself. We were shedding our old skin to don a new one. I had not seen Arne since we had set sail. He had much to do. We had animals on board. Without the luxury of a leisurely boarding they were anxious and he and Siggi, along with the other men had been making them comfortable. Odin, the bull we had taken from the Saxons had been the easiest to load. For that I was grateful. If he had chosen to be awkward then the drekar might be a pile of burned ash being covered by the blackened remains of the fire snake.

The only part of the drekar not encumbered with bodies, animals or barrels was around the steering board. I had space two paces by the width of the drekar. Sven, Halsten, Eidel and I would rarely move from this space. This first day would be the last time that all four of us were awake and on watch at the same time. From now on one or two of us would be asleep all the time. The four ship's boys would sleep when their watch master slept. I just had Fótr. Eidel had Folki. Eidel and Halsten were the most nervous of the four of us. They had not been at sea for over a year. I was confident they would manage but Sven and I had arranged the night watches for the first seven days to be ours.

Sven brought me some water and dried seal meat. As I ate Eidel took the steering board. We all needed to have the feel of the drekar. "Sven, when you have eaten and made water then you can sleep. I will wake you in the night. Make sure Tostig sleeps too."

He laughed, "Was I ever as excited as he is, Captain?"

I nodded, "All of you were."

He nodded, "I will have him clear the ash from the larboard side of our new home. That should tire him out."

He went to find Tostig, "How does she feel, Eidel?"

"Different from the snekke. It is as though she is a woman grown. She does not make quick movements but she knows her mind."

"Aye." I pointed to the southwest. The sun was setting. "Before you turn in for the night light the pot and hang it from the stern. I have no doubt that we will lose the snekke at some time but let us not make it the first night eh?"

"Aye."

I picked up the new tally stick I had brought. I took my seax and cut a mark at the top. By the time we reached the far side of the world, there would be forty or fifty such cuts.

When darkness fell Arne joined me. He pointed along the drekar. It was as though the ship was alive. Families filled the drekar right up to the bow. The ship's deck seemed to move as some slept beneath blankets while others spoke to each other. "All is well, brother?"

Arne nodded, "Odin seems to calm the others. He is well named. So long as he remains in a good mood then we will have no problem from the animals."

"The problem will not be the animals. It will be the people. They have to endure this for day after day. You and Gytha will need to keep them occupied. The voyage we made from Larswick to Føroyar and Føroyar to the land we just left was over quickly compared with this one. "

He put his arm around my shoulder. "Do not fret, brother. I know the weight you bear. I will take all that I can from your shoulders. Until we reach this new land of yours then you lead the clan and we serve you."

Darkness fell. I could still see, in the north, a faint glow which flickered. The mountain was still wreaking havoc. It was only then that I saw the snekke. Padraig had her two lengths from us. Any closer and we would have risked a collision. The people slept. There was just Fótr, Eidel and I awake. I turned to Halsten, "Sleep while you can. My brother and I take this watch. I will have Sven wake you at dawn. Sven will give you this compass and the hourglass. If we have the sun then we can begin to plot our course."

He nodded and pointed to Fal and Folki. Both were curled up in two tiny balls. "And hopefully they will be a little calmer on the morrow eh?"

Soon my former ship's boys were asleep. Fótr and I were left alone with the sound of the sea rushing along the side of the drekar and the snap of sheets and stays. We sailed into darkness. We saw no stars. I was steering with the wind. We had marks on the gunwale and by keeping the steering board between them we knew that we were steering a straight course. I suspected that the smoke from the mountain still obscured the sky. Ash still fell. The wind was from the north.

Fótr was seated upon my chest. His own was much smaller. We were silent. I was listening to the ship and I knew not what he was thinking. My little brother was deeper than both Arne and myself. He was much younger than we were. When our mother had borne us, she had been younger. Fótr was a late child and she had treated him differently to us. She seemed to cling to him as a child. He suddenly said, "Our mother will now be buried beneath the fire snake."

I did not turn but nodded, "Aye, I dare say she will. Her body will be safe from any who would disturb it."

"She was a Christian," I said nothing. "Edmund told me once that Christians had to be buried in holy ground." He sighed, "I know not what makes holy ground but I do not think that the holes we dug for them were holy."

"You may be right." I was just filling the silence for Fótr had something he needed to talk through and this was a good time to do so.

"What I mean is that if she is covered by the blackened bones of the fire snake then she will be trapped there for all time."

"Perhaps, except that she is not alone. Her father is with her. He stayed with her all the time she lived with us. That shows great love."

"But she should be in heaven! Her heaven! It is not Valhalla. Will she be there?"

He wanted an answer I could not give. I would not lie to him. "When we found Edmund, he told us that he had heard our mother's confession and he confessed to us. I do not understand the idea but the followers of the White Christ believe that if you confess before you die then you go to heaven. Perhaps our mother is with her god now." I did not say that it should have been a priest who heard the confession. Edmund seemed happy that just saying the words granted him entry to heaven.

Fótr said, "Thank you, Erik. You have eased my troubled mind." I heard him stand. "I kept this. Was that wrong?"

I turned and saw that he had the wooden cross my mother kept around her neck. We had not found it when we had buried her and Arne had made a cross from two pieces of wood. "You took it from her?"

"After she was dead, I took it from her fingers. I just wanted something to remind me of her. When we had the storm and I thought we were going to die I held it and I heard her voice. It brought me comfort."

"Good, then keep it. A sailor needs all the luck he can manage."

The rest of our watch continued in silence. We had no way to measure time but when Fótr began to nod off I woke Sven and gave him the compass to hang around his neck. "The wind has not changed. The course is still south. We keep this course until I wake and then I will decide whither we go."

"Aye, Captain."

"Come Fótr, we brothers will share the bear fur. He will guard us both."

I was more tired than I thought for as soon as my head touched the fur and I wrapped it around us I was asleep. For the first three days we kept a course heading south and then the wind changed. We had had no sun for the ash cloud had followed us. The ash became less and less. Then the wind changed to come from the north and west. I gave Arne the bad news. "We had this last time. We may need to tack to make progress. I had hoped to sail west but that will have to wait and as we have neither sun nor stars, I cannot place us. The wind for the last few days aided us and took us further south than we might have hoped. Do you feel the air? It is already less cold."

He shook his head, "It is still cold or that might be that I miss hot food. We are in your hands."

We could still make good progress south for we could use the wind from the north but it meant we crabbed our way. When I could I eased the steering board to take us towards the southwest but, generally, we headed south by southwest. At some point, we would need to head west. We would have to use oars. I was waiting until the wind came from the south and west. I knew it would come and then, by rowing into the wind we would close with the hidden lands of the west. Then we would tack. I wanted to delay tacking for as long as possible. We invited collision with the snekke.

We had been sailing for eight days when the wind swung around to stall us. "Oars! Reef the sail!"

We had worked out that we could manage six oars on each side. We could double crew them. That would leave us men to take over. This was the first time we had run out the oars and we did not manage it smoothly. It took Gytha to restore order for it was the women and the children who caused the confusion. When the men were at the oars, I began a chant. We would not sing it for long. We just used two verses to get the rhythm.

The Clan of the Fox has no king
We will not bow nor kiss a ring
We fled our home to start anew
We are strong in heart though we are few
The Clan of the Fox has no king
We will not bow nor kiss a ring
We fled our home to start anew
We are strong in heart though we are few

The women had never heard the song. It told them who we were. I used the hourglass to keep a record of the time we rowed. We changed rowers after an hour. In all, we rowed for four hours. I deemed that we had made some progress south and west. "In oars! Lower the sail!" The snekke, as I knew well, did not need oars. She could tack and turn and still keep pace with us. North and south were somewhat uncertain directions without the sun but the light in the morning and the evening told us where east and west lay. The sun was lowering in the sky. There was cloud cover but an occasional shaft of sunlight told us where lay the west. Using the wind which was sent by the gods we headed south again.

All three watch keeners were awake. "We keep heading south. I know that we head towards an empty ocean but you need to trust me. Once the water feels warm then we will head west even if that means sailing north and west. We need some sun and I pray that the Allfather sends it to us."

Three days later and the wind had veered back to blow directly from the west. We could sail south and west once more. Even better was the fact that the Allfather answered our prayers. He sent the sun. It brightened the spirits of all of those on board. The clouds we had contained moisture and we had had rain. Those with seal skins had not suffered but some of the women and children had had to live with wet clothes. The sun allowed them to dry their clothes. The rain had, of course, topped up our barrels. I was confident that we would not run out of water. We had augmented our diet with fish. We would not starve. The snekke had also managed well and those on board were in good spirits. The day the sun came out felt like a wedding day. If we had had beer then it would have been perfect!

Now that we could use the compass, I was much happier. Our position was not precise but by using it and recording the position of the sun we could monitor our progress across the ocean. I still had the record I had taken in the snekke. Only I could read my notations but life was never perfect and we all had to make adjustments. The sun shone for the next three days. Our progress was steady. The last of our grain would be fed to the animals and we had rationed it so that it would last for fifty days. I hoped to make landfall before then. I had decided to risk the deer island with the warriors. I knew there was grazing and the warriors had not seemed particularly threatening.

Eidel had grown into his role. All of his experience came back to help him and I allowed him to take a night watch. It made life easier for me. I had felt like a bat, only coming out at night! Halsten was less confident. He always had been. We developed a routine now that I was awake during the day. Gytha, Arne and Snorri came to see me and they were filled with questions. The further south we went the more the air became warmer. The furthest south any of them had lived had been Larswick. I believed we were enjoying weather which was as warm as Larswick and I knew it would get warmer. They were curious how much warmer it would get.

I told them and then mentioned the biting insects. Gytha had questioned me about them when we had still been in the knarr hall. We knew of such insects. They plagued the land of the Picts and they were bearable. Arne and Snorri had dismissed them as an irrelevance. I saw their faces when Gytha probed me further.

"They are insects, Erik. A warrior bears such things."

Fótr was off duty too and he sat by me, "Tell them, Fótr, of the insects."

"There are so many that your head and face turn black with them Your arms are black too. They each bite so that your head swells with the red bites. Dreng suffered worst of all. He was ill." He looked at me, "Could the bites have killed him?"

I shook my head, "I know not."

Gytha smiled at Arne, "And that is why we listen to Erik. You said that when you ate garlic they did not bite as much?"

"Aye."

"I am assuming it grows freely in this land?"

"We found it in the dark and shady places."

"Then my women and I will seek it out when we land. People can eat it but I think I can make a salve. Did you see any of the fragrant herbs we had in Larswick?"

"I saw none but then we only explored part of one island."

"There will be other herbs which grow in this new world. We will find them. And you say there are honey bees?" I nodded. "Then the plants which the bees use will be the ones we use to ward off the biting insects. We use nature to fight the insects."

We had a period of twelve days when the weather remained the same. Some days sunny and some cloudy, occasional showers and the wind, generally coming towards us. Our progress was slow. Then the weather changed. When we had been at sea for twenty-eight days according to my tally stick, I saw, to the north and east, clouds. I wondered if it was our island then dismissed it. The wind began to turn so that it came from the north and east. While Arne took this as a good sign, for it meant we travelled faster, I feared it for the black clouds would herald a storm.

Halsten was steering and I went to him. "Turn so that we sail west. We will take advantage of this wind. I will tell Padraig." I went to the stern and made the signal for the snekke to close up to us. "How fare your passengers?"

"They are happy."

"There is a storm coming. I will turn west and make as much progress as we can. If we are separated, I will shorten sail to help you find us."

"Aye, captain."

"Rek this is about the place we saw the geese. It seems like a lifetime ago!"

Rek shouted, "For Dreng it is!"

He was right. Dreng had seen the geese but he had not reached his home. He was a reminder of the dangers we faced. I warned my brother of the storm and what it would mean. I took my seal cape and donned it. "If you wish to rig the sail over the passengers then do so. It might keep the bairns safe and make the women less fearful. I know that we had to bale for long periods in the snekke to keep her afloat. Padraig and his people will work hard. The sail might send the water over the side."

Arne decided that it was worth trying and he and the men set to organizing it. I had my ship's boys stand by the sheets and stays. Rather than risk losing the sail or having our mast damaged, I would reef it. The problem was one of timing. At the moment the wind was serving us and whipping us along the waves. I wanted to cover as much distance as we could. I had Halsten on the steering board and Eidel watching the snekke. The storm closed with us during a long day. We had the sail ready but not rigged. It was the late afternoon when the first drops fell and they were huge ones.

Arne shouted, "Rig the sail!"

I watched the pennant at the masthead. It was horizontal and stiff. The wind was coming from directly astern. From the light in the west that meant we were sailing due west. Then the rain began. It did not fall, it plummeted. There were hailstones mixed in with it and we heard the rumble of thunder.

"Reef the sail!" Sven helped the boys to do it faster than I had ever seen it done.

I glanced astern and saw that Padraig's sail was already reefed. I could not hear them but I saw Rek handing around containers to help them to bale. Thanks to our seal hunts the one thing we had plenty of was seal oil. I lit the lantern and hung it from the stern. We did not need it yet but by the time we did then I might be too busy to do so. We barely had the sail reefed before the heart of the storm struck us. It was a wild motion. The prow seemed to dive into troughs and a deluge of water cascaded from the waves behind. I feared for the snekke although we had endured a similar storm and we had survived. Some of the younger women screamed as the ship lurched. I heard Gytha's voice commanding order. It worked.

I joined Halsten at the steering board. It would take two of us to hold her. The snekke had been easier. We had been right to rig the spare sail for rivers of water poured over the sides. That was water we would have had to bale. The storm raged for two days. I never left the steering board but I was helped by the other three helmsmen. Lightning struck the seas around us but we were spared. I think others managed some sleep in those two days but I did not. We lost a sheep overboard and would have lost a child had Gandálfr not been quick-witted enough to grab him as he slid towards the gunwale. From then on, the women held their children even tighter.

I knew that the storm was abating. The motion became easier. The rain had stopped in the night but the waves were so high that we had to endure as much wetness as we had when it had rained. It was as I glanced astern to see the light that I realized I could not see the snekke. *'Jötnar'* had disappeared during the storm. When dawn broke and the seas calmed, we looked out on an empty ocean.

Chapter 15

I had the sail half lowered and sent Fótr up the mast to see what he could. He sat there until noon but saw nothing. I sent Tostig up to relieve him. The wind was once more from the northwest and we had resumed our crabbing course south and west. I had the sail lowered just half way. Arne came to me as the sun began to set ahead of us and Sven lit the lamp. "Do we turn and search for him?"

I shook my head, "He could be ahead of us or to the north or the south. We envisaged this happening. That is why Rek is with him. He has my maps and Rek will know the place we seek. If we became separated, we would meet at the first land we found. The land of the deer."

"Were there not warriors there?"

"Aye, and they know that. This time they have two warriors with them. When I was there, I had four boys. This time they know what to expect." I could tell that he wanted a different answer. "Arne, this is not like losing men on land. There are no paths here to follow. The only signs we might find would be wreckage if they have sunk. Remember when I followed the drekar in the snekke, heading for Larswick? I became separated but all was well. You must trust our people. We are sailors and we can sail."

He nodded, "We have lost enough warriors already. We cannot afford to lose these two as well."

"And we will not. Lower the sail. Tostig, scan the horizon one more time and then descend. Their fate lies with Ran and in the skills of Padraig, Aed, and Rek!"

The loss of the snekke cast a dark mood on the whole of our ship. The two families were popular. My cousin, Helga, was also on board. Snorri's grandchildren were with them. I felt eyes staring daggers at me. Gytha sought me out. "You did the right thing. My daughter is not drowned. Her spirit is still in this world but the ocean is so vast that I cannot see her."

"Her husband is a good sailor."

"I know and you are too. Your achievement is even greater than we thought. You did this in a tiny snekke. I feel humbled by what you did."

I began to blush. I was not used to such compliments. "It is just what I do."

She shook her head, "You are too modest but I am glad you are our leader on the sea. I sleep better and feel safer."

Each day we had taken to having a lookout at the masthead. All of us were desperate to see the snekke once more. As the days progressed and we saw an empty ocean then hope was lost. Then, one-morning, Tostig shouted, "Captain I spy a bank of cloud on the water."

Fog! It was an even greater enemy than a storm. It masked rocks, "Keep a watch on it. Crew, take a reef. Let us edge into this fogbank."

We were soon in the damp air. Over the past six days, the air had become much warmer and I knew we were closing with the land. We had seen more seabirds but this fog was a disaster. I remembered the rocks which ringed the islands along which we had sailed. When we entered the fog, I had Tostig join the other boys. They clung to the prow peering into the murk.

It was Fal who spied the rocks, "Rocks and white water to larboard!"

I put the steering board hard over. The movement was so violent that two women fell over and the cow mooed in terror.

"Take in another reef!"

The fog lasted a day and we edged our nervous way through it. Once again, I did without sleep. I was on watch at dawn when the sun rose and burned through the fog ahead of us. I sent Fótr up to the masthead. He had no sooner reached it than he shouted, "Land ahead."

I could not believe it. We had reached the new world sooner than when we had sailed the snekke. It must have been the time we rowed with oars and, perhaps, the fiery mountain had helped us too. Everyone gathered along the sides for their first glimpse of their new home. The sun began to burn away the fog and, as I glanced astern to see our wake, I also spied land to the south and east. The land ahead was not the land we had visited.

"Prepare to come about. Let loose the sail!"

Arne looked at me incredulously, "We have found land! Would you go home?"

Pointing ahead I said, "That island I do not know." Turning I said, "I believe that is the land we first found but I must sail around it to ascertain the truth of it."

"But there is land ahead!"

I shook my head. I was captain and this was my decision. "And the land behind us is closer. Besides Padraig might be there. We have to investigate." I sighed, "Brother until I say we are at the island of the bear then you must trust me."

He gave me a nod, "And I do. That you have found land after the storm, the fog and so many days at sea astounds me. Of course, I will trust you."

I waved over Sven and Fótr. "Fótr, to the masthead. I believe this land ahead is the land we first spied. I think we missed it in the fog. I intend to sail east and then south. The others can watch for rocks I wish you two to look at the land. You know that which we seek."

Fótr was bubbling with excitement, "Aye, brother. I believe it is. I feel it in my heart!"

"Then see it with your eye!"

"Aye."

"Ship's boys, keep watch for rocks."

I did not recognize the land but then I had never seen the north coast and as the land slipped away to the south then we were sailing along the north part of the island. Tostig and Fótr both shouted at the same time, "Open water ahead!"

I began to ease the steering board over slowly. The land looked like the one we had landed upon but, as it was mainly trees, it was hard to tell. By noon we had seen two tendrils of smoke and the dark-skinned warriors fishing. Their appearance drew many to the steerboard side. I had to shout at them to make them return to their places. This was not the place to overbalance the drekar. It was late afternoon when Fótr suddenly shouted, "Captain I see the beach where we landed. It lies off the steerboard bow."

Sven jumped up on the gunwale and grabbed the forestay. "It is, Captain. It is the tiny beach we used!"

"Eidel, take the steerboard."

I joined Sven. I looked for the snekke but there was no sign of it. "The beach is too small for us."

He nodded, "But we have found it."

"There is no sign of the snekke. If Rek sees this he will recognize it. They may land."

"Captain, close with the shore and I will swim and leave a message."

"Are you certain?"

"Aye, Captain, I am not afraid."

"Then tell them we sail south and look for a better anchorage. Shorten sail. Eidel head close to shore." I took a piece of my charcoal and gave it to him. He slipped off his clothes and stood on the gunwale. With the sail raised we slowed and halted just forty paces from the shore. Sven dived in and swam ashore. I looked for any warriors who might surprise him but there were none.

He returned and we pulled him up. He grinned, "It was good to have land beneath my feet again!"

"Hoist the sail!"

We left the beach and I wondered if the snekke was behind us, ahead of us or lying at the bottom of the ocean! We had cast the bones and they would lie where they fell. I could do nothing about this. The Norns had spun and the threads of my friends and cousins were beyond my control. The island, for now, I knew it to be an island, prevented the wind from having a great effect and we sailed gently down the coast. Fótr shouted, "Smoke ahead!"

Was this the camp of some of the barbarians? We were safe from them aboard our drekar but the fact that land was so close made everyone on the drekar wish to step ashore. There was a small headland which jutted out and there were trees which hid the fire. I had a theory about these people. The houses we had seen by the shore had been temporary. Perhaps, in the hot months, the biting insects inland drove them to the shore. This might be a camp of warriors waiting to ambush us. I put the steering board over so that we were more than two hundred paces from the shore. "Take in a reef."

As we edged around, I saw that the snekke was drawn up on the beach. Helga and Maren were cooking. Of the three men, there was no sign. I saw that this was a long beach and we could land. I clutched the blue stone. Gytha was aboard us but the Allfather had guided us here. We had landfall. We had crossed the Unending Sea.

"Take up the sail! We are here!"

I put the board over and headed the prow to the sand. We slid gently onto the shingle and sand. Tostig, Fal, Faramir, and Fótr leapt ashore and ran with ropes to tie us to the trees. "Run out the gangplanks over the prow!" Turning to Sven, Halsten and Eidel I said, "We have achieved what we set out to do. Well done. I thank you."

Eidel shook his head, "Sven has done this before but I am in awe of you Captain; through the storm and the fog, when the winds were against us you never lost faith. You trusted your own judgment. I can never be a navigator. I will be a warrior; find a wife and make young warriors!" He spread his arms around him, "This land smells good!"

He was right. There was a wholesome smell from the shore. This land felt right. This would not be our home but we could camp here and, in the spring, leave for our island of the bear!

Helga and Maren, with their children in their arms, came to greet us. Arne, Snorri, and Gytha were the first to disembark. I waited while the clan trooped past me. The men, to a one, clasped my arm as they passed me. No words were said for none were needed. I saw in their eyes that they were grateful. None had sailed so far from land before and they were pleased to be alive and away from the fiery mountain.

"Fótr, Tostig, let us take Odin ashore. The others will follow. Fal, put another gangplank so that it will bear Odin's weight. I would not wet him! He might think we try to baptize him." I slipped a halter over his huge neck and spoke to him as I did so. "A new land for you. I fear that you will not enjoy the biting insects but you will get to use your tail."

His snort made me laugh. He might be a Saxon bull but he had a Viking heart. Behind me, Tostig and Fótr were moving the cow and calf. I hoped that the sheep and two pigs would choose to come of their own volition. We had no ram and, unless we found one in this new land, we would have no more. The two sheep we had would just be kept for their wool but we believed that the pigs would produce young.

The two gangplanks creaked when Odin and I stepped on to them but they held. We moved down slowly and it gave me the chance to see the clan. Some struggled to keep their feet. The land would appear to be moving. Added to that was the fact that the sand was soft. It would take some time. I led the bull to the grass which grew beneath the trees. It was spring grass. I had no doubt it would be a little salty but the animals would not mind that. Fótr handed me the hammer and the metal stake. I drove it into the ground. The cow and calf would stay close to the bull.

That done I took out Gytha's blue stone and kissed it. "Thank you Ran, thank you Allfather, thank you the spirit of my father." I was not arrogant enough to believe that I could have made the journey without their help.

I wanted just to lie beneath the trees and sleep but I was the captain. Our journey was not over. This was a waypoint. I had to ensure that my ship was sound and that we were prepared for the next part of the voyage. I saw that Tostig was reunited with his sister. "Fótr, Folki, Fal come with me."

We went aboard the drekar. I found the water barrels. As I had expected one was completely empty and one was half empty. The third one had also been broached. In a perfectly ordered world, we would take all of them ashore and empty then refill them. This was not a perfect world. "Take the empty one ashore. I am certain that Rek and the others will have found water. Empty the half empty barrel and let the animals drink it. Take their trough."

Left alone on the drekar, I began to move the smaller barrels we would use to fill the large ones closer to the prow. That done I began to examine the ropes for damage. I clambered up the mast to look at the sail. It would need a little stitching but that could wait until we reached the Isle of the Bear. I reached the mast fish. We had been lucky. We could have suffered much worse. My voyage on the snekke had prepared me. If I had not renewed all that I could we might now be pieces of driftwood.

I had not heard Gytha and Arne return aboard. As I turned, they smiled and my aunt embraced me, "The one who worked

Across the Seas

the hardest to bring us here is the only one working still. While the rest of the clan laughs and enjoys the sun, you still walk your deck alone."

I shrugged, "We have yet to reach our destination. Remember that I know there are warriors on this island and now that I have seen its size the numbers may be enough to cause us trouble."

Gytha gave Arne a knowing look and he looked a little shamefaced. I guessed words had already been exchanged, "Brother, you are right. We are here to consult. You are the only one who can advise. What do we do now?"

Gytha nodded, "The mark of a good leader. He knows when to be a follower. I will leave you. The women will make our camp homely."

When she had gone Arne said, "You know each time she speaks I feel like a little boy."

I laughed, "I know what you mean but I am glad that she is so. As for my advice? We need the water barrels to be filled. There is hunting on this island and that will give us food. The animals need to recover. Given all of that, I would say we need to spend seven nights here but…"

"There is a but?"

"But will the warriors who live on this island allow that? It is less than a year since we were here last. They will remember us. You will need to fortify the camp. I have begun to check the drekar. I also need to check the snekke but those two actions will just take a day or so."

"We will start to make the camp defensible. Come, the clan would like to thank you."

"Thank me?" I was confused. "I just did that which I was supposed to."

He put a huge arm around me, "Aye brother. That is all you did." He shook his head, "The other voyagers who discovered new land found rocks covered in ice and snow. They found a land riven by fire snakes. You find this. I think, as does the clan, that you did more than you were supposed to!"

As I reached the top of the gangplank Arne stood back, for the clan were gathered on the beach and they began to cheer and chant my name. I felt humbled. I walked down the gangplank and men patted my back. Some of the pats made me wince. I saw

Across the Seas

some of the younger, unmarried women flash their eyes at me. I walked through them, smiling and red-faced. I went into the trees. I needed to make water. I could feel the heat from the land already. We had enjoyed a breeze from the sea. It was hard to believe that less than forty days ago we had been freezing in our fjord. We had made a mighty journey already. I did not retrace my steps. I went into the woods until I found a game trail and I followed that in the direction of the beach. It led me to a small stream. I cupped my hand to taste the water. It was good. The stream led, not to the beach, but a small shingle and rock covered outfall. I was fifty paces east of the camp. I walked back. Already I saw that there was a fire and the women were making food.

As I reached it, I saw Fótr and waved him over. "There are small barrels on the drekar. Roll the empty barrel back to the ship. Bring the small barrels. If you walk along the beach you will find a stream. The Allfather has made it so that it will fill the barrels."

Fal said, "Can we not enjoy the time ashore?"

Fótr snapped, "Are you a child? Our captain works and so do we."

I pointed to the tree line, "See Fal, the other men hew down trees to make us strong. They build a wall to keep us safe. The women cook. The only ones who do nothing are those who have seen less than five summers. We are the Clan of the Fox. This is what we do. We use our wits to survive."

I went to Gytha as the boys began to roll the empty barrel back to the ship. It would be good to have sweet water once more. Gytha was organizing the cooking. I pointed to the boys, "They are going to fill the water barrels. There is a stream yonder."

She nodded, "Good. You girls," she pointed to four who had seen about twelve summers, "take these pots and fill them with water." Giggling, they ran off and Gytha smiled, "This will be the start of the education of my son and his cousin. You should think about taking a wife. You could have any of the unmarried women, you know."

"I know but I am not ready."

"The clan needs warriors. You should be married." She suddenly stared into my eyes. "What a fool am I? Your dream. It comes to me! Now I see. Forgive a foolish old lady." She looked up at the sky, "The Norns spin and I, of all people, should have known that. You are wise, Erik the Navigator. Follow your heart for it knows its own course."

At the time I did not know what she meant. Gytha was wise beyond words. She could listen and she knew more than any person I had ever met. Before I could dwell on her words, I heard a shout as Padraig, Aed, and Rek returned. They had one of the local deer hanging from a spear. They had hunted

I hurried to them. I wondered if Arne might be upset for, after dropping the carcass they ran, not to him and the other men but to me. "Captain, we thought we had lost you!"

"I am just pleased that you live. Tell me all." I needed to know what had happened so that we could avoid it in future.

"When the storm came, we found it difficult to stay close to you. Sometimes we almost rammed the stern and, when we hung back a little, we lost you. After the storm had died, we looked for your sail but found none. We decided to follow the last course you had taken. We found the island. It was the north coast we found but Rek recognized it. I knew you could not land the drekar at the beach Rek said had been your home and so we sailed until we reached here. We arrived barely in time for a fog came from the east. It enveloped us. I confess, Captain, that I feared the island was enchanted. I had never seen fog descend so quickly and to be so dense. Then, yesterday, it cleared. We decided to go hunting."

Arne had joined us. He asked, "And did you see signs of the locals?"

"We crossed their trail but none of us was skilled enough at tracking to know how fresh were the prints."

"We will have a palisade up by dark. Tomorrow we hunt and we seek the warriors."

I looked at him, "We seek them?"

"Better we find them before they surprise us. You are the sailor and you have done your part. I am the warrior and I will now do mine. We need seven days. Let us make it a safe seven days." He turned, "Warriors, fetch your weapons, helmets, and shields from the ships, tomorrow we hunt!"

I brought my bear fur ashore and found somewhere beneath the trees. This land was not as warm as the land in which we would settle although it felt hot compared with the land of ice and fire. The hunt enabled the women to make a more interesting stew than we might have expected. With shellfish, deer heart and kidney as well as some salted seal meat and greens from the river, we dined well.

I sat, not with Arne, but my crew and that of the snekke. It was not that I did not wish to sit with Arne, Siggi, and Snorri but the eight of us around Padraig's fire had much to speak about. It was Aed who came up with a solution to our becoming separated. "It seems to me, Captain, that even if the storm had not driven us apart then the fog would. I have never seen it so thick. Had we taken down our sail and been towed by you then we would have been like a sea anchor. We would have kept you more stable and kept closer to you."

"Aye, but we would have risked snapping the tow."

Aed looked at Padraig, "Not if we used two tow ropes. One from the larboard quarter and one from the steerboard quarter."

We spent some time speaking of what we had each learned. It was not just that they had learned about the snekke and sailing. They had discovered something about themselves and their families. Padraig said, "I think that Aed and I are lucky in our women. They kept the children safe and did not complain. The Saxon women we knew would not have coped."

"We are a hardy clan and you two have augmented it. Our blood is all the stronger for it."

"And you should be thinking of your blood, Erik. When do you take a wife?"

They all looked at me. Was the whole clan debating my lack of wife or my apparent lack of interest in women? "When I found that piece of driftwood it set my course, Aed. When our clan has a new home with wooden walls and a roof; when we have defences against enemies and we sail no more then I will seek a bride. There is no rush. The girls who are of an age are already married. Should I marry a widow just to have children? I think not."

They seemed satisfied with my answer. As we ate Fótr said, "Sven, Halsten and Eidel are seeking brides. The three are seen as heroes by the unmarried women. When we went to fetch the water Salbjǫrg Bennisdotter spoke to Kolla Asbjornsdotter, and they were speaking of Sven and Eidel. They thought we heard them not but our shipmates have been casting their eyes upon them."

"That is good. We are few in number now. We have more women than men and we need to reverse that trend."

I went to check that the ships were secured to the land. I already had plans for the next day. We would, it there was little wind, lower the sail on the drekar and stitch it where necessary. We could remove the one from the snekke and repair that on the beach. Arne had already told me that he planned on taking all of the men to hunt and explore the land around. We would have to be the guards for the camp. I went to my chest and took out my helmet, sword, and arrows. I took my bow from its place at the stern and I went ashore. I would not need my shield. It was the only one which remained on the drekar.

I laid my weapons on the bear fur and lay down. Our ships were safe. An enemy would need to clamber over a palisade and get through a sleeping clan. They could not do that for Arne had four men watching the woods.

The next day Arne led the men out early. Gytha took the women who had older children to forage. We were left with the mothers who had babies, Padraig, Aed, and my five ship's boys. First, we took down the snekke's sail and laid it on the beach. There was still a breeze and so we left the drekar. The sail of the snekke was not badly damaged. We would not need to use the spare yet. We stitched it and then replaced it. The women arrived back at noon and so, while I waited for the wind to drop, which I guessed would be at noon, I sent the boys to forage for kindling.

Gytha looked pleased with herself. "We have honey for we found a bees' nest. Smoke works with these bees as it does with the bees at home." She grinned and looked twenty years younger, "I can make you the mead I promised you when we left Larswick!"

All of the women had their spirits similarly uplifted. On the voyage, they had just kept their children and babies occupied.

Now they could help the clan and make that which we needed. Inactivity does not sit well with our people. They had foraged not only honey but also greens and wild garlic. Gytha sent the older children to collect more shellfish. I had the traps we had made for lobsters. I took them and walked along the line of stones which made an arm of the small bay in which we camped. I put stones in the bottom of the two of them and then lowered them into the water. I tied the two ropes around rocks.

Walking back told me that the wind had dropped sufficiently. The boys were not back from their foraging. They were exploring. It would not take this long to collect wood. "Padraig, Aed, let us look at the drekar's sail,"

I took off my seal skin boots and leather jerkin. With no ship's boys, the three of us would need to climb the mast and examine the sail on the yard. We pulled on the rope and hoisted the yard and sail. I noticed, immediately, that there were two tears. Each was the length of my arm. Not dangerous now, if we had a storm they might shred and we would lose the sail. "You two fetch the needles. I will climb the mast and examine the yard."

It was some years since I had been the ship's boy working under the watchful eye of Ulf North Star. The lessons I had learned had not been in vain and I scurried up the mast and grabbed the top of the mast. The cords close to the pennant were in good condition. I worked my way along the larboard side and they were also in good condition. It was as I made my way steerboard that I saw one had sheared. It would be easy to repair. I was pleased. The voyage could have been more damaging. It was as I looked up to the north and west that I saw them. There were four canoes and each held six warriors. They were coming around the headland and were less than a mile away.

Chapter 16

"Arm! Arm! Skrælings!" I slid down the backstay. "Padraig, they come by sea. Get the women on board the drekar. Aed, fetch my weapons!" My words must have carried for the five boys appeared from the woods. They dropped their kindling by the fire and raced up the gangplank. Rek looked accusingly at Tostig, "Sorry Captain, Tostig wandered off and we had to seek him!"

"Time for recriminations later. Get your weapons. They come by sea. We cannot defend the camp but we can defend the drekar."

Aed ran up the plank encumbered with my bow, two swords, and my arrows. I had more arrows in my chest. Gytha led the women and children on board. I saw that Helga had her sword with her. The boats were now closing with us. Padraig shooed the last four women on board. It was then that the animals began to low. We could not afford for them to be taken.

"Boys, use your slings and your bows. Discourage them. If they land, we must go to fight them." I had three warriors and five boys against twenty-four skræling. It would not end well.

I nocked an arrow. I had metal tips on them. The skrælings had animal skins only. Any warriors I hit would be wounded. I aimed, not at the one at the front of the boat but the one at the back. The last time we had fought them I had noticed that they used no steering board. The one at the back used his paddle to steer. I sent my arrow and it plunged down and struck him on the shoulder. His paddle dropped and the boat slewed around. Arrows and stones were sent from the drekar and the skrælings turned to head towards our camp. I nocked another arrow and sent it into the right side of a warrior. A third arrow hit one in the back and then the boats slid onto the beach. "Folki and Fal, guard the women. The rest of you we go to save our animals. I picked up my sword and grabbed my shield. I had been wrong. I did need it.

I saw that the first warriors were dragging their boats on to the beach. I reached the sand as they did so. I saw that they wore hide breeks and each carried a stone club and stone tipped spear. I saw two bows. We could not hesitate.

"Clan of the Fox!" I roared our war cry for I wanted Arne and the hunters to hear it. The others joined in with the shout. The skrælings turned. Eight had landed. Our stones and arrows had accounted for six and two of their boats had yet to land. I did not hesitate.

I ran at three of them. One sent an arrow my way. It struck my shield and bounced off. A spear was rammed at my head and I blocked it. I swung my sword in a scything motion as the stone club hit my shield. My sword bit into flesh and, as I dragged it, the edge sawed through the man's guts. I punched blindly with my shield and was rewarded when it hit the club armed warrior in the face. The third rammed his spear at me. I brought down my sword and hacked off the end. He looked down in surprise at the stump he held. He was even more surprised when I pushed my sword up into his guts. Padraig and Aed were good warriors. Armed with a sword and a seax they had already dispatched two when I went to the aid of Fótr and Tostig. The two were brave but they had not yet fought with the swords they carried. Rek had a bow and he sent an arrow into the skræling who had knocked Tostig to the ground.

The other boats had landed and, although I hacked through the arm of one of those trying to kill my brother and Aed killed the one hit by an arrow, we would soon be overwhelmed. It was then that I heard, from the woods, "Clan of the Fox!" Arne led our warriors who raced from the woods. The surprise was complete. The skrælings were given no opportunity to surrender. They were butchered where they stood.

I ran to Tostig. The blow he had taken from the stone club had broken his arm. Even as I knelt by him Gytha hurried to his side. "Go, this is my work. You have saved the clan again!"

Arne wiped his sword on the breeks of a dead warrior. He shook his head, "I am sorry! This is all my fault! Snorri counselled me to come back sooner but the hunting was so good that…"

Sheathing my sword, I shook my head, "This is *wyrd*. The Norns were spinning. Tostig was also distracted but all is well. He has a broken arm. The animals are safe as are our women."

"If the roles were reversed then I would be angry. Can you not rise to anger?"

I laughed, "A sailor has to endure much that he cannot help. Perhaps it is in my nature to make the best of what I have."

He knelt down and picked up a stone club and a spearhead, "If this is all that they have then we need not fear them."

"Yet they broke Tostig's arm. They are fearless. Even when our weapons cut them down, they kept attacking." I wandered to the water's edge. I now saw that their boats were made of bark wrapped around a wooden frame. They were very light but, at the same time, flimsy. I could see why they were just used around their coasts. "We can burn these."

"Aye." He looked north. "I wonder if there are more of them?"

"We will know tomorrow. It will take until then for them to realize these are not returning. If they have more men then they will all come."

"You think they know where we are?"

"If these were scouts it would have been one boat. You did not see their settlement when you hunted?"

"No."

"Then they saw our drekar when we passed."

"Siggi, take half the men and fetch the Butar deer."

Siggi waved and left us, "Butar deer?"

He laughed, "Siggi said they were the ugliest deer he had ever seen. He said they were the Butar Beer Belly of the deer kingdom!" He shrugged, "It honours Butar and is better than calling them deer!"

It was late in the afternoon when Siggi returned. The hunters had done well. We had ten carcasses to butcher. Even had we wanted to leave we would not be able to until we had dealt with our booty. While the animals were skinned and butchered, I returned to the drekar. The sewing was even more imperative. It was as we stitched that I realized I had lost three arrows for they lay in the bottom of the bay with dead skrælings. Until our forge was lit then I could not replace them. I now saw that I might need to use stone tips as the skrælings did. The metal tips would need to be recovered and that meant just using them on land. I was learning.

Arne had eight guards watch over us that night. Before I retired, I went to speak with Tostig. He was asleep. Gytha said, "I gave him something to make him sleep. He wished to apologize to you."

"He has no reason to."

"He has. He went out a boy. He is the same age as Fótr but Fótr is a man. Today my son grew. He ceased to be a boy. A broken left arm is a small price to pay. I would thank you and Rek for you saved his life."

"We are too few in number to lose any."

For the next two days, we woke to rain, mist, and fog. The air was still warmer than back in the land of ice and fire and even Orkneyjar but it cast a damper on the mood. We had much to occupy us. The meat had to be dried and salted. Bones were boiled. Marrow was extracted. The hooves were melted down for glue. The hides were tanned. With warriors to protect them foragers collected more honey and greens. Gytha would not be able to make the honey until we landed at our final destination. We began to pack the drekar and the snekke. When we found that there were squirrels which lived close to the camp then the warriors and the boys hunted them. It was not just for the meat, it was for their fur. They were easier to hunt in the rain. After the rain stopped, we had cloudy and dull days. In all, we spent nine days at the camp and then we decided to leave. It was Gytha who determined the time. She woke one morning and said that she had dreamed and her dream disturbed her. That was enough for us. We were all keen to get to the land of the deer, now Butar deer.

We had barely loaded the last barrel when Rek, who was atop the mast shouted, "Skrælings! Some have bows!"

I looked to the west and saw ten of the bark boats. With five and six men on each boat, they could have hurt us. Had they caught us on the beach there would have been a battle. I believe we would have won but the cost might have been high. Once more it was the Navigator who commanded. "Cast off. Padraig, follow us. Lower the sail and run out five oars on each side." My brother looked at me. "Trust me, brother!" The bark boats were less than four hundred paces from us. "Gytha, have the women and children take cover. They have bows with them."

"You heard Erik, obey him!"

"Larboard oars, row!" We began to turn so that we were facing the boats. The wind began to fill the sail. "Steerboard row." I began to sing and to stamp my foot on the deck. I would give them their rhythm.

The Clan of the Fox has no king
We will not bow nor kiss a ring
We fled our home to start anew
We are strong in heart though we are few
The Clan of the Fox has no king
We will not bow nor kiss a ring
We fled our home to start anew
We are strong in heart though we are few

The drekar surged forward. The skrælings were in for a shock. They had never seen, let alone fought such a ship as our drekar. We had painted *'Njörðr'* before we had left the land of ice and fire. The god's red and black face looked terrifying. When we had landed, I had checked the prow and it was undamaged. When I had thought they used wooden boats I had been worried. Now I was not. We ploughed into them. They crunched as they were destroyed and the warriors screamed as the hull rode over them. The bow rode over one boat and sank two more. The oars smashed into the skrælings. The ship's boys hurled their slings at those in the bark boats which lay further away. I put the steering board over to take us through the three boats to larboard. I would head out to sea where the wind from the west would make us fly. Padraig had taken the snekke to larboard of us. "In oars." As the wind took us, I looked in our wake and saw that just four bark boats remained afloat. Survivors were being dragged into them. The skrælings would remember the dragon ship and they would fear it.

We headed south. This time I knew there was land to the south west of us. More importantly so did Rek and the crew of *'Jötnar'*. "Tighten the fore and backstays. Replace the oars on the mast fish." I opened the chest and took out the hourglass. It was still overcast and we might not need it but I would have it close in any case. Without the sun our course was not as accurate as I would have liked. I erred on the side of caution and headed south and west when I could. The wind was a cool one and came from the north and west. It suited us for it kept us moving steadily down the coast. We could not see the coast but I knew it lay to the west of us. I also knew that there were people there and I wanted to avoid them. I did not know if these skrælings spoke with each other but I did not wish to take a chance. Perhaps they had some means of communication which we did not use. When we had examined the dead warriors before we had let the sea have them, we had seen that they looked nothing like us. They were smaller and the warriors had fewer muscles than we did. Their hair was black. I knew of no Viking with black hair. I knew that we would have to learn to talk to them at some time. That would involve taking a slave. That was how my mother had learned to speak Norse.

I was also confident that it would take roughly three days to reach our destination. That would allow us two days before we needed to head west. By my reckoning that would bring us close to where we had repaired the snekke. I knew there were people close to the island but there was nothing we could do about it. Sven, Halsten and Eidel joined me at the steering board. Eidel shook his head, "Those skrælings, are they, men? I have seen nothing like them."

"I am guessing that they are men. They are just a different type from us." I took the compass from around my neck. "We sail due south for two days. If you have to err then err to steerboard, always steerboard. There is land there."

Sven nodded, "I have seen it, my friends."

"We will head for the coast after two days." They seemed happy. I gave the compass to Sven and then went to my fur which lay on the deck by the steering board. Tostig came to join me along with my little brother, Fótr. Tostig had his left arm in a sling. His mother had splinted it. He had every chance that it would heal and be straight. I had known warriors who had had an arm broken and it had been badly set. They could still hold a shield but that was all.

"How is the arm?"

"It aches, Captain, but my mother said I deserved it. She is angry with me."

I laughed, "Your mother is not angry. You made a mistake."

"But it could have cost the clan dear."

"It is part of growing up. You make a mistake and you learn from it. Your brother Siggi fell while climbing a mast on his first voyage. He has never fallen since. It is how we learn and grow. The land we are sailing towards is, like those skrælings we fought, different. It is unlike anything you have seen before."

He nodded towards the north, "But I have been on an island like the one we sail to."

Fótr shook his head, "It is three or four days south and it is much hotter. The island is smaller too. My brother is right Tostig. He was nearly killed by a bear. There may be other such creatures on the island."

He looked at his bandage, "And I have one arm!"

Fótr said, "Fear not, we are family and we will watch out for you."

"And now I will sleep. You two can chat away but Fótr and I have the middle watch again!"

I slept easily for I knew that the spirits had sent the dream to Gytha. We were meant to go to the island of the deer. What we would do after that I did not know. The Norns were still spinning. Tostig had a broken arm and that was for a reason. Only the Norns knew.

I put the steering board over two days later. We had lost the clouds and we had sun. The wind veered a little to come from the north and east. We travelled quicker. I did not wish to sail beyond our island. We struck the coast at noon and I turned the steering board to parallel the rock-lined land. Fótr was on the yard and he sought the islands where we had repaired our snekke. I had Fal watching the snekke astern. This was not the time to lose contact. Our people lined the side but they now took it in turns. They had learned.

Snorri and Arne joined me, "There are enough trees here to build a thousand ships."

Snorri looked at my brother, "And we have enough crew for how many more ships?"

"You are right. I am trying to run. First, we need to walk. Erik, when did you leave the island?"

I closed my eyes and counted back. "It would be about this time, Skerpla. That is *wyrd*. Why do you ask?"

"So that we have a better of what to expect. Were the deer rutting?" I shook my head. "Good. This is a new world and I wondered if their seasons followed our pattern. We have a month to clear some land of trees and stumps and use the new plough to plant our barley and oats. If the deer were not rutting then it is as it was in Larswick. There will be young deer. I have a mind to catch a couple."

"Catch wild deer? Why?"

"It was something Gytha said. She thought we could tame them. Perhaps use them for milk or to breed from. It would save hunting. We could harvest them like our own animals."

I was not the only one who had grown and changed.

Snorri said, "That is a long process. It will not happen overnight."

"If my brother is right, and I have no reason to disbelieve him, then we have a whole island to make our own. Unlike the land of ice and fire, there are other islands and lands we can use when we need to. My son is almost two summers old. By the time he has seen ten then we will be ready to take over another island. Perhaps we might risk a war with these skrælings. I saw nothing in them to make me fear that they could hurt us."

The Norns were spinning!

Knowing we were so close to the island of the bear I went without sleep. The light was hung from our stern and I shouted to Padraig to shorten sail. We did the same. The sea was a little lively and I did not want to miss the island. The land was so close that I could smell it. With the wind from the west, it felt as though we were about to crash onto the rocks. We kept a good lookout. Tostig could not race up the sheets but he had two eyes and he used them. When dawn broke, I spied the land to the northwest and the island where we had repaired our snekke just ahead. The journey had taken longer than I had thought but seeing the tiny spit of land told Sven, Fótr and I exactly where we were. I turned and shouted over the stern. "Release your sail. The island should be some miles ahead."

Padraig waved and I looked to the land. There was smoke. The skrælings were there. They would see us for whilst the snekke might be hard to see no one could miss a drekar. The dots of land soon clarified into the islands we had used before when we had repaired the snekke. Arne and Siggi became excited when they saw the first island loom up out of the sea. I shook my head, "That is not the Isle of the Bear."

"But it is not inhabited!"

"I know Siggi but it is not explored yet. Is there water? Are there deer? Is there an anchorage we can use? I know that there is water, deer and an anchorage on the Isle of the Bear. We are at sea and I still command cuz."

He grinned, cheerfully, "Aye, Erik!"

We sailed on until I saw the bay ahead of us. The island we had briefly used looked reassuringly the same. The skrælings had not colonized it. There was no smoke. I saw no sign of bark boats. I had the sail reefed and side oars on each side manned as we edged around the southern coast and into the bay.

"Back water!" Fótr, Fal, and Folki leapt into the shallows and ran with the lines to tie us to the rocks.

I heard Fótr shout, "The blackened stones from our fire are still here! It is as though we have just left."

I laughed and turned to Arne, "Well brother, I have guided the clan to our new home. Once more you lead the clan!"

He came to me and picked me up, "There is no other Viking could have sailed all the way across the Unending Ocean and found this island. Do you wish to be the first ashore?"

I shook my head, "No brother, that honour is yours. I have a ship to secure and then to unload. This is our home and it is up to you and the others to make it so!"

This time there was real excitement as the clan went ashore. This was our new home. The land of ice and fire had not impressed them but this looked, by comparison, to be paradise. There was no smell of brimstone. The air was warm and the sea was blue. The sand was yellow and not black and the land was covered in a carpet of green. My ship's boys, Tostig included, did me great honour. They stayed by my side. Fótr smiled and said, cheerfully, "What orders, Captain?"

"First we take Odin ashore and the other animals and then I will ask my brother to have men take the barrels and their chests ashore. I am afraid we will, once again, have the joyous task of shovelling the deck clear of Odin and his fellows."

Fótr nodded, "And we serve a god. It will stand us in good stead."

I led the bull down the gangplank. I would not tether him for there was nowhere he could go. The cow, calf, sheep and pigs happily followed. I fetched my chest and then shouted, "Arne, we have barrels to move and chests!"

His voice came from the forest, "We come!"

It took until the middle of the afternoon to shift the barrels and chests. The water barrels were almost full and they were hard to move. The dung was piled in a heap. It attracted flies and when Arne and the warriors had moved their chests, he ordered the clan to shift it into the forest. I knew that we would soon hew trees to make our halls and clear the ground. It would be then that the dung would become gold. Until then it was a nuisance. It was almost dark by the time we had removed the deck. I could smell food cooking on the fires and Gytha came to me, "Erik you and your boys have done enough. Leave the rest until the morrow. Come and eat." She glowered and glared at my brother's back, "The jarl takes advantage of you! Come. I have saved choice cuts for you." To make sure I could not escape she linked me, "You have a good eye, Erik. This land is perfect. There may be bears but the warriors can hunt them. We are like a stronghold. The sea protects us and we have all that we need here. You were guided well."

I smiled at her, "When we found it, I thought you had led us here."

"No, nephew, it was the spirits but I am honoured that they took my form. They could have used your mother's!"

"No, Gytha, we both know that my mother would never send me here and besides she was Christian."

"And I am glad that you did not follow her down that path!"

Chapter 17

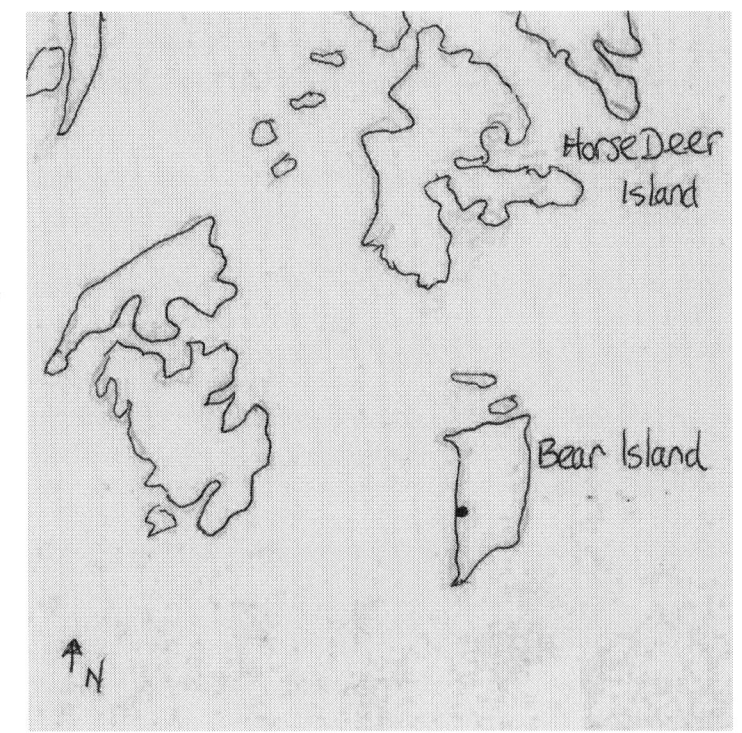

It took us longer to unload the drekar than it had to load her. That was because I only had Sven and my ship's boys to do so. The men were hewing trees and clearing the land. I asked them to cut down the pines first for we could make pine tar. We would need to clear the stumps if we were to plough the land. That they did but it meant they were further away from the camp than we would have liked. Arne left eight men to cut down the trees at the beach so that we could build one hall there. We had the whole island to ourselves and had no need to be confined to one place. Arne, Siggi, and Snorri explored the island during the first few days. I was not insulted that they did not take my word for

Across the Seas

what we had found. I had not tramped every animal trail. Barrels and chests began to pile up on the beach. I did not like the disorder, every sailor is tidy, but we could do little about it. Then we shifted the sacks of scrap metal. We left the sacks on the beach and then loaded the hull with stones to give her ballast. That helped to clear the land around our hall of stones. What we did not have was turf. There had been turf on the island with Butar's deer but this island was heavily forested.

Padraig and Aed became the clan's fishermen. Each day they took their lobster traps and laid them. The put their nets across the bay and they used their lines to catch fish. We would build a small fishing boat but that was a task for the future.

On the third day, while we had a break for food and water, I spoke to Gytha about the problem. "We have no turf for our halls, volva."

She nodded and smiled, "We used turf on Orkneyjar for that was all that we had. Here we have so many trees that we can use those for the walls and the roof. It means we do not need to dig deep holes for the foundations. You watch, Erik the Navigator, the halls will rise before your eyes!"

She was right. Once we had the drekar loaded with ballast and the deck replaced we were done. When all that was completed, we tethered the two ships fore and after. There were two ropes at the bows of each ship and two at the stern. They were firmly attached to huge trees which we would leave to stand as natural bollards. They were not for timber. They were our anchors. That done we left our two ships alone. There was still work to be done to them but shelter was more important. Black clouds appeared from the seas to the east. My ship's boys and I joined the men building the beach hall. This would be where we would all sleep for a moon or two. The climate was so clement that I was certain we could sleep out of doors if we wished. Snorri returned to supervise the building of the hall. He was now the oldest man in the clan and the wisest. The men had cleared many trees.

Snorri looked at the land we had cleared. "We need not remove the stumps. There is little to be gained from the effort. First, we split all of the trees into two and divide them. We need two thirds to be longer than the other third. Set to."

It was not complicated work, it was just hard. It took a whole day to sort and trim the wood. As the afternoon turned to dusk Snorri showed us how to cut a notch towards the end of the split trunks so that we could lay them alternatively and build up the walls. "That is for tomorrow."

We heard Arne and the others coming back through the woods. As he approached, he was shaking his head, "We need more axes and tools. Taking out stumps damages them more than I would have expected."

"We have the scrap metal and we have the anvil. We could build the forge on the beach and begin to melt the iron. I am no smith but I can melt metal."

Harald of Dyroy was one of our biggest warriors and he had an affinity with metal. He saw Arne looking at him, "If Erik the Navigator can melt the iron then I can try to make tools."

Melting iron was the work for any but making moulds and pouring molten iron was the task for someone who knew what they were doing. Our store of iron was precious. We could not replace it. Our days of raiding for cereal, iron, and slaves were over. Our new world meant a new life. We had to think differently.

I saw that Gytha had a large pot out on the fire. She smiled as I approached her, "I begin to brew mead, Erik. We have found more hives. We will not take all that the bees produce but we will make mead! By Heyannir we can hold a feast and thank the Allfather for our new home."

The next day while Sven and I chose the best place for the anvil, Fótr and the boys emptied the sacks. It was as they emptied them, I saw the black sand from the land of ice and fire. I remembered that the black stone from which they were formed had been hard. "Pile the black sand up together. Harald of Dyroy may well be able to use that to make his moulds."

When that was done, we built a kiln to melt the iron. It was as we were building it that Gytha came to us. "You will need to build a bread oven and a kiln to make our pots. They can all be in this area. It is far enough away from the hall that we do not risk a fire."

I nodded, "We do not have enough stones here."

"And we do not need the kilns yet but we will need them." She pointed to the skies. The black clouds which had been approaching were almost overhead. "This looks like one of the storms we endured at sea." Smiling she said, "You will need your capes."

A warrior ignored a volva's warnings at his peril. We left the iron kiln and fetched our capes. Our chests were now ashore and under the eaves of the trees. "Come, we need to find stones." We had barely stepped into the trees when Odin unleashed a storm upon us. Padraig and Aed left their fishing and ran to the shelter of the half-finished hall. There was a canopy of leaves above us but, even so, the rain found a way through. Before we had walked four hundred paces the ground began to turn to a leafy, muddy morass. The wind made the mighty trees sway. I prayed that our ropes held our ships to the shore. They had to for we could do nothing about it now.

I headed for the place Arne and the men were clearing the trees. It was close to a stream. When we planted crops, we would be able to water them in times of drought. We had no drought in the land of ice and fire, Larswick and Orkneyjar but this was a new land. We had to be prepared for any disaster. Farming was hard. It was why we were always ready to raid. Here we could not raid. When we reached the clearing that our men had made, I saw them all sheltering beneath the trees. They did not have their seal skin capes and they huddled under the thicker branches. Arne smiled. He had to shout above the wind and the sound of the rain, "Ever prepared, little brother. What brings you here?"

I cupped my hands to shout back, "Gytha needs more stones for a bread oven and a clay oven."

Harald of Dyroy was close by, "You have finished the smithy?"

I nodded, "We can begin to melt the iron whenever you are ready. We have black sand from the land of ice and fire to make your moulds."

Arne pointed to the skies. "There will be no melting of the iron for a few days yet. As for stones? There are plenty here. You will be doing us a favour if you take them."

I nodded, "We will have to build a cart. We have wheels back at the drekar. I will go and fetch them." I turned to Sven and the others, "You have seal skin capes and hoods. They cannot hew wood but you can collect the stones. Make piles of them here. Cut the wood for the cart."

We had had carts on Larswick. We had never needed them in the land of ice and fire but the four wheels were still there. We had brought them ashore. I would just need two of them. Back at the camp, the rain was so hard that all work had ceased. Snorri had taken the spare sail and rigged it over the half-finished walls of the hall. The women children and builders sheltered. I saw the two ships in the bay. I was thankful we had chosen this narrow inlet. The two ships rose and fell alarmingly but they were held. Had this been an open bay, such as the one on the Isle of Butar's Deer, then they might have been torn from their moorings. As it was, I still worried that they might be damaged.

Snorri came to the beach with me while I collected the two wheels. He pointed to the distant islands to the west. The land was shrouded in rain and we could see nothing. "You chose the best place for a camp. Look." I saw huge waves rolling towards the islands. When they hit it they seemed to engulf it. "I am guessing that the eastern shore of this island is suffering just as badly! Had we been on the eastern side of the Island of the Bear then we would have lost the ships already."

As I headed the half a mile or so back to the clearing, I thought on that decision I had made more than a year ago. Had that been the Norns? Snorri was right. This was the most sheltered anchorage we could have found. Before I had set off, I had picked up a dozen or so of the nails we had made. We would need them.

The rain had not abated but the wood for the cart, roughly hewn by the men, was ready to be assembled. The boys were working their way across the clearing fetching the stones which had been dragged to the surface when the stumps of the trees had been removed. Arne, Siggi and I built the cart. It allowed us to talk.

"How long, brother, to clear the trees?"

He laughed, "How long is a piece of rope? We need to clear a larger area than this. We picked a higher piece of ground so that it would be well drained but crops need sunlight. I think that in half a moon we will have cleared enough ground to spread the animal dung and then, a week later plant our crops but we will still be hewing trees."

Siggi nodded, "And taking the timber to the beach to build the second hall. This is where we need horses or oxen. I suppose we could use Odin. He has given Freja another calf. He can work too." The voyage had not harmed the animals and both the sow and the cow were carrying young.

The cart was crudely made. Only the wheels looked finished. We had not smoothed the timber but it would enable us to haul the stones more easily.

"Sven, begin to load the cart."

With the stones laid in the cart, I took Fótr back with me. He helped me to push the cart along the track back to the camp. Already our footsteps had begun to make the game trail into a human path. Soon the wheel ruts would mark it as the domain of men. "You will stay at the beach. You can help to unload the cart and then sort the stones. It will make it easier to build."

I swapped with Sven after two trips and I helped to move the stones across the clearing. By the middle of the afternoon, we had completed the movement but the rain did not look like stopping. Arne had taken the men back not long after noon when it became clear that they would get no more work done that day. The clearing was in a sorry state. Our boots had churned up the freshly turned soil. As soon as we left, I knew that the birds would be down to feast on the worms!

The rain stopped after dark but the winds did not abate for two days. Arne and the men returned to their work and we could begin to build the kilns and ovens. Before we did that Sven and I waded out to the ships and added two more ropes to the drekar and one to the snekke. The moorings had held but there was little point in taking risks.

The storm acted as a spur and the hall was finished by the time the winds had ceased blowing. We had not had enough turf for walls but we were able to find enough grassy sods for the roof. Sand was put inside to cover the stumps and some of the smaller stones and shingle laid to make a floor. It would compact down and, eventually, we might put down a wooden floor but we had a roof and we had a fire. Our hall was built.

Harald of Dyroy returned for I was ready to melt the iron. Those were long days. The storm had gone and the temperature rose. We almost prayed for a breeze to cool us down. I worked wearing just my breeks as did Sven and Fótr. Helga smeared seal oil on our backs and chests to stop them becoming red. Harold of Dyroy made his moulds. We learned from our mistakes. Some of the first iron we melted was contaminated with impurities. We had to put it to one side. We would use it but not for axes and weapons. It was adequate enough to make nails and hunting arrows or for strengthening shields.

The start of Sólmánuður meant we could plough the new fields. We were still clearing around it but it could be ploughed. We had brought the plough from Maevesfjörður and we had made a harness from some of the deer hides. We had never used Odin to pull anything. As I had been the one to bring him back from the land of the Saxons Gytha suggested that I should be the one to lead him. A Gytha suggestion was an order from any other. I was not certain what to do. I had never ploughed. I had rarely seen anyone ploughing. Benni was our farmer and he came with me to offer advice.

Benni was just a little younger than Snorri. He was a kind man and he was patient, "All we need to do is turn the deeper soil over and mix the animal dung into it. Digging out the roots and removing the stones has done the hard work for us. Just keep the bull moving and we will see what we can cover."

Odin began well enough and we soon covered the length of the field four times. Then he became bored or tired or, perhaps, just awkward.

Benni shrugged, "We will just have to wait."

It was Fótr who had the idea. He went into the woods and brought out a handful of some longer strands of grass. He stood before Odin and waved the grass. Intrigued, Odin moved forward and started to chew. Fótr walked backward and we managed another half a length before he stopped again. I could have used a goad but Fótr's method was working. Tostig and Rek quickly joined Fótr and soon he worked happily knowing he would be rewarded every half-length or so. More than half the field had been ploughed when he decided he had had enough. Arne and Benni were satisfied. It meant we could finish the ploughing the next day and then begin to sow the day after. We hoped for a quick crop. The air was much warmer. Men worked in breeks and kyrtles. The women needed shade from the sun. We had not yet needed to hunt and Arne decided to wait until the second hall was erected before we did so. Padraig and Aed had been successful in fishing and now spent each day making a fishing boat. It was smaller than the snekke and broader in the beam. Our new home was, so far, everything that the clan had hoped.

Once the seeds were in the ground we waited. We had planted half the field with oats and half with barley. We still had some seed left and Benni advised us to clear a second, smaller field, for a later crop. We began work on the second hall. We left enough space between the two longhouses so that we could have a walkway and we used the lessons learned in the building of the first. The young were sent into the woods to collect grass and turf. There was not a huge amount but there would be enough to give a roof. Having built the beach hall the second went up much more quickly. We had enough timber hewn to make floorboards for the first hall.

Benni asked if he could have a house built close to the fields. He and his family were farmers. It coincided with the first wedding on the island. Eidel Eidelsson and Salbjǫrg Bennisdotter decided to be wed. I wondered, after, if that was the reason why Benni and his sons asked for their own home. We began the work on the house while the women prepared for the wedding. This was a propitious moment for the clan. Their children would be the first children of Bear Island. I was pleased for Eidel had been a ship's boy. What I was less pleased about was the attention I received for I was still unmarried and I had seen twenty-three summers. Arne's eldest was three years old and I did not even have a woman. Gytha silenced the questions and the attention returned to the couple. The wedding was delayed until Salbjǫrg's father and the rest of her family moved into their farmhouse. The couple then took Benni's place in the longhouse. We had missed the longest day by just a few days but Gytha's first batch of mead was ready and so we celebrated. That month was a glorious month. With two halls and a farm built we had more room and there were fewer arguments. The sow gave birth to eight piglets and we saw the shoots begin to grow in the field. Benni ran all the way to the halls to tell us the news. Arne decided that it was a sign and he took half the men to hunt.

I did not join them for Padraig's boat was finished and I was honoured when they asked me to go on their first trip. We still had the large hooks we had made but never used. We had some strong fishing line and we sailed to the west of the island. Padraig had built the fishing boat to the design used by his own people. It had a smaller hull a pace from the larboard side. It was attached to the main hull. He called it an outrigger. It gave the boat more stability and did not appear to slow it down. They had used deer hide for the sail. It did not look pretty but it was tough and, as they said, they did not need speed. They wanted something which was strong and would last them.

We did not sail far out to sea but we went as far as the darker waters. We had seen fish with what looked like a sword and a sail on their backs. We had seen them between our island and the Isle of Butar's Deer. They had never taken our bait. Aed had the idea of towing our hooks behind us and to bait them with fish they had caught the previous day. By using the sail, we could move quickly and, Aed thought, replicate the movement of fish. He thought the sails made the fish we hunted a predator.

Aed and Padraig were true fishermen. I was not. I was a sailor and there is a difference. They spied the seabirds diving on the open water and they headed for them. Padraig saw the distinctive sail and we sailed towards it. The birds scattered as we sailed through them. We saw sardines in the water. Aed nodded. He would remember this place. We had no smaller nets. We could make one and dine well. We had made the hooks with large fish in mind. If they took the bait the only way they could remove the hook would be to have it ripped from their mouth. I thought we were going too fast but the fishermen were happy with the speed. The wind was with us and we fairly flew. We had three lines out and two were successful. Two of the sailfish clamped their jaws around the fish we had used for bait. The fish thrashed around to break free but they were hooked. Aed put the steering board over and we slowed. We headed for the shore tacking from side to side. The fish with the sails did our work for us. The hooks tore their mouths and as they thrashed to free themselves, they became weaker. By the time we neared our island, they were dead in the water. It took the three of us to haul each fish on board. They were as long as a large child and far heavier. We took the hooks from their mouths. They worked. We had similar bone we could use to make more.

As we headed into the bay Aed said, "If we put a net on the outrigger we can use it to store fish. If we have four hooks then we can increase the chances of success."

When we carried the two fish ashore the women, children and men working around the halls gathered to stare in amazement at the wondrous creatures. The feast that night was the first time we ate the pink flesh of the sailfish. It was not the last for there is nothing a Viking likes more than a meaty fish and this one was superior even to the salmon we hunted.

Arne turned to me as he washed the fish down with the last of his mead, "You are truly favoured by the gods to have brought us to this idyllic island. The Isle of the Bear is perfect."

I nodded, "And what of the biting insects?"

"True they are an inconvenience but only in the woods and Gytha's salve makes them bearable. The fires from the kilns and the smithy keep them from the halls. It is good."

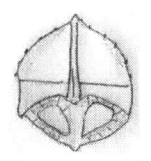

Chapter 18

By Tvímánuður the barley and the corn were growing so quickly that many thought the soil must be enchanted. Eidel was to become a father and Maren had given birth to another son. The cow had calved and we had a male to follow Odin. When our foragers found the red berries ripening and, having tasted them, judged them to be delicious then we took to the woods to forage. Arne made certain that there was a warrior with each group of women and children. Rek's father had died and so Rek went with his mother and sisters. He was now considered a warrior. I sent Fótr with them and I accompanied Dreng's mother, Ada, and her children. I had told her that I would be their foster father and I had tried to do so. I took my bow. The bushes grew along the game trails. I guessed the animals found them attractive and that should have been a warning but we had had such an easy time since we had landed that we thought we were safe.

We spread out along the different trails. We wanted to collect as many as we could. I followed Rek and Fótr. Rek's sisters were almost women and I think they would rather have had two more eligible young warriors like Sven and Halsten. My two helmsmen were seen as the best of the young men left in the clan. Dreng had a sister and a brother. Neither had seen more than ten summers and they were happy for me to accompany them. Dreng's mother had lost a husband and a son. The sun had gone from her world and she did not move as quickly as Rek and Fótr. She had two children left and she kept them close to her. I did not mind. It was pleasant to be in the woods and collect such a bounty. We had woven baskets into which the fruit was placed. I carried the basket. The laughter of the two children contrasted with the silence of their mother.

As the two young people headed deeper into the forest and Ada picked the odd fruit or two, I took the bull by the horns.

"Dreng loved this land, Ada. His spirit is here. Can you not feel it?"

She shook her head. She had only seen twenty-eight summers herself. She had given birth to Dreng when she was about thirteen. She looked older than her years. "Erik, I know you mean well but I have no husband and my first born lies dead at the bottom of the Unending Sea."

"Yet Egilleif and young Ebbe live."

"Without a father. And I have a bed without my husband."

"There are men without wives."

"They are boys. Sven and Halsten are but a little older than Dreng. You are the only man who has no wife." She suddenly stopped and, taking my hand, looked at me, "Would you marry me, Erik the Navigator? I would have you for you are a good man."

The Norns were weaving well or the Allfather was testing me. I shook my head, "That is not in my future. Gytha has dreamed." I realized how that would sound. She would think I was making an excuse. "I would be marrying you out of sympathy and that is not what you want. I will care for you and your children. I will raise your son as a warrior but I will not lie with you."

She smiled and I realized that was the first smile I had seen in a long time. "As I said, Erik, you are a good man."

Just then there was a roar from ahead. I knew the sound. It was a bear. In one motion I unslung my bow and grabbed an arrow, "Egilleif and Ebbe come here now!"

From ahead I heard screams. Fótr shouted, urgently, "Erik!"

"Stay here!" I ran down the trail. Rek and his family were twenty paces from us but the twisting game trail had hidden them from us. Even as I arrived, I saw that Fótr was on the ground as was Rek's mother and Rek was advancing towards the bear with his sword drawn, "No Rek!"

My words were wasted. He bravely ran towards the bear, leading with his sword. I had an arrow nocked but no target. Rek lunged and his sword sank into the bear's side. It was not a killing blow and she raked him with her claw. The side of his head was peeled away. My ship's boy died instantly. As his body fell, I sent an arrow into the chest of the bear and, running closer, nocked and sent another. One must have hurt her for she ran. Of Rek's sisters, there was no sign. I nocked another arrow. Rek was dead. As I neared her, I saw that Rek's mother had had her throat ripped out. Looking up I saw Reginleif and Rjúpa, Rek's sisters coming from the woods. "Your mother and brother are dead. I was too late." I fearfully turned over Fótr's body. He murmured. He was alive. I looked and saw a lump as big as a cockerel's stone on the side of his head, "Fótr, it is Erik!"

He opened his eyes, "The bear! Why am I not dead?"

"Because the Allfather watched over you. Rek is dead."

Siggi ran through the woods to us with Gandálfr and Benni. They had their swords drawn. Siggi took in the horror and shook his head, "We came when we heard the shout."

"As did I but we were too late. The Norns. It was a bear. Rek wounded her and she has two arrows in her. Fótr, stay here with the girls. Others will come. We will follow this beast and finish her."

"I will come!"

Siggi shook his head, "You are wounded cuz, listen to your brother and stay here. Erik, you have the bow, you lead."

The trail was easy to follow. She had broken branches in her flight and there were specks of blood. She was not bleeding heavily but she was hurt. She would be a dangerous prey. I deduced that she must have been the mate of the one I had killed. I wondered if there were cubs. Then I realized that had there been cubs they would have been with her. She was alone. The ground began to rise and the bear left the trail. I held up my hand. There were rocks above us. Bears liked to use caves. If they had no caves then they built themselves a den. I waved my bow to the left and right. I was the youngest of the four of us but I had killed a bear. I could smell the bear as I worked my way through the shrubs and bushes. I saw that these were the same bushes which bore the fruit. These had been stripped bare. I had an arrow nocked and I was listening as well as looking. The ground rose a little. I had seen this tiny knoll when I had sailed around the island but as the trails did not lead to it, the area remained unexplored. There were no trees upon it. It was rock. The bushes were scrubby.

I saw two fallen rocks to the side of me. They rose as high as my shoulder. I placed my bow and arrow upon them and clambered up. I saw the entrance to the cave. It was thirty paces from me. Of the bear, there was no sign.

"Siggi, I see the cave. Approach and I will watch for it."

"Aye."

"If she attacks, she will be wild for she is hurt. Head or heart are your targets!" I had four arrows left. I had only brought a few for I did not think we would need them to collect berries! I chose the best of the arrows I had left. This one had a good tip. I hoped that, if we killed the bear, then I would be able to retrieve the two which were embedded within her. I also hoped that my three companions had good edges to their swords.

The wind was from behind us. Bears might have poor eyesight but their sense of smell is perfect. When Siggi and the others were less than ten paces from the entrance she must have caught a whiff of them. With a roar, she burst from her cave. She was moving fast for a bear with a sword wound and two arrows sticking in her. I sent one towards her head. Gandálfr whipped his sword before him and it made her rear. The back of her paw caught him a blow and he tumbled backward. My arrow hit her in the chest. The beast was above my three clan brothers. I sent another arrow and it hit the bear in the shoulder. Benni lunged at a leg at the same time as Siggi thrust upwards. He managed to cut into the inside of her thigh. As she raised her arms and roared, I sent an arrow into her neck. I am not sure which of us struck the mortal blow but the she-bear fell forward, spraying the three of them with her blood.

I jumped down from the rock and ran towards the cave. The other three stood in shock as the bear pumped her lifeblood down the slope. I dropped my bow and drew my sword. I clambered over the bear and into the cave. If there were cubs then I had to spare them a slow and lingering death. Inside was the smell of death. There was just enough light from the outside to show me the two rotting corpses that were the she-bears cubs. From the smell, they had been dead for many months, perhaps a year. I wondered if I had inadvertently caused their deaths when I had killed their father? Had he been hunting to provide for them? Or was there another bear yet remaining? I would never know.

I went back outside My three companions were examining the bear. We heard noise from the track. Arne shouted, "Where are you?"

"We are here. Climb the slope!"

Siggi looked up at me, "And you killed the he-bear alone." He shook his head, "The Allfather truly favours you. We should call you Erik Bear Killer."

Gandálfr, who was bleeding, said, "Do you wish the fur?"

"No, Siggi killed it. I will have her teeth. It will remind me how lucky we were."

Arne and half a dozen of our warriors arrived. "It is dead?"

"It is, brother. Those berries were expensively bought."

He nodded, "*Wyrd*. It is the Norns. They spin and we are powerless to do anything about it. All are well here?"

"Aye."

"Then let us get this beast back to the halls." He looked up at the cave as the others slid their spears beneath it. "Are there more?"

I shook my head, "Not in this cave. If I was the leader of the clan, I would examine every part of this island to see what else lies here. I should have done so and it has cost me one of my crew. Rek and Dreng are both dead and it is because of this island. Perhaps it is cursed."

Arne put his arm around me and led me away from the others, "Do not speak like that. The island is not cursed and I do not want you to put those thoughts into the heads of others. Do you understand?"

I nodded.

It was dark by the time we managed to drag and carry the bear back to the hall. I saw that Gytha had the two girls in the hall. Fótr was just staring into the fire. Arne said, Go and speak with our brother. This is terrifying for him."

He looked up as I approached, "It is dead?" I nodded. "I thought I could be like you and I could slay the beast. It just got Rek killed. He tried to save me when the bear hit me."

"Had you not tried to kill the bear then it would have attacked Rek anyway. He had a glorious death. He is in Valhalla now and our father is thanking him for his action." I pointed to the hall. "We now have a responsibility. Until they are married, we have to watch over Reginleif and Rjúpa."

He shook his head, "I am not capable of that."

"You are," I remembered Arne's words. I swept my arm around the open space before the halls. The clan was there and some were looking at the bear but most were looking at us. "The clan look to us. We are the brothers of the jarl. You and I found this island. If they doubt us then they doubt Arne. We cannot let our brother down."

He shook his head, "I would not let Arne down. How do you look so brave?"

"It is an act. Inside I feel as you do but we are Vikings. We are alive and so are many of the clan. Now there are just three of us left from the crew of *'Jötnar'*. That binds us. We must be strong for one another."

"I will try." He stood. "I will go and speak with Reginleif and Rjúpa." He went into the hall and I could hear the Norns spinning.

Gytha took charge when it came to the burial of the dead. We had no cemetery yet and she decided that we needed one. We headed to the eastern side of the island with the two bodies. Rek had his sword with him. He had been so proud when he had taken it from the dead Dane he had killed. Gytha found a piece of headland with no trees and just a couple of scrubby bushes. "We will clear this land of bushes and this will be where we shall bury our dead. They will face the morning sun and our home in the east."

We soon cleared the bushes. As with the rest of the island, we found rocks below the surface. That suited us for we lined the sides of the grave with them. The mother and her son were put in one grave. Curled up as they were in the womb, we placed Rek's sword in his hands and covered both of their faces with his shield. Then each member of the clan deposited soil on the top. We walked around until there was a mound. After standing in silence we headed back to our halls and the setting sun.

Our lives changed that day. Although there were no more bears on the island, Arne and the warriors discovered that it was now a less friendly place. The berries which had cost the lives of the mother and her son were used to brew a wine. It proved to be a potent brew. Vikings like their ale and mead. Each warrior who drank it put from their thoughts the two deaths. Vikings looked forward not back.

By the end of Tvímánuður, our cereal was growing well and Benni had used Odin the bull to plough the second field. We sowed that one too. We had now learned where we could gather greens and Gytha had organized a vegetable plot close to the halls. It was more sheltered there and easier for us to pick them. Seafood and fish formed our staple diet. The sea teemed with them. As well as lobsters we found all manner of crabs, mussels, clams, and scallops. We allowed the deer to grow. We would cull them close to the rutting season. The two new babies born at the end of Tvímánuður seemed to lighten the spirits, especially of the women. The men were more stoical about the deaths. For my part, I had remembered my promise to Ada. I might not be able to give her comfort but I could give her children skills. I taught Egilleif and Ebbe how to use a bow and a sword. I taught them how to make arrows. Ada could teach them other skills. I took them both with me on the fishing boat. Padraig and Aed were happy for me to use it. I helped the two of them to make hide jerkins. We had no more sealskin and so I helped them to make hide boots. In short, I did all that Ebbe or Dreng might have done. It was not onerous. I liked it. They called me a foster father. Ada smiled more. She even tried to make me more affectionate. She would touch my hand when we were close. For some reason, I could not respond and I did not know why.

At Haustmánuður we harvested our crops. It was ten times the yield of the one on the island of ice and fire. We had enough for a winter of bread and beer. The bread ovens were lit and beer was brewed. When the first of the bread was baked, we drank mead and the berry beer we called Rek's Blood. It was a heady brew. There were a couple of fights. They only resulted in blows and a bloody nose. Arne ended them but they also resulted in a liaison. I did not drink as much as the others. I saw Fótr and the elder of Rek's sisters, Reginleif, heading off, hand in hand towards the forest. Fótr now had a beard and they were of an age but I did not want them rushing into something. I followed. They were loud and I was not. I saw them head for a clearing. We had been thinning the forest and they found a patch which had been warmed by the sun. They lay down and Fótr began to stroke Reginleif's hair.

I stepped out from behind a tree and they both jumped to their feet, "Brother I…"

I held up my hand, "There is nothing untoward here. You came for peace and quiet. I understand that. However, this is the forest and it is a dangerous place." I looked at Fótr. "We would not wish anything to happen to Reginleif would we? She and her sister are in our care. We are responsible." I stared hard at him and he nodded. "Now if you wish to be as one then you need to seek the permission of the one who is responsible."

He frowned and said, "That would be you!"

"Aye, little brother, it would. What say we go back to the hall and tomorrow, when your breath does not smell of wine the two of you can speak to me and tell me that which is in your heart."

They rose and walked back to the hall. As we neared them, I saw Gytha watching us. They scurried past her and she smiled, "You take your responsibilities seriously. They are both young. Nothing would have happened." She linked my arm and led me towards the feasting. "I worry that you take everything too seriously. You are young. Live."

"But what of your dream; my dream?"

"What will happen will happen. You need not fear for the future. All of your present prepares you for the future. Your father, mother, Edmund are the work of Urðr, your past. Verðandi she weaves what we do each day. That is the now. It is what happens this day and what you do. Skuld is the mischievous one for she plots for the future. She has spun with her sisters and tied your thread to…" she shrugged, "I know not." She nodded with her head towards Ada who was sitting by the bay and she was alone. "She needs comfort. She needs a man. There is no harm and no dishonour, Erik, what is it they are calling you now? Bear Killer."

I shook my head, "I am still happy to be Erik the Navigator. I will go and speak to her. I do not like to see people unhappy."

I went to the rock upon which she sat. The sun was setting in the west. It was a special place to watch the sun setting for it disappeared over the land but illuminated the sea. It looked as

Across the Seas

though the sea was on fire. She turned as I neared her. I smiled, "It is good to watch the sunset in the west and over land. Who would have thought it?"

She nodded, "You. When all of us believed you were foolish and then lost you held on to your dream. My son believed in you." She shivered.

"Are you cold?" I put my arm around her and she snuggled into me.

"No, it is just that I thought someone was walking over my grave." She smiled. "It was a phrase my grandmother used to use." She squeezed my arm and looked fearful, "Is it the spirits? Is it Dreng?"

I thought about it and nodded, "It could be. He and the other boys often sat on this rock to watch the sunset. Perhaps his spirit is here. Gytha believes that whatever killed him came from this island."

"Just like Dómhilda and her son Rek."

"The bear is dead."

She whispered, "I do not wish to be alone this night. I would have you lie with me."

"I cannot be your man. It is not you, it is…" I tapped my head, "something in here."

"I am a woman and I have needs. You are a man. That is all that this is." She smiled, "For my part, I love you for you have done that which you promised and cared for my family. There are no bonds binding you."

I felt the hairs on the back of my neck prickling. I looked around and saw Gytha looking at me. She was smiling and she nodded. I stood and took Ada's arm. "Come. I will try to give you comfort but I know nothing."

She smiled and there was a glint in her eye, "Fear not. I know enough for both of us." She led me to her sleeping fur. There were no others in the hall. She took off her tunic and I saw why she had shivered. She was naked. She held her hand up and I took it.

I woke in the middle of the night. I needed to make water. The hall was filled with sleeping bodies. Ada just murmured in her sleep but did not wake. Slipping on my breeks I headed outside. I saw the back of the night sentry. He was standing by the fire. I went to the trees and made water. As I headed back to the hall the sentry turned and I saw it was Arne. He was smiling.

"I thought to take a turn as sentry this night. You are now a man."

"How..."

"The whole clan knows. It is good. There were some warriors who thought you preferred the company of men. I knew that was not true."

I shook my head, "I will not be marrying Ada. She knows this."

"Of course. No one expects you to. We all know that the Allfather has chosen you. Your seed will be in Ada. Perhaps she will be fruitful and bear a son. I would like a nephew but when you walk around tomorrow no one will judge you. If I am any judge Ada will become a different person now. She will become the woman she was before Ebbe died. Her life can begin anew."

I said nothing. The whole clan knew and yet only Gytha had spoken. I stared out to sea.

Arne said, "The summer is done and soon we will have winter. When the new grass comes, I would take men to the other islands. In the fullness of time, we will need more land and more animals. Let us plan earlier this time eh?"

I nodded. The Norns were spinning.

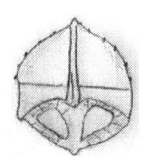

Chapter 19

When Fótr and Reginleif came to see me, at noon when I returned from checking the lobster pots, I had already made my mind up what to say. Fótr drew himself up. He was getting as tall as me. "We would be wed, brother. You are her foster father and I must ask you."

I nodded, "You are both young and this is a big decision." I let my words hang in the air, like a sword about to descend. "You both wish this?"

Reginleif nodded and gripped Fótr's arm, "We both wish it." She smiled, "My mother was not old, Erik the Navigator. She had but fourteen years with my father. I am a woman now and I would have children. Fótr is a good man and he tried to save me and my mother. He was a friend of my brother. This is meant to be. Let us try to find some happiness."

"Then when it is the winter solstice you shall be wed."

They both looked disappointed. Reginleif more than my brother. "But that is four moons away."

"And in four moons you will both be a little older and I hope, wiser. I have made my decision."

Fótr said, "This is good. We will have the long days of winter to lie together."

"Until then you do not misuse my trust."

Gytha smiled when I told her. This is good for the clan. You are making it stronger. And Ada is now a different woman. I saw her this morning and she was laughing. Her children have seen a difference. You are a healer as well as a navigator."

"My brother would have us explore the other islands."

"That is good."

I was surprised. I had thought our volva would have wished us to stay together. She seemed to read my thoughts, "The clan is growing. Remember Orkneyjar?" I nodded. "We two families were the only ones for many miles. Here we live in each other's laps. It might create conflict. I am happy to live like this but look at Benni. He chose the woods. He likes the solitude even though his daughter lives here with Eidel. There will be others and that means we must spread. Your brother is a good leader. He is making the right decisions."

What I knew was the sea. There I was comfortable. Perhaps it would be good to sail the snekke around the islands. Then I realized that I would only have Fótr with me. Sven was now married and had asked Arne if he could build a house on the western side of the island. He would be a hunter. My world was changing.

Even by Mörsugur, we had had no snow and although the air was cooler, we had had neither frost nor sleet. Even stranger was the fact that we still had daylight for hours each day. Even Gytha was perplexed and pleased at the same time. Our second crop was growing. We would have a spring harvest. Our routine was upset and we had to rethink it. Instead of hiding in our halls to keep warm we could continue to work. We began to clear, in the month before Mörsugur, another field closer to our hall. It kept the men warm, hewing the trees and it provided kindling. The logs were stored. We had yet to decide upon a use for them. Some men wished a knarr. There were some who wished us to trade but with whom? I joined the men to cut down the trees and I used one of the newly forged axes. Some men favoured building a second drekar while others spoke of building small halls for everyone. Arne showed his wisdom by remaining silent and allowing others to argue for him.

We put some of the logs to immediate use. We built a barn for the animals. We had shared a hall with them on the land of ice and fire but here we had no need. There were no cattle thieves here. There were no wolves to take them in the night. Once we had cleared the trees and begun to remove the stumps Arne divided the men into two and I joined Snorri to build the barn. Egilleif and Ebbe, along with Fótr joined me. Fótr now had a good beard and Ebbe had taken to simulating him. As we split some of the trees to make planks, he asked Fótr, "When you are married will you be a farmer?"

"I will be as my brother, Erik, I will be a sailor. There are islands to explore out there and the jarl wishes us to do so when the new grass comes."

I had been thinking about this, "It may be, Fótr, that we can do that sooner. This clement weather has taken us all by surprise. This may be a land free from ice and snow. The days might not be as short here as they were even at Larswick. We have yet to reach the winter solstice. When we do I will decide. We might sail then." I smiled, "Of course, you being a married man may not wish that!"

He had been teased by the other men and knew how to respond, "We will only sail in the hours of daylight. Being away in the day will make Reginleif even happier to see me when I return."

"Foster father, could I come with you? My sister helps the women and my mother. I am coming to the age of a man."

"Of course. It was remiss of me not to invite you. Just because I am your foster father does not mean that you have to follow me. You may not wish to be a sailor."

He hefted some branches on his back and began to carry them to the woodpile, "You are more than a sailor, foster father." He dropped them and returned. "You are a warrior. You slew as many men in the battle with the Danes as did the jarl. You slew one bear alone and helped to kill a second. You are a man to follow."

Fótr had finished placing the wedges in the trunk and he stood, with his hands on his hips, stretching his back, "He is right, brother. Arne is the jarl but you are the one the young men try to copy." He pointed to the bear's teeth necklace I wore around my neck. I had drilled each tooth and threaded them onto a piece of thin hide. "Each time they see the teeth it is a reminder that you were the one who drove the bear from my body. You were the one who saved the girls."

"Then perhaps I should not wear it." I had chosen to wear it not as a badge of honour but a reminder to myself of how parlous life was. Rek had died because of the bear. I wanted the teeth to help me respect nature. I did so at sea but on the land, I knew that I had been reckless and that had been Rek's undoing. He had tried to copy me.

"It matters not. They will still emulate you."

That evening, as I lay in Ada's arms, I told her that Ebbe had asked to sail with me. "That is good. He will be safe with you."

"Sailing with me cost Dreng his life."

"Aye I know but that was The Sisters." She snuggled into me and began to nibble my ear. "I have news."

I nodded absentmindedly. Most of Ada's news was the gossip from the cheese making or the shellfish cleaning. "Aye?"

"I am with child. You are to be a father."

I sat bolt upright, "What?"

Laughing, she pulled me down to lie with her again, "The bairn will be born at Sólmánuður. Perhaps he will arrive in this world on that most propitious of days, the summer solstice."

"Are you happy about this? We are not wed."

"Of course, I am happy. I chose you. You did not choose me. In fact, you went out of your way to reject me! I am the envy of many of the women. There are other widows who wish men. I was the one chose the last warrior."

I had planned none of this. When I had chosen Dreng all those years before then my thread and Ada's had been woven together. Her husband had died and the Norns had spun us closer. Dreng's death had not severed the thread, it had tightened it. *Wyrd*.

Once we had built the barn we went hunting. The rutting season was on and there would be weakened stags who could be culled. There were older animals who might not survive the winter. Arne left six men to watch the halls and the rest of us took bows and spears to hunt Butar's deer. We had not hunted them but we knew where they were. The sounds of the rut drew us. We had no dogs and that was a pity. Dogs would have helped us. Instead, we used the boys and the young men as hounds. Ebbe and Fótr were given fire hardened ash spears and they were sent to the flanks of our hunting party. They would drive the animals into our trap in the middle. Gytha had spoken to the hunters before we set out. She had spun a spell to protect us. We all remembered the bear. "Kill only the weak. The deer on this island are ours. We husband them as we do our cows and pigs. You will need to show strength and intelligence. You are the Clan of the Fox and you are clever!" Perhaps Arne should have spoken but the words, coming from a volva, seemed more powerful.

Fótr and Ebbe wore hide jerkins. They also had hide caps. I warned them of the dangers of charging deer. Fótr had laughed, "Brother, I helped you after one nearly killed you. You need not fear. I respect the deer and I will watch Ebbe."

We left before dawn for the days were a little shorter than they had been. Arne led us so that we approached the herd from the west. The wind blew their musky smell towards us and we were between them and the scrubland they used for protection. I had my yew bow. The arrowheads had been recovered from the bear and I had used some of the poorer metal to increase my metal-tipped arrows to thirty. I had made a hide bag for them and I wore it around my waist. My skill with the bow and the power of the yew made me the envy of the younger warriors. Others had bows but most had spears.

We heard the clash of heads as the males rutted. With no predators to fear and no other men on the island, we could afford to take our time and watch where we placed each foot. We were in a long line. The boys on the flanks had ten paces between them but the warriors in the middle had just five. All could see Arne. We kept moving closer. The archers each had an arrow nocked. The deer were just fifty paces from us when one old female raised her head and sniffed. We had to attack now while they were unaware of our presence. Arne raised his spear and then brought it down. I sent my arrow into the side of the old doe's head as the boys on the flanks began a clamour. They were boys and they had been reckless. They had advanced beyond the herd so that panic set in and the deer just ran in every direction. I prayed that Ebbe and Fótr had shown discretion. Then I had to concentrate as one stag, wounded already from the rut, led some females towards us. Arne and Siggi took down the male with their spears. I saw only young and I held my arrow. Then I saw an older male and it was limping. It still had heart and it gamely limped towards us.

I had an arrow nocked already. The tip was one I had used to kill the bear. I had named it Bear Heart. I aimed at the stag's head. It lumbered towards me. Deer had thick skulls and my arrow would struggle to penetrate it but the eye was a target. I

Across the Seas

allowed the deer to close with me. The animal had widened eyes and its mouth was open. This was one angry deer. I waited until the animal was five paces from me. I released and prepared to dive to the side. The Allfather guided Bear Heart and my arrow flew straight and true into the eye. The metal tip struck the brain of the beast and it died instantly. Its dying hooves carried it closer and it sighed its death at my feet. I knelt and touched its skull, "You had a warrior's death. It was brave and it was quick. I pray for such a death!"

I turned and looked at Siggi and Arne. My brother shook his head, "We are the brothers of the blade but you either have more courage than any man I know or you have the death wish! What if your arrow had missed?"

"Then you would have to be the foster father to Ada's unborn son and I would be in the Otherworld!"

He shook his head and Siggi clapped me on the back. "I am glad that you are in this clan. You give us more to speak of than any other warrior! Life is never dull with you cuz!"

Fótr and Ebbe were unharmed although Gandálfr's son Leif had been knocked to the ground and had a bloody coxcomb. His father had little sympathy for him, "You are as clumsy as your mother. Perhaps I should bring her next time!" He was raising his son a Viking.

The hunt meant that when the solstice came, we had plenty of meat for the feast. Fótr and Reginleif were married and the clan ate better than they ever had. Unlike the winters at Larswick and the land of ice and fire, here there was plenty to eat. We had daylight. We had berry wine and ale. We had bread from our ovens. We had lobsters and crabs. We even had that most luxurious of foods, honeyed oatcakes. Life was good.

I stood with Arne watching our little brother take his bride to their sleeping fur. As they disappeared, we went outside. Darkness was creeping from the east but we had hours of daylight. "We have had a good half year or more here brother and Fótr is married." He put a huge hand on my shoulder, "And you are to be a father. The Allfather has been kind. We have paid a price but that is the Allfather's weregeld. I am jarl and I need to think of the future. Since we came to this land there have been five babies born, four of them boys. Yours is one of six who will be born when the days lengthen. We do not need the land yet but this island will not hold us all. We need another island and, one day, we will have to sail to the mainland."

For all we knew the distant land we saw on clear days could be an island but if it was then it was an island as big as Hibernia. It was a mainland to us!

"And you wish me to explore the islands?"

"I intend to plough the new field in Þorri. It does not smell like snow. Then we will clear another field and build small halls for those who wish them. You would rather sail, would you not?"

"Of course, but there is danger."

"Not to you! I have never known such a good navigator as you."

"I do not fear the sea but there are warriors out there. There are skrælings. I can evade them but what if my voyage brings them to us?"

"I have thought of this. That day will come. If we hide on this island it will come. They came to attack us on the island of Butar's Deer. If it comes sooner than we expect then we can defend this island. As you showed on the island of Butar's Deer we can use the drekar. If we bloody the noses of these skrælings then it will make it easier for us to live on the mainland. If you meet them then I would have a slave."

"That might guarantee that they will come!"

"As we learned at Larswick if we can speak their words then we might be able to tell them what we wish. You have brought us to good land. Let us hold on to it."

As we returned indoors, I felt the breeze at my back. It was the Norns. I would do as my brother said. He was jarl but I did not think that it would end well.

The months of Mörsugur, Þorri and Gói were a revelation. Some of the days were warmer than a summer's day in the land of ice and fire. The trees did not grow but the ground remained reasonably warm. Gytha was a clever woman. She said that it was because we were closer to the sea. Certainly, when we had a clear day, we could see snow on the hilltops to the west. The weather was so clement that Fótr and I introduced Ebbe to the snekke. It had not been used since we arrived and so we used

Þorri to clean the hull and replace the sheets and stays. I rebuilt the steering board withy. We took her out on a quiet day. Fótr could teach Ebbe how to be a sailor. I decided I would manage with just two crew. There were others who would have happily come but I wanted just two that I could rely on.

I sailed us around the island. It gave me the chance to see the two tiny islands to the northwest of us. They were too small for us to use. There would be little game and I saw no watercourses. The same was true of the island to the east of us. What all three islands provided was a safe anchorage should we have winds which stopped us landing at Bear Bay. We had named it Bear Bay in honour of the bear I had slain there. It took all day to circumnavigate the island for we were patient with Ebbe who was all fingers and thumbs. The snekke was not like the fishing boat. It responded instantly to the slightest movement. When we had had five crew and all that we needed to sail across the ocean then the snekke had been heavier. With just three and no cargo, she barely touched the water. As we lowered the sail to scull into the bay I said, "Well Ebbe, do you still want to come to sea with your foster father?"

"Aye but I fear I have let you down this day. Was my brother as poor as I was?"

"He started much younger. The six boys I had as my first crew learned together. They covered for each other. Ask Fótr what he was like."

My brother nodded, "I did not know a sheet from a stay. I moved too suddenly and almost upset the boat." He shook his head, "I am just glad that the others were all patient with me. You will learn. I hope to learn how to use my brother's compass and hourglass. I would be a navigator too."

As we pulled the snekke up onto the beach I said, "You would explore?"

He pointed south, "The land keeps going. Do you not wish to see what is there?"

I smiled, "I wish to find a waterfall first." They both stared at me as though I had taken leave of my senses. "Let us say that first I want to walk this land and find a waterfall which came into my head when I dreamed. Gytha saw it too. Skuld planted it there and it does not do to upset a Norn." I turned to Ebbe, "That is why I have not married your mother. She deserves to be married but when I explore the land to the west I may not return."

They both looked shocked, "You cannot mean that brother. We will be with you."

"Unless I find a river which heads inland then I will be on foot. A snekke, no matter how lively, cannot sail up a waterfall." I saw from their faces that they were confused and did not understand my words. I tied the snekke to the mooring post we had driven into the sand. "Anyway, we have first to explore the islands. Now that we have sailed around this island then I can tell my brother that we are ready."

Arne was delighted with my news. He and the other men had cleared two more areas for crops. We had saved seed from the first crops and Benni thought that we could plant by Gói. Such an event was unheard of. Benni had advised just using each field for three years and then giving them a year to lie fallow. Arne and the others would clear two fields a year. I knew then that within three years we would need another island. We would have to leave woods for the animals. I saw now why there was an urgency about his decision to send me to the islands.

It took some days to prepare all that we needed for our voyage. Ebbe needed weapons. Rek had had a good cape and I gave that to him. Arne had a spare short sword and that became Ebbe's first weapon. We salted our own fish and deer meat in small barrels. We now had the luxury of beer and so we took one of those. We had found a dead fawn in the woods. It had died of some natural cause. We did not eat the meat for fear it was poisoned but I took the skin for although the hide was of little use to protect its wearer, I could use it for map making. The cloak we had used the last time was finished. The charts I had made lay in my chest. I cut the skin into manageable sections and I took that and charcoal with me.

It was Einmánuður when we left our island home. Ada was now visibly pregnant. She helped me to organize the three of us. She wove her own spells into her woven wool. She bound our hair and her own into it. I knew it was not as powerful as Gytha's magic but it was comforting and the three of us kept it close to our hearts. The night before we left, Ada and I cuddled,

"My son has told me of your dream of a waterfall. I am a Viking woman. I can endure the hardships of the land. You need not fear that I would hinder you in your quest."

I kissed her on the forehead, "And that is the trouble, Ada, I know not what my quest is. I dreamed the waterfall and I fell. That is all. I could have dreamed my own death. That death may be necessary for the survival of the clan. When the day comes for me to explore the land then I will choose to go alone."

"That shows great honour as well as a love of the clan."

"My father began this clan. Arne is making it great. Whatever I can do I will do for the clan and for my blood."

"I am content and I know that you will return."

"You are a volva?"

"All the women of this clan have powers, Erik. I knew when Dreng died. That was why I was not as upset as you might have expected me to be. I know that you and my son will return from the islands."

Gytha, Snorri, Arne, and Siggi came to see us off. They said little but their presence did me great honour. I climbed aboard and said. "We may be away for seven days. I have spied six large islands. I intend to explore the ones which are as big as Bear Island or bigger. Watch for my smoke on the islands. If you see no smoke then it means I have found people."

Gytha raised her arm, "May the Allfather protect you!"

We set sail and headed for the islands we had used to escape from the skrælings.

Chapter 20

As we neared the island, I had time to examine it more carefully. The last time we had been fleeing for our lives and I had just been concerned with escaping from the warriors who pursued us. Now I saw a pair of islands. They had fjords and hills which were higher than on the Island of the Bear. Sailing around was not as easy as I had expected. There were many bays but often they had rocks just below the surface. It was getting on to dark when we reached the western side and I headed for an inlet which looked as though it had a beach. It proved to be a mudbank. This was not an auspicious start. Luckily the tide was on its way in and we were able to reach the shoreline where there was a sliver of sand. We pulled the boat up out of the water.

"Do we light a fire, foster father?"

I shook my head. "There is a high piece of ground yonder. Tomorrow morning, we will climb it and see what we can see. If I spy no sign of skræling we will light a signal fire. They would not expect to see one yet."

I quickly sketched what I had seen that day and it was fresh in my memory. It was Fótr who saw the creatures after which we named the island. He spied foxes not long after the sun had set. They were not red, they were silver grey. We called it the Silver-Grey Fox Island. We took it as a good sign for we were the Clan of the Fox.

I slept fitfully. With just three of us, it would be hard to keep a watch and I did not wish Ebbe to have the responsibility. The result was that I woke early. I took my bow and my arrow bag and headed for the top of the island. There was enough light to see and I made my way up the animal trail. The east and the rising sun lay on the other side of the jumble of stones and rocks which topped the hill. It was as I was climbing that I noticed what looked like the hand of man. I spied what I would have called, on Orkneyjar, a grave. It was a grassy knoll which looked like an upturned boat. The grave did not look recent but it made me wary.

I reached the top as the sun rose and bathed me in sunlight. I touched my blue stone, "Thank you for this dawn, Allfather." I saw that the other island lay not far to the north of me. The channel looked shallow. I turned a full circle. I saw no tendril of smoke. I spied animals moving. I even saw a number of whales close to Bear Island but I saw neither smoke nor signs of man. The only evidence was a grave. I knew the others would worry when they found me absent. I descended and as I did so I saw other mounds. It looked like a burial ground. It faced west. Our graves faced east. Was this a place that some ancient people had used as a cemetery? Was it a holy place and would our presence anger those peoples?

The other two were peering anxiously up at me as I arrived. "We will eat and then light a fire on the top of this island. I do not think there are men here now but I believe that once, there were."

Later, as we built the fire, Ebbe asked, "Why do you think that men lived here once?"

I pointed to the mounds which could be clearly seen, "They look like graves but I cannot see any clearings lower down and the trails we climbed only had my boot prints. However, if we invite an attack by skrælings when I light the fire then I may have to eat my own words!"

We lit the fire and watched the smoke from the dampish wood rise as a signal to our clan. I saw no movement. I saw no angry warriors rushing to slay us. I had brought my skin and charcoal. I took the opportunity to make the map I had begun even more accurate. It was noon by the time we returned to the drekar and set sail. This time we could see the mainland and I saw fires burning. We were too far away to make them out clearly but I am certain I saw the bark boats close to the land.

We headed north for the long narrow island which lay closest to the mainland. I headed towards the western side of it. This time it was dark when we reached it. I had misjudged the length of the day and the fact that the land to the west hid the sun sooner. We had to edge into a beach. Fótr was much better now at spotting where it was safe to land. We grated on to sand and then pulled the snekke up. It was another cold meal. The boats I had seen had been a warning and I would heed it.

We all rose at the same time the next morning and, as the sun rose, we walked towards the centre of the island. As luck would have it, we were at the narrowest part of the island. South of us, it looked to be a narrow, rocky sprawl of scrub, spindly trees, and long grasses. We headed north. It soon became obvious that not only were there no people on this island there were few animals. We saw little evidence of trails or dung. What we did see was the smoke from settlements along the coast of the mainland. We were not fleeing this time and we had the opportunity to study the land. We used the scrubby low berry bushes to keep us hidden from view. It looked like the skræling lived by the beaches. I saw fish racks with drying fish. I saw animal skins. This time Fótr and I saw women and children. We had not seen so many of them before. They also wore animal skins. They were too far away to see clearly but each group appeared to be no more than ten or twenty people. I kept us hidden below the skyline. When we saw the northern channel, we knew we had explored the whole island. This was not worth colonizing. Perhaps one farmer and his family might make a living but it was too close to the skrælings. Added to that we had seen no water. The bark boats could easily cross the narrow stretch of sea. We were hours away from our snekke. Although it was risky, I had promised a fire each day and I would keep my word. We lit one on the beach. The smoke rose. I hoped it would be seen.

We headed back to our snekke and this time, when we reached it, I lit a fire. This was not a signal fire. It was a fire for food. We would have a hot meal. We gathered shellfish and added salted deer meat to the stew. As we ate Fótr pointed east. The largest island we had seen lay there. Once we had explored that one it left just the islands to the north and east of us. "This island looks close to the land. I fear there may be people there."

I shook my head. "It is close to Bear Island. I am certain that we would have seen smoke if there were villages."

"It lies to the north of our home, brother. There is high ground between us. It looks to have plenty of trees."

He was right of course and it would be a mistake to make assumptions. "Tomorrow we sail east. We will not have to fight winds. We leave before dawn and we use the winds. Let us reach there before noon. That way we can not only see any smoke we will smell fires if there are people there. We do not have to explore every blade of grass on every island. Our brother just wishes to know if can settle the islands easily or will we have to fight."

Our decision to leave early was justified. Not only was the tide in our favour and carried us east quicker, as the sun came up ahead of us, we looked back and saw skrælings on the beach where we had camped. They must have seen our smoke and, as we were so close to them, investigated. It was a warning. The large island loomed up ahead of us and we managed to reach it before noon. We saw no smoke and that was a relief. We also found a sandy beach immediately. We landed and with weapons at the ready headed inland.

We quickly discovered that this island teemed with game. We found their dung. As we progressed through the forest along their trails, we smelled them. When we heard them, we crept. The wind was in our faces and brought their musky smell to us. The thinning bushes allowed us to get close to them. We spied them and they were a shock. We found that the deer we discovered were different from the Butar deer. These were bigger and had the most solid looking antlers I had ever seen. A boy could have carved one to make a shield! They had a head like a horse. Perhaps they were a type of horse but when I looked, I saw them grazing the trees and bushes as well as shrubs. We named then horse deer.

I was tempted to hunt them but they looked too big for the three of us and I would not risk Ada's son. We kept climbing and I was glad that we did for we found the blackened remains of fires. The fires had been lit in the last months. We found the remains of butchered animals. There were bones which had been split and the marrow removed. The breaks were clean. A weapon or tool had been used. That put me on my guard. We crossed to the eastern side and found another fire on the beach. The discarded shells were clear evidence that the skrælings used this island. We would light no fire. They might not occupy it all of the time but they visited Horse Deer Island and that was enough. We headed back to our snekke and had a fireless meal.

Ebbe shook his head. "Those deer were bigger than Odin!"

He was right. They had been higher in the shoulder and one of the stags we had seen looked to be close to his weight. "One of them would feed the clan for seven days!"

"Aye Fótr but the fires tell us that skrælings come to this island. The mainland is just a short way to the north. They might not live here but they use it for hunting. We have been lucky thus far and I am glad that we have but one island left. We have valuable information to give to our brother."

The next morning, we sailed south towards our island and then took the prevailing wind west to the island which looked to be marginally smaller than our own. It soon became clear that it was considerably smaller than our own. What I had taken for one large island was, in fact, a series of smaller islands around a larger one. Even the larger one was deceptive. There were many small inlets and bays which cut into it. We landed on one of the few beaches we found. We managed to walk across the island in less time than it took to walk from our hall to the cave of the black bear. There was little sign of game trails. If there were animals, they were not the horse deer. We confidently lit a fire. This time our people would know that we were returning. I spied islands to the north of us but there were closer to the ocean and looked to be small. We now knew our world and its boundaries.

We left at dawn and had to tack against the winds to round the southern tip of Bear Island. I saw boys on the southeastern tip fishing and they waved. They would return to the halls and tell the clan that we were returning. The last mile or so was quicker for we had the wind behind us and the snekke flew. Arne. Snorri and Siggi awaited me on the beach. I could see that they were eager for news.

We pulled the snekke on to the beach, "You two empty the boat and then moor it in the shallows. You have done well. Ebbe, you can be my crew any time."

"Thank you foster father."

As they obeyed me, I walked with the other three towards the halls, "We saw smoke from all but one island. There were skrælings?"

"There were signs that they hunt there. There are a huge species of deer on the island. I think they travel there to hunt it. That is the only island worth colonizing. The mainland might be a better place but there are many skrælings who camp by the beaches and inlets."

Snorri asked, "Camped?"

"I saw no houses. There were boats and there were fires. Although I saw no dwellings I am guessing that even a skræling would wish a roof. They may make homes in the same manner as they build boats."

He stroked his beard. "Perhaps they travel there in the summer. The biting insects did not seem as bad at Þorri. In fact, they hardly bothered us."

Arne said, "That was when we had many fires burning and the smoke drove them away. You have done well, brother. There is no need to think of sailing to this Horse Deer Island yet for we have yet to hew down the trees here."

"There is something else. When we camped on the long thin island closest to the mainland, they sent boats to try to take us. I think they will hunt us and fight us. They will not wish us to take their horse deer."

"You know more about these waters than any and I will heed your advice brother. We will keep watch and we will make our homes defensible but I do not fear these skrælings."

It was the wrong thing to say for the Norns were spinning.

We settled into a routine now that we were back on the land. Ebbe sometimes went with Padraig and Aed to fish. It was good practice for him. Fótr and I joined the other warriors in hunting and hewing trees to clear for fields. Snorri was right. The biting insects seemed to hide in winter. As the days became longer and warmer so they began to bite more. Gytha's salve and the wild garlic we ate helped to negate the effect of their bites. Four more warriors decided to build farms close to the newly cleared fields. Arne knew that we had, at most, two years left on this island as a clan. We shared all that we produced but, soon, men would want to reap the benefit of their own hard work. That would be when we needed more land.

Some men missed the trading we had enjoyed at Larswick while others missed the raiding. Young men trained to be warriors but they had yet to be blooded. Sven and Fótr were the exceptions. Even Eidel, Halsten, and Stig had little battle experience. Our tales of the skrælings and their attack on Deer Island just made them want to go to war. We had not enough metal to make mail and so the younger warriors used tanned deer hide. We still melted iron to make weapons and we still produced slag. The slag was taken and hammered into crude discs to cover their hide jerkins. There was enough wood to make shields. It was not willow but we found wood which split as easily and the younger ones were shown by the older warriors how to alternate layers and then cover them in hide to make a good shield.

 I was almost domesticated. I was foster father to the brothers and sisters of Rek and Dreng. I was about to become a father myself. As Ada grew, I felt our child kicking inside her. Ada seemed to enjoy my hand on the unborn babe. She bore great affection towards me, I could see that but I still yearned for the waterfall. Only Gytha knew of the skræling maid I had seen. She still haunted my dreams and yet I had never seen her in real life. The spirits sent her to me. Why?

 My son was born on the most propitious day of the year. It was the summer solstice. Gytha beamed as though it was her grandson she bore when she came from the birthing house with my son, Lars Eriksson. "Here is the son of our navigator! He is healthy and he screams like a warrior! It is good."

 Wrapped in a birthing cloth she handed him to me. He was red and looked too big to have lived in Ada. "Ada is well?"

 "She is well and it shows you have a good heart that you ask after her." Gytha leaned in. "I have dreamed and I see great events in Lars Eriksson's life. He will not outdo his father but he will be a jarl when he grows." She stroked his bloody head, "You and I will not see that greatness for we shall be in the Otherworld but it is *wyrd*."

 That was a disappointment. We all died but I had wanted to see my son grow. That, it seemed, would be denied me.

 We celebrated the solstice every year but that year, after our first year on the island and with a new warrior in the clan, we celebrated more than ever. It was a joyous time. When three days later Reginleif told my brother that she was with child we seemed to have a perfect world. We should have known that the Norns do not like to see men happy. They were spinning.

As the summer progressed, we hunted and fished. We prepared for a winter which we knew would be benign. We planted winter barley, knowing it would grow. We watched our crops grow. We now had four cows. With Odin and his son Thor, we had two bulls who could pull the plough. We had milk for cheese. Our pig herd had grown and the only disappointment was that we lost our two sheep. The Allfather had been kind.

We had so much hide that I was able to make a spare sail for the snekke. Although heavier than the woollen ones we normally used, a hide sail was more robust. There were fewer places for it to tear. We also made one for the fishing boat. We had now developed a technique to make it easier to hunt the fish with the sail. We took *'Jötnar'* out at the same time. We used spears to stab the thrashing fish and land them quicker. We were able to put the dead fish in our snekke and we managed to harvest more fish that way. The salt pans we had made when we first arrived produced enough salt for us to preserve all the fish we caught. We knew that the winters would be mild enough for us to fish then too. We would never starve here in the new world.

My son grew. By Tvímánuður he was big enough to hold his head up and look at me. He was so helpless and yet I saw, in his eyes, determination. Gytha's prophesy was a good one. The longhouse was a good place for him to grow. The other mothers and the babies just a little older than he meant that there were always eyes upon him. I did not envy Benni and his family living so far from the hall but they enjoyed the solitude. His daughter, Eidel's wife was also with child. When his grandson was born would he wish to be close to him?

Despite the fact this land was nothing like the lands in which we had lived before, we kept the same rituals. Gormánuður meant we harvested the crops and burned the bones of the animals. On Orkneyjar we had done this because not all of the animals would survive the winter. Although that would not happen here, we did it anyway. Benni and his family, as well as Sven and the others who lived far from the hall, came for the feast. He and his wife would see their daughter! Our old sow was no longer fertile and so she was slaughtered. We had young females. Her meat was a luxury. The berries which had cost lives the previous years had been gathered and brewed Rek's Blood. We had the bounty of ale and we celebrated. Some of the last year's wine still remained and that was a heady and potent brew. The day of the feast obliged us by being like the days in Larswick when the leaves fell. The air became still and a sea fog edged close to the beach. Our feet crunched the leaves which had turned red and fallen. It was a beautiful evening.

The whole clan was crowded into our two halls and it was joyous. Arne's wife, Freja, was with child again and it seemed a good sign. We sang songs of our past and we celebrated our dead. Our father was honoured for we were here in this new world because of his vision. Benni drank more than most. His eldest son, Benni Bennison, had recently become a father and Benni had the happy look of a grandfather. His daughter was with child and the old farmer celebrated. Snorri and Gytha had also become grandparents for the third time. Siggi was to be a father again. It had been a good feast.

We all rose late. Sven and Gandálfr did not have far to travel to reach their homes. Benni had the longest journey and he and his family left first. I rose and wandered down to the bay. I looked west. There was a mist over the islands and land there. The air was still. The water looked so flat that I swear I believed I could walk upon it. Our boats would not be setting off to fish. There was not enough breeze. That was a good thing. We would all take a day off.

Sven, Gandálfr, Faramir, and Folkman all left to walk the short distance to their homes. It was fortunate that we were still saying goodbye for Leif Bennison came racing through the woods. Leif had seen just nine summers. He was Benni's last child. His clothes were torn. How could that be for he had left us but an hour earlier?

"Skrælings! They have killed my family! They are coming here!"

I reacted the first, "Women and children to the halls! Men arm yourselves!" The Norns had been spinning. The calm and the fog of the feast day had helped them to cross the water. Wind and waves normally protected us and our guard was down. I ran into the hall to grab my shield, helmet, sword, bow, and arrows. I had mail but I did not think I would have enough time to don it. I saw Arne, Snorri and the others donning theirs. As I ran out, I shouted, "Warriors to me!"

Until the mailed warriors emerged, I would take charge. It was the young warriors who followed me. All had a sword. Some had helmets and most had a shield. I pointed to the boys with slings and bows. "Stand behind us. The rest of you, shield wall!" Padraig and Aed had shields and they joined me. Sven did not and he stood behind me. Fótr did not have one either and he, Tostig and Ebbe flanked Sven. Eidel, Halsten, and Stig each had shields. They were also in the front rank. Six men were not a huge number but there were ten behind us and ten boys with slings and bows. I laid down my shield and nocked an arrow. We faced the trail. The two halls and the barn were behind us. If Arne and the others did not reach us before we were attacked then we could take shelter with the walls at our backs.

The skrælings were hard to see. They were dark of skin and wore animal skins. It was their movement attracted my attention. I saw shapes running through the woods. There were many of them.

"Shields!" The five shields came up and my companions squeezed in closer to one another. The skrælings were racing quickly. They moved like racing deer. I sent an arrow at one when he was a hundred paces from me. My arrow struck him in the chest and threw him back. I nocked and released a second which hit another in the arm. It made them become a little more cautious. I saw them unsling their bows. I laid my bow down, and, drawing my sword, picked up my shield. It allowed our line to spread and afford protection for those behind. Their arrows came towards me for I had slain two of their men. It allowed our slingers and bowmen to unleash stones and arrows at them. Their arrows cracked into our shields.

From behind me, I heard, "Clan of the Fox! Let us go to war." We had fifteen mailed warriors joining us. It gave me hope. The hope was dashed when the skrælings realized that their arrows were having little effect and they charged us. I counted at least forty of them. I shouted, "Brace! Those with spears hold them at bay until the jarl reaches us!" The ones behind us poked their spears over our shoulders.

I knew the skræling spears would either be stone or fire hardened. They could not hurt a shield. Deadlier weapons were the stone axes which they held. They could break an arm. The others had spears and four skrælings discovered that their stone spears shattered on wood while our metalheads killed. I hacked across the middle of the warrior before me. He fell screaming his life away as he tried to hold in his guts. A warrior ran at me and lunged at my head. I lowered my helmet and the stone head slid off it. When I lifted my head I rammed my sword into his throat and up into his skull. These skrælings did not fight as we did. They fought as a mob, as individuals. The boys at the side had to fight. I shouted, "Break wall!" I needed Fótr, Sven and the others to join in our attack. I felt their weight move from behind us as I slashed across the head of a small warrior.

Then, from my right, I heard Arne, "Clan of the Fox! Kill them all! None shall survive!" he had forgotten that which he had said months ago. We needed a prisoner.

The pressure from our fore began to ease as our mailed warriors hacked and chopped their way into flesh that had no protection. Our spears and swords stabbed and slashed. The skræling warriors had no answer to our attack and they ran!

"After them! Let none escape."

I handed my shield to Sven and sheathed my sword as Padraig and Aed slew the last men before us. I sheathed my sword and picked up my bow. "Keep in pairs. Fótr and Ebbe with me."

Our mailed men were slower than we were. We knew this island and the skrælings did not. Some tried to run where there was no trail. I saw Snorri hack one down. Even as I nocked an arrow and hit one in the back I was working out where they had left their bark boats. They would be heading for them. We passed the bodies of Benni and his family. Two dead skrælings showed that the farmer and his family had put up a fight. I knew that they had to have arrived on our west coast. There was only one beach there and it lay beyond the cave of the black bear. I pointed my bow west and led Fótr and Ebbe to cut them off. There was a game trail. We ran through virgin woods and emerged on the small trail. The fallen leaves showed that no one had been down it lately. Arne was right we had to kill as many of them as we could but I knew we needed a prisoner. We had to find out how to speak to them. Once we reached the mainland they would be as leaves on the tree. We would not be able to fight them all.

When we crested the rise and emerged from the trees, I saw, five hundred paces from us, their boats were drawn up on the beach. Two boys guarded them. "If we can I would take them, prisoner. Take no chances. Wound them if you must."

"Aye, brother!"

Even as we descended, I saw the first of those who had fled reach the boats. There were just two of them. They dragged one boat into the shallows. Then they waited. We covered another two hundred paces and reached the sand by the time they had done that. I nocked an arrow and kept running. We were not yet seen. When we were just one hundred and fifty paces, they spotted us. It was long range but the four of them obliged me by standing close together. My arrow hit one of the boys in the leg. It pinned it to the boat. The two warriors ran at us. From the right, I saw more warriors emerging from the woods and running to the boats. I sent another arrow into the chest of the warrior who ran at me. Fótr and Ebbe, both armed with swords ran at the other. I nocked another arrow. My brother and foster son did not hesitate. Ebbe ducked beneath the swinging axe and slashed the warrior's thigh. At the same time, Fótr rammed his sword up under the arm of the warrior and slew him. The boy who was not wounded had courage. As I switched my aim to the skrælings running towards the boats, the boy ran with his axe at Fótr and Ebbe. I had eight arrows left and each one found a mark. Behind me, I heard a cry. I did not dare turn around for the skrælings were closing with me. I sent my last arrow to hit one in the shoulder and then drew my sword and Raedwulf's dagger. A huge warrior with what looked like feathers hanging from his head ran at me with a stone dagger and axe. I blocked the axe with my sword and the stone knife with my dagger. He was a bigger warrior than I was and he tried to push me down. I pulled back my head and butted him. I broke and burst his nose. I smashed his teeth. I saw his eyes glaze. As he reeled I slashed first, across his middle with my sword and then, across his throat with my dagger. He fell dead.

Arne and the others slaughtered the last of the skrælings. The only one who remained was pinned to the bark boat. I shouted, "Do not approach him. Leave him to me." I sheathed my weapons and walked towards him. My arrow had driven through his leg and deep into the frame of the back boat and he could not wrench it free. He saw me coming and he drew a short stone knife. It might cut my arm but my hide jerkin would stop it doing serious damage. I held my arms open, "Surrender and I will not hurt you!"

He shouted something back and waved his knife. I took off my helmet and shook my head. He seemed to see the bear teeth and he lowered his dagger. In two strides I reached him. I took the knife from his hand and pitched it into the sea. I hated to do it but I had to break off the arrow and pull his leg away. He screamed and then passed out. I took a spare bowstring from my pouch and tied it above the wound. I slung him over my shoulder.

Arne had taken off his helmet and walked towards me. "Why did you not kill him?"

"He is but a boy and we need to speak their words. He can be our slave and learn our words. When he is healed, we can send him back to his people."

"Send him back?"

"Aye, we will need to talk with them. Look how many they sent here. There must be ten times that number on the mainland."

"We killed them all."

"Aye brother and lost almost a whole family. It will not harm us and is worth trying."

He nodded, "You are right and you are wise."

Siggi ran up to us, "Come quickly, my father is wounded."

Arne shouted, "Pile up the bark boats on the beach. Fetch all the bodies here. We will show these skrælings the folly of fighting Vikings!"

Snorri lay in the forest. Close by were the bodies of two skrælings. He had his back to a tree. His leg had been pierced by a stone spear. He gave us a wry smile, "They may have primitive weapons but, by the Allfather, they hurt. I fear the spear has hurt the bone!"

We all knew what that meant. My uncle would be lame.

Arne said, "It is about time you became the wise old man of the clan. Your sons, Siggi and Tostig, can now do the fighting for you."

He looked at the boy slung over my shoulder, "You have caught one?"

Arne nodded, "My brother is a fisherman and hopes to make this one tame!" He shook his head, "Take my uncle back to the halls and we will burn the bodies."

I sent Ebbe ahead to warn Gytha and her volva. Neither of the wounds was likely to cause death but the sooner Gytha could start to heal him the better. Ada was nursing our son by the water when we arrived. All the women stared at the young boy. He had still to awake. Gytha nodded and smiled, "Once again, Erik the Navigator, you show your wisdom. You were the only one to think of saving one of them." I bowed. She turned to her husband, "And this, Snorri Long Fingers, is the Allfather's way of telling you to hang up your sword."

While her women worked on the boy she probed and poked her husband. I went to Ada and our son, "All is well?"

She smiled, "It is because you live."

When Gytha had finished with Snorri, she kissed him. "You will never walk without the aid of a stick, my husband. You will have to become a singer of songs."

"Then that is a skill I will have to learn as I have a voice like Butar's deer in season!"

"Now let us see to this young skræling." She used salted water and vinegar to clean out the wound and then she packed it with moss mixed with honey and some of her herbs. She wrapped it up and bound it with a bandage. "Your arrow was clean, Erik, but I fear he will never run. You chipped the bone. He has a wound like my husband." She suddenly stared up at the sky and clutched her amulet. "Gytha, you are an old fool. This is the Norns. They have given my husband and this skræling the same wound. You need not sing songs husband. You can learn the words of this skræling and teach him ours. Erik, you took this thrall…"

"And I give him, gladly, to you Snorri Long Fingers."

Even as he nodded the boy opened his eyes and pointing at my neck said something in a hushed voice. He pointed at the teeth of the bear. The Norns were spinning.

Epilogue

The fire burned all day and all night. The pall of smoke and the fact that their warriors did not return would tell the skrælings what had happened. The next day we took Benni and his family to the cemetery at the eastern end of the island. As the sun came up we buried Benni and his family. Eidel now had a foster son, Leif Bennison. The ship's boy was now a man, he would soon be a father and he had his wife's brother to care for. The men had died with weapons in their hands. They would be in Valhalla. Snorri, that most patient of men, tried to tame the skræling. I just felt the hairs on the back of my neck as they tingled. I was part of this. The boy would lead me to my waterfall and, perhaps, the maid I had seen. Our world would never be the same.

The End

Norse Calendar

Gormánuður October 14th - November 13th
Ýlir November 14th - December 13th
Mörsugur December 14th - January 12th
Þorri - January 13th - February 11th
Gói - February 12th - March 13th
Einmánuður - March 14th - April 13th
Harpa April 14th - May 13th
Skerpla - May 14th - June 12th
Sólmánuður - June 13th - July 12th
Heyannir - July 13th - August 14th
Tvímánuður - August 15th - September 14th
Haustmánuður September 15th-October 13th

Glossary

Afen- River Avon
Afon Hafron- River Severn in Welsh
Àird Rosain – Ardrossan (On the Clyde Estuary)
Balley Chashtal -Castleton (Isle of Man)
Bebbanburgh- Bamburgh Castle, Northumbria also known as Din Guardi in the ancient tongue
Beck- a stream
Beinn na bhFadhla- Benbecula in the Outer Hebrides
Blót – a blood sacrifice made by a jarl
Bondi- Viking farmers who fight
Bjarnarøy –Great Bernera (Bear Island)
Byrnie- a mail or leather shirt reaching down to the knees
Càrdainn Ros -Cardross (Argyll)
Chape- the tip of a scabbard
Cyninges-tūn – Coniston. It means the estate of the king (Cumbria)
Dùn Èideann –Edinburgh (Gaelic)
Drekar- a Dragon ship (a Viking warship) pl. drekar
Duboglassio –Douglas, Isle of Man
Dun Holme- Durham
Dún Lethglaise - Downpatrick (Northern Ireland)
Dyrøy –Jura (Inner Hebrides)
Dyflin- Old Norse for Dublin
Eoforwic- Saxon for York
Føroyar- Faroe Islands
Fey- having second sight
Firkin- a barrel containing eight gallons (usually beer)
Fret-a sea mist
Fyrd-the Saxon levy
Gaill- Irish for foreigners
Galdramenn- wizard
Hersey- Isle of Arran
Hersir- a Viking landowner and minor noble. It ranks below a jarl
Hí- Iona (Gaelic)
Hjáp - Shap- Cumbria (Norse for stone circle)
Hoggs or Hogging- when the pressure of the wind causes the stern or the bow to droop

Hrams-a – Ramsey, Isle of Man
Hundred- Saxon military organization. (One hundred men from an area-led by a thegn or gesith)
Hwitebi - Norse for Whitby, North Yorkshire
Jarl- Norse earl or lord
Joro-goddess of the earth
kjerringa - Old Woman- the solid block in which the mast rested
Knarr- a merchant ship or a coastal vessel
Kyrtle-woven top
Ljoðhús- Lewis
Lochlannach – Irish for Northerners (Vikings)
Lough- Irish lake
Lundenburh/Lundenburgh- the walled burh built around the old Roman fort
Lundenwic - London
Mast fish- two large racks on a ship designed to store the mast when not required
Midden- a place where they dumped human waste
Miklagård - Constantinople
Njoror- God of the sea
Nithing- A man without honour (Saxon)
Odin- The "All Father" God of war, also associated with wisdom, poetry, and magic (The Ruler of the gods).
Orkneyjar-Orkney
Ran- Goddess of the sea
Roof rock- slate
Saami- the people who live in what is now Northern Norway/Sweden
Samhain- a Celtic festival of the dead between 31st October and 1st November (Halloween)
Scree- loose rocks in a glacial valley
Seax – short sword
Sennight- seven nights- a week
Sheerstrake- the uppermost strake in the hull
Sheet- a rope fastened to the lower corner of a sail
Shroud- a rope from the masthead to the hull amidships
Skræling -Barbarian

Skeggox – an axe with a shorter beard on one side of the blade
Skíð -the Isle of Skye
Skreið- stockfish (any fish which is preserved)
Smoky Bay- Reykjavik
Snekke- a small warship
Stad- Norse settlement
Stays- ropes running from the mast-head to the bow
Strake- the wood on the side of a drekar
Suðreyjar – Southern Hebrides (Islay)
Syllingar Insula, Syllingar- Scilly Isles
Tarn- small lake (Norse)
The Norns- The three sisters who weave webs of intrigue for men
Thing-Norse for a parliament or a debate (Tynwald in the Isle of Man)
Thor's day- Thursday
Threttanessa- a drekar with 13 oars on each side.
Thrall- slave
Trenail- a round wooden peg used to secure strakes
Tynwald- the Parliament on the Isle of Man
Úlfarrberg- Helvellyn
Úlfarrland- Cumbria
Úlfarrston- Ulverston
Ullr-Norse God of Hunting
Ulfheonar-an elite Norse warrior who wore a wolf skin over his armour
Veisafjǫrðr – Wexford (Ireland)
Volva- a witch or healing woman in Norse culture
Waeclinga Straet- Watling Street (A5)
Walhaz -Norse for the Welsh (foreigners)
Waite- a Viking word for farm
Withy- the mechanism connecting the steering board to the ship
Woden's day- Wednesday
Wulfhere-Old English for Wolf Army
Wyddfa-Snowdon
Wykinglo- Wicklow (Ireland)
Wyrd- Fate

Across the Seas

Wyrme- Norse for Dragon
Yard- a timber from which the sail is suspended
Ynys Enlli- Bardsey Island
Ynys Môn-Anglesey

Across the Seas

Historical Note

I tell lies for a living. I am a writer and this book is very a 'what if' sort of book. We now know that the Vikings reached further south in mainland America than we thought. Just how far is debatable. The evidence we have is from the sagas. Vinland was named after a fruit which could be brewed into wine was discovered. It does not necessarily mean grapes. King Harald Finehair did drive many Vikings west but I cannot believe that they would choose to live on a volcanic island.

I have my clan reaching Newfoundland and sailing down the coast of Nova Scotia. The island I call Bear Island is Isle Au Haut off the Maine coast. Grey Fox island and (Horse) Deer Island can also be found there. The Indigenous people, the Mi'kmaq, inhabited the northeastern coast of America. In the summer they would migrate to the coast and in winter, when there were fewer flies, they would retreat back to the hinterland. The maps are how Erik might have mapped them. Butar's deer are caribou and the horse deer are moose. Both were native to the region.

For the voyage, I used the records of single-handed sailings and rowing of the Atlantic.

The Vikings were a complicated people. Forget movies where they wear horned helmets and spend all their time pillaging. They did pillage and they could be cruel but they were also traders and explorers. The discovery of Iceland and after that Greenland and America has been put down to the attempt by King Harald Finehair to create a Viking Empire. True Vikings never liked kings. Rather than be taxed they sought new lands. Iceland was empty and bare but they made it their home.

http://www.hurstwic.org/history/articles/daily_living/text/Demographics.htm is a good website with some interesting stats. In 1000 AD 75% of Vikings were under 50 and under 15s represented half! A boy was considered a fully-grown man by the time he was 16. A man could be a judge at the age of 12. Helgi and Bergr were 10 and 12 when they avenged their father by killing his killer. We cannot imagine their world.

The compass I refer to was used in the Viking times. There is a Timewatch programme made by the BBC in which Robin

Knox Johnston uses the compass to sail from Norway to Iceland. He was just half a mile out when he arrived.

I used the following books for research:

- Vikings- Life and Legends -British Museum
- Saxon, Norman and Viking by Terence Wise (Osprey)
- The Vikings (Osprey) -Ian Heath
- Byzantine Armies 668-1118 (Osprey)-Ian Heath
- Romano-Byzantine Armies 4th-9th Century (Osprey) -David Nicholle
- The Walls of Constantinople AD 324-1453 (Osprey) -Stephen Turnbull
- Viking Longship (Osprey) - Keith Durham
- The Vikings in England Anglo-Danish Project
- Anglo Saxon Thegn AD 449-1066- Mark Harrison (Osprey)
- Viking Hersir- 793-1066 AD - Mark Harrison (Osprey)
- Hadrian's Wall- David Breeze (English Heritage)
- National Geographic- March 2017
- Time Life Seafarers-The Vikings Robert Wernick

Griff Hosker
February 2019

Other books by Griff Hosker

If you enjoyed reading this book, then why not read another one by the author?

Ancient History

The Sword of Cartimandua Series (Germania and Britannia 50 A.D. – 128 A.D.)
Ulpius Felix- Roman Warrior (prequel)
Book 1 The Sword of Cartimandua
Book 2 The Horse Warriors
Book 3 Invasion Caledonia
Book 4 Roman Retreat
Book 5 Revolt of the Red Witch
Book 6 Druid's Gold
Book 7 Trajan's Hunters
Book 8 The Last Frontier
Book 9 Hero of Rome
Book 10 Roman Hawk
Book 11 Roman Treachery
Book 12 Roman Wall
Book 13 Roman Courage

The Aelfraed Series (Britain and Byzantium 1050 A.D. - 1085 A.D.
Book 1 Housecarl
Book 2 Outlaw
Book 3 Varangian

The Wolf Warrior series (Britain in the late 6th Century)
Book 1 Saxon Dawn
Book 2 Saxon Revenge
Book 3 Saxon England
Book 4 Saxon Blood
Book 5 Saxon Slayer

Book 6 Saxon Slaughter
Book 7 Saxon Bane
Book 8 Saxon Fall: Rise of the Warlord
Book 9 Saxon Throne
Book 10 Saxon Sword

The Dragon Heart Series
Book 1 Viking Slave
Book 2 Viking Warrior
Book 3 Viking Jarl
Book 4 Viking Kingdom
Book 5 Viking Wolf
Book 6 Viking War
Book 7 Viking Sword
Book 8 Viking Wrath
Book 9 Viking Raid
Book 10 Viking Legend
Book 11 Viking Vengeance
Book 12 Viking Dragon
Book 13 Viking Treasure
Book 14 Viking Enemy
Book 15 Viking Witch
Book 16 Viking Blood
Book 17 Viking Weregeld
Book 18 Viking Storm
Book 19 Viking Warband
Book 20 Viking Shadow
Book 21 Viking Legacy
Book 22 Viking Clan

The Norman Genesis Series
Hrolf the Viking
Horseman
The Battle for a Home
Revenge of the Franks
The Land of the Northmen
Ragnvald Hrolfsson
Brothers in Blood
Lord of Rouen

Drekar in the Seine
Duke of Normandy

New World Series
Blood on the Blade
Across the Seas

The Anarchy Series England 1120-1180
English Knight
Knight of the Empress
Northern Knight
Baron of the North
Earl
King Henry's Champion
The King is Dead
Warlord of the North
Enemy at the Gate
The Fallen Crown
Warlord's War
Kingmaker
Henry II
Crusader
The Welsh Marches
Irish War
Poisonous Plots
The Princes' Revolt
Earl Marshal

Border Knight 1182-1300
Sword for Hire
Return of the Knight
Baron's War
Magna Carta
Welsh Wars
Henry III

Struggle for a Crown 1360- 1485
Blood on the Crown
To Murder A King

The Throne

Modern History

The Napoleonic Horseman Series
Book 1 Chasseur a Cheval
Book 2 Napoleon's Guard
Book 3 British Light Dragoon
Book 4 Soldier Spy
Book 5 1808: The Road to A Coruña
Waterloo

The Lucky Jack American Civil War series
Rebel Raiders
Confederate Rangers
The Road to Gettysburg

The British Ace Series
1914
1915 Fokker Scourge
1916 Angels over the Somme
1917 Eagles Fall
1918 We will remember them
From Arctic Snow to Desert Sand
Wings over Persia

Combined Operations series 1940-1945
Commando
Raider
Behind Enemy Lines
Dieppe
Toehold in Europe
Sword Beach
Breakout
The Battle for Antwerp
King Tiger
Beyond the Rhine
Korea

Other Books
Carnage at Cannes (a thriller)
Great Granny's Ghost (Aimed at 9-14-year-old young people)
Adventure at 63-Backpacking to Istanbul

For more information on all of the books then please visit the author's web site at www.griffhosker.com where there is a link to contact him.

Printed in Great Britain
by Amazon